"Liar," he mumbled in a caressing voice. "You have known ever since you stood me up two years ago."

"I wonder what would have happened if I hadn't."

"This is what would have happened, before the day was out, Aphrodite," he murmured in her ear. Then he lowered his head and kissed her gently on the lips, holding her in a warm, tender, embrace. "But as two years have passed since then, and you are a confirmed Jezebel, this is what will happen now," he added.

Then he embraced her much more vigorously and left her breathless...

Fawcett Crest Books
by Joan Smith:

THE DEVIOUS DUCHESS

LADY MADELINE'S FOLLY

LOVE BADE ME WELCOME

ROYAL REVELS

TRUE LADY

Babe

Joan Smith

FAWCETT CREST • NEW YORK

A Fawcett Crest Book
Published by Ballantine Books
Copyright © 1980 by Joan Smith

ISBN 0-449-21142-8

Manufactured in the United States of America

First Fawcett Crest Edition: February 1980
First Ballantine Books Edition: July 1986

One

Lady Withers sat in her elegant Crimson Saloon, frowning into a glass of ratafia. She was still young and considered handsome. She had a doting husband, three children, and an active social life. She enjoyed good health and excellent credit, but still the frown was quite pronounced.

"What has got you in the hips?" her brother asked, not greatly interested.

"What am I *ever* plagued about these days? It is Lady Barbara, of course."

"What has the hellion done to set the town on its ear today?" he asked, with a little of smile of anticipation that took the harsh edge from his face. As one of London's more eligible bachelors, Lord Clivedon was accustomed to hear himself called handsome, though he was not precisely so. He was dark of complexion, with features more rugged than refined, but when he smiled, he created an illusion of handsomeness. A well-cut jacket was on his shoulders, a well-tied cravate at his neck, and blindingly polished Hessians on his feet.

"I don't know that she has stirred yet *today*—it's only ten-thirty, and after being out till four this morning, I expect she is still in her bed."

"Four, eh? A bit dashing for a young lady. Are you in possession of the sordid details, or must I wait and hear them at my club?"

"Do they discuss her at the clubs? How shabby!" his sister exclaimed, with a *tsk* of annoyance. Lady Withers was an enemy to shabbiness—physical, mental, moral, and most particularly social. She was every bit as elegant as her brother in her toilette, and somewhat more pretty.

"Regularly. I believe the bet currently on the books has to do with some Austrian colonel she is playing with. One of the riffraff who came over after Waterloo. Hasn't the money to get home, I expect. The odds are two to one she'll have him. I've placed a pony she won't. I've made a thousand pounds on her already this Season. She never does marry 'em."

"He is a perfectly *wretched* person, Larry. You've no idea. He ran off with some chit in Austria, which is why he is here. There was a regular brouhaha. I had it of Princess Esterhazy, the Austrian ambassador's wife, who had it of the Duchesse de Sagan in a letter from Vienna. It was Fannie Atwood's cracker-brained scheme of going to Paris after Waterloo that put her in touch with all these seedy foreigners she hangs out with nowadays. She seldom associates with Englishmen anymore, and naturally Lady Barbara meets them as well. The colonel you spoke of is not at all the thing, and you must do something."

"*I?*" Clivedon asked, astonished. "The girl is nothing to me. She is only a connection."

"She is a third cousin on her father's side, but more importantly, the relationship is *known*. I can't tell you how often some cat twits me about her doings. I am mortified ten times a day with her. And there is no forceful *male* relative to get a rein on her, you see. That is exactly the trouble. Her parents both dead, the mother's relatives, if she has any, are in France. It is that wretched French streak that makes her so impossible."

6

"And attractive," he added, with a maddening smile.

Agnes cast a curious look on her brother. "Of course she is monstrously pretty."

"No other male relatives, you say—surely old Manfred, her father's heir, is closer to her than we are."

"He is closer to the grave than anything else. He couldn't begin to manage her. The thing is, Larry, I have decided to take her myself. No, don't stare! It must be done. I am convinced we shall deal very well together, for I used to like Barbara amazingly before she started running wild. It is Fannie Atwood's foolish notion of treating her as if she were a forty-year-old widow like herself that leads the girl astray. Letting her set up that sky-blue phaeton and wild team you couldn't handle yourself, I daresay, and wearing *such* gowns. If Barbara had someone to take a motherly interest in her, she might be led to propriety. Anyway, Fannie is a perfect ninny-hammer, and why her father ever left her in the woman's care is a perfect mystery, except of course that he was sweet on Fannie himself and thought they might marry. Of equal mystery is why Fannie took her on."

"Not much mystery there. Fannie is forever outrunning the grocer, and needed the money. She won't agree to it."

"I think she will, and I mean to ask her, before Barbara's reputation is completely in shreds. If she runs off with this Colonel Gentz, for instance . . ."

"She won't. She's thoughtless, not mindless."

"She will do something shatter-brained, and I mean to reclaim her before she does."

"It will never fadge. Fanny is her legal guardian, and closer to her than we are. You would have to wade through the courts and prove her immoral or something equally distasteful to us all, and harmful to Barbara as well. It cannot be done."

"Well, it can, for Fannie is marrying that Count Bagstorff person, and the upshot will be that she drags Barbara off to Austria with them on the honeymoon, and if *that* is not immoral, it should be. And once they get her out of England, you know, where *none* of us know what is going on, it is but an instant till they fleece her of her fortune by one means or another."

Clivedon's eyes flew to his sister, bright with interest. "I hadn't heard Fannie was leaving the country."

"I know, Larry, and that is why I asked you here today. I ran into Fannie at a rout last night, and she told me—I *think* she was hinting—that Barbara is not at all eager to go with her to Austria. I daresay Bagstorff has been rolling his eyes at the girl, for he is only after Fannie's money, of course, only she is too infatuated to see it. So it is the perfect time to do it."

Clivedon sat considering the matter a moment. "You couldn't handle her, sis. She is too hot at hand for you."

"Oh no—I am sure with tact and tenderness . . ."

"Tact?" he asked, staring. *"Tenderness?* You're mad. She is not a child. She's been on the town for five years."

"Not that long, surely!" Lady Withers exclaimed. This came perilously close to shabbiness, to delay so long in nabbing a husband.

"At least five. I'm not sure it isn't six years. Of course she has traveled a good bit. She was in Vienna in '14, and in Paris in '15, and missed a few Seasons. She was here for the royal visit of the Czar and the King of Prussia, and that was not the year of her come-out either. She was already carrying on with the Czar and Metternich at that time, an accomplished flirt. She damned near stole Wellington away from Caro Lamb in Paris, and—well, she had a fling with Byron before either of those events. She's been out since '13 at least."

"I didn't realize you kept such close track of her," Lady Withers said.

"Oh yes. Did I not mention she is a good source of income from betting at the clubs?"

"Tell me, Larry, was there ever a wager to the effect that Lord Clivedon might be brought up to scratch? About two years ago . . ." Agnes asked, with a searching look.

"As a matter of fact, there was. I made five hundred,

8

illegally, by getting Hobson to lay a wager for me," he answered, with a pleasant smile.

She sighed wearily. "Perhaps you're right. She is past reclaiming. She spent a year at Devonshire House before ever she did make her bows, and that cannot have done her any good. If she is a quarter of a century old, there's no point of thinking of finding her a match."

"She's twenty-three."

"She is well-dowered too. I think I *will* try my hand at it."

"No, I'll take her," he said, in a voice that was firm yet nonchalant.

"You! You cannot mean . . ."

"No, Widgeon! I am not such a fool as you seem to take me for. In my position, I will hardly marry a lady who has made herself the talk of London—and several other cities."

"I shouldn't think a little scandal would bother you much. I seem to recall hearing rumors of a duel not too long ago."

"Unfounded. We settled the matter at Jackson's Parlor," he replied, slightly pink around the collar.

"Still, matters that require settling in such a fashion usually involve a little scandal."

"Babe does not deal in little scandals. She causes Gargantuan ones. Lady Angela tells me she has lately been seen at Mrs. Duncan's place gambling, and that is no better than a dive nowadays. Next thing we hear she'll be opening her own den."

It was, strangely, the only decent name in this account that caused Lady Withers to complain. "Oh, dear! It's true, then. You *are* dangling after Lady Angela."

"Do you women never think of *anything* but marriage?" he asked petulantly. "You will not see me caught by either a prude or a hellcat this season."

"I confess it is a relief," she confided. "Not that I have a *word* to say against Lady Angela. How could anyone? She is perfectly charming and gracious, and of course, totally moral. Almost excessively so. But how shall you take

9

Barbara, if not in marriage? How shabby that sounds. Somehow, one always ends up sounding horrid when the girl is discussed. You cannot take her to your house—a bachelor's establishment."

"I wouldn't let her anywhere near it. She'd have the saloon full of rackety foreigners and bailiffs. We have an unseemly quantity of relatives, however, every one of them *except* Babe tiresomely respectable. I'll think of someone. When is Fannie marrying this foreigner?"

"Not for a month, but she leaves for Dorset for a house party soon, in company with Bagstorff and likely Colonel Gentz as well. The pair of them run tame at Portland Place. It was Gentz Barbara was with last night at some embassy party, and Fannie not even with her. My husband was there."

"Till four?" Clivedon asked her, with a teasing smile.

"Certainly not, but she was still going strong at two, and you may be sure she wasn't home till hours afterward."

"I'll see what I can do. Fannie may be happy enough to be rid of her. Folks usually are."

"Yes, when she was with the Harrows last year, while Fannie made a dash to Paris, you know, and left her behind, Mrs. Harrow was delighted to see the last of her. But of course she has those two long-toothed daughters of her own, and I expect that was what her complaints were all about. It's rather sad, really. So spoiled in so many ways, with her looks and her father's fortune, and yet no one to take a lasting interest in her. Really, I wouldn't mind at all, Larry, to try my hand at it."

"I would mind for you. Three squawlers are enough for you to see to. I'll handle Babe."

"I couldn't take her immediately. Boo has thrown out the measles, and Nickie will be bound to follow, but in a week or so I could do it." Her brother arose. "Larry—handle her gently," she suggested.

"With Tact and Tenderness," he agreed blandly, then added in a livelier tone, "and of course a chair and a whip, for my own protection."

10

Two

Lady Barbara Manfred lay back against a lace-edged pillow in her canopied bed and rubbed her eyes. They were large, deep blue eyes, heavily fringed. Pale blonde hair streamed over her pillow, perfectly straight hair, fine like silken threads. The face was delicate, cast in a classical mold. There was nothing childish about it. Even in her early teens, she had looked like a woman. Today she looked pale and tired as well, after a series of late nights. She glanced to the window, where a pigeon had perched on the ledge. She looked beyond it to the spreading beech. It always reminded her of home—Drumbeig. There was a beech-clad hill visible from her window there, in the northernmost part of the Cotswolds, in Oxfordshire. So long ago it seemed, when she had used to live with her parents. For how long had she lived this stupid, boring life, being battened on one person after another who didn't want her? Going to parties and routs and to any foreign country where excitement offered. Looking for—what?

What was it she wanted? Excitement? Not really. She

was bored even with excitement. Surely that was the hall-mark of disillusionment. But she was not quite desperate yet. She still hoped, and kept on looking, for something. Some anchor for her wandering life. Someone to love, and to love her. Her mind roamed over her various beaux, with Colonel Gentz slightly in the forefront. He was hand-some and amusing, and a fortune hunter. Not Theodor. She supposed he would trail her to Austria, but she would be rid of him there, leave him behind when she came home to England. She wished she didn't have to go to Austria at all.

"Morning, mum," the maid said, coming in with a heavy silver tray, on which a cup of cocoa steamed. Poor Mary, lugging that heavy tray all the way up from the kitchen, only for a cup of cocoa.

"Put it here," Barbara said, then on impulse called, "Thank you, Mary," after the retreating form. The girl looked over her shoulder, surprised at the courtesy. She must be kinder to servants. Lately she found herself slip-ping into Fannie's habit of treating them like machines. At home the servants were all her friends. At Drumbeig, she would know all about Mary, whether she had a beau and sisters. She didn't even know if this Mary was mar-ried or single. She sipped her cocoa slowly, disliking the cloying sweetness of it. She'd have coffee or tea the next morning. She really should eat something too. She used to eat monumental breakfasts at home with Papa, and never gained an ounce. She was becoming too thin, she thought, looking at her arms. Papa used to call her Rapunzel, his little princess, and pinch her arms, telling her even a princess had to eat. How did one fall into these habits—doing what others did, only because others did so? There was no other reason she had switched to cocoa except that Fannie liked it. She hadn't done a lot of things till she came to Fannie. Hadn't stayed up till three or four and slept till noon. But then, you had to fit yourself into a household.

And Fannie was very nice. She was never so happy as when she was with Fannie. She was sometimes parted from her, for Fannie went to places she did not like to take a young lady, and when she was with such people as the Harrows, she realized how much she loved Fannie. She was lively and gay, with a large circle of friends. Of course she was a little raffish as well, but she was kind to herself, and that was not an easy quality to find in anyone.

She set aside the cup and pulled her bell cord. "The mauve suit, if you please, Harper," she said to her dresser, who came in immediately. "It doesn't match my eyes, but it will match the circles under them. God, I look hagged. What is my cousin doing? Is she up yet?"

"Yes, milady. She has company belowstairs. A gentleman."

How cold Harper was. With her two years and still called her milady, and answered questions in a monosyllable if she could. There was no friendly gossiping; no sharing of secrets. But Harper was an excellent dresser, particularly capable in the realm of hair. Barbara's ruler-straight hair was a problem to her, and she valued Harper highly. "Count Bagstorff is here already?" she asked.

"No, milady. It's not the count. It's Lord Clivedon. He's been there half an hour."

"Clivedon?" she asked, surprised. "What the devil can *he* want? Is he asking for me?"

"No, milady. They haven't asked you to be called."

"Oh." Lady Barbara's lips formed into a pout. She considered hurrying up her toilette and descending uninvited to greet Clivedon. The urge was all to do so. There was something in him that intrigued her, even while she half disliked him. He was toplofty, had a very good opinion of himself. She hunched her shoulders with petulant impatience, but when she had her hair dressed, she said, "Braid it, please, Harper. I'll wear it up in braids today."

This was the most time-consuming coiffure she used. It was usually the style chosen for riding or rough outings, where her other do's were likely to come unhinged. Her hair was widely praised, but this fine straight hair was also a nuisance. The reason she asked for braids today

13

had nothing to do with riding; she did it to force herself to stay abovestairs. While Harper worked on her hair, brushing it out, Barbara leaned towards the mirror, smoothing a concealing cream on the circles under her eyes. Why should she satisfy him to think she was chasing after him? He had thought it two years ago—conceited oaf. He had expected her to run after him and beg forgiveness after that foolish incident at Richmond Park, when she was supposed to meet him, but had gone off to another party instead, and had a delightful time too. Much she cared if he pokered up that evening at the ball, and pretended not to see her. She had caught him looking at her a dozen times. He had not honored her with any gallantry after that. It was odd how vivid the memory was still, and she had left plenty of men waiting since!

"Hurry up, Harper. Never mind the braids. Just pin it up quickly."

Harper was a wizard, and a swift one too, but when Lady Barbara glided down the stairs five minutes later, she found her cousin Fannie sitting alone, looking nervous.

"Babe, the most astonishing thing," she said, "what Clivedon has proposed."

"Proposed! You can't mean it!" Barbara exclaimed, and could actually feel her cheeks blanch. Her heart was fluttering fiercely. She didn't know whether she was frightened or thrilled, but she knew she was deeply affected. "What did you tell him?" she asked, walking quickly forward.

"Why I didn't tell him anything, till I have discussed it with you, to find out what you think of having him for your guardian. After I marry Bagstorff and go to Austria, you know. You have said you dislike the thought of going with us, and we plan to stay for a year. I rather thought Lady Withers——"

"Guardian!" Barbara asked, blinking. *"Guardian!* Is that all? How should he be my guardian?"

"Why, outside of old Manfred, he is your closest rela-

14

tive in England, my pet, and *such* good *ton*. He means to put you up with his sister, I expect."

The matter was discussed for an hour, while a variety of emotions washed over Lady Barbara, none of them quite so powerful as that first wave of shock. She considered the matter coolly. She really did not *want* to tag along on Fannie's honeymoon, but still, it hurt to see how clear it was that Fannie didn't want it either. "It might be better, as it will get you away from Gentz, and you have said often enough you don't mean to have him," Fannie mentioned, more than once. It was more usual for her to urge a match with Gentz.

There were other excuses too. "Clivedon is excellent *ton*," was often heard. Much Fannie cared about *ton!* "You always seemd to like Lady Withers very well, and really, she is not a prude, like the Harrows. I will not consign you to the Harrows again." After considerable talk, Babe agreed.

"Very well," she said, in a voice more cheerful than mere resignation. She had some hope for pleasure in the scheme. Clivedon was a broad-minded gentleman, who would not expect her to act any differently than she did now. He was certainly no prude—quite the contrary. And she liked Lady Withers. It would do, she supposed. She wondered where the idea had come from. Fannie, she thought, had been as surprised as herself.

The exchange of guardians was hastily arranged, with all parties in agreement. After two visits from solicitors and three from accountants, Lord Clivedon stood in custody of Lady Barbara and her fortune till her twenty-fifth birthday, two years away. She expected every hour he would call to discuss it with her. Two mornings she stayed in for the purpose, but he did not come, nor did Lady Withers. On the third day, he sent a note that his carriage would call at Portland Place the next morning to remove her to his custody. She waited at the window, planning a sharp remark at his cavalier treatment. When it was only a footman who came to the door, she was not only disappointed, but furiously angry. How *dare* he treat her so

15

poorly? Not a call, not a note, not even coming in person to convey her to Lady Withers' home. And Lady Withers no better. Why had not *she* come?

She turned to Fannie with a certain sparkle in her eye. "I've changed my mind, Fannie. I'm not going," she said, and sat down, folding her arms on her heaving bosom.

"Not going! Babe—it is too late for not going. The papers are signed. You *must* go."

"I will not. If he thinks to treat me like this . . ."

"But I go to Burrell's house party, my dear, and you are not expected. Indeed, it is not a place I would take a young lady at all."

"You planned to take me four days ago!"

"Well, I didn't *like* it. The papers are all signed. He is your guardian. You *must* go."

"I don't have to do anything I don't want to."

"To be sure, you do not, Babe, only Clivedon will create a wicked row if I take you to Burrell's. He mentioned they are not the sort of people . . . Not to say . . ."

Barbara fixed her with a challenging eye. "What did he say? You don't mean to sit there and tell me he had the *insolence* to criticize your—our friends, and you didn't tell me."

"Not in the least. He was very civil. I daresay he didn't mean to be so bossy at all, but it is always Clivedon's way, you must know. Oh, *do* go on, Babe, you are giving me the headache, and Bagstorff is coming in ten minutes."

"All right. All right, I'll *go*, but . . ." She looked to Fannie, dear Fannie, whom she thought loved her, but all she saw on the face was distress, and an eagerness to be rid of her. Nothing would be the same once she married Bagstorff. "Good-bye, Fannie," she said, in a rather tight voice. "Thank you for everything. It's been nice. I'll come to see you soon. When do you return from Burrell's?"

"Nothing is decided, dear. Clivedon thought it would be nice to be married in the country, and I rather think it would."

"Will you not be back before your wedding? Oh, Fannie, I must attend your wedding!"

16

"We'll be in touch, love," Fannie said impatiently, and took her elbow to pilot her to the door, close it after her, and go back to the sofa, feeling strangely guilty and lonesome. She *liked* Babe, but Clivedon was quite right. A newly married lady would be too busy to handle her. Her thoughts wandered more happily to Count Bagstorff.

Three

Lady Barbara would not have been at all surprised had she been required to wait while her trunks were strapped onto the carriage, but this indignity, at least, was spared her. The carriage moved forward as soon as the footman had closed the door and resumed his position. Lady Withers' house was close by on Cavendish Square. When the carriage crossed Oxford Street, Barbara realized this was not where she was being taken. It proceeded straight to Grosvenor Square, to Clivedon's own handsome residence. She settled down somewhat then, imagining a sort of welcome party awaited her at the home of her new guardian. That was well done of him. She had only been in his house twice, attending two large balls two years ago, before he had turned chilly towards her. She had never been one of the intimate circle of Clivedon's friends. It was generally considered the toniest circle in town. Not so dashing as the old Devonshire House set, where Barbara had been a sort of pet in her very youth. The duchess, Georgiana, had doted on her, but she was long dead. Nor did she enjoy any favor with Caroline

Lamb after competing with her for a few beaux. Nothing lingered from those old days but the softly drawling voice used by the duchess and copied by the rest. The duchess's lisp and habit of using many French phrases had not survived a month. She turned mentally from the past to the present. She must improve, live up to the higher standards of Clivedon's set. It would be good for her, this change. Really, she had been slipping into questionable company lately. All a result of Bagstorff's influence.

She was smiling as she entered the door of the residence, preparing her prettiest speech of thanks. The smile faded as she was led into an empty chamber to await his lordship. The room's elegance was her only welcome; there was no party. What could it mean? Did he think to have her live here, with himself? He had some maiden aunt keeping house for him, she knew, but still, it seemed a little smokey. She hunched her shoulders, dismissing it. If Clivedon thought it suitable, then it must be acceptable. Odd Fannie had said it would not do; Fannie was not overly nice in her notions of propriety.

After five minutes, a servant brought her wine and biscuits, which she ignored. "Please tell Lord Clivedon I am waiting," she said.

"His lordship knows, milady. He will be here presently," she was told.

She waited another ten minutes before his unhurried steps approached the doorway. "Ah, Lady Barbara, sorry to keep you waiting," he said, in a voice that did not sound sorry, or try to. "I had the devil of a time with my cravate this morning. I am trying the Olbadeston," he added, patting his cravate. "I see you have been entertained during my absence." His eyes glanced off the untouched glass of wine, the biscuits, their careful pattern not disturbed on the plate.

"Good morning Clivedon. Kind of you to worry about me, but in future, when you wish to *entertain* me, I will just drop the hint that an empty room and stale biscuit is not the way to set about it," she answered sharply.

"Stale?" he asked, lifting his brows. "Shocking! Do permit me to apologize." He picked one up and tried it. Though he made no comment, there was a crisp sound indicating freshness as he bit in. "Try your luck again," he said, passing the plate.

"I did not come here for a biscuit!" she answered, feeling control was slipping from her fingers. "Furthermore, I don't think I should be here at all, taking up residence in a bachelor's establishment."

"Do you object? Do you know, it occurred to me you might, so I have arranged with a female relative of mine to house you. Lady Withers would have been here to guard your reputation this morning as well, but unfortunately one of her children has got a swelling or spot, or some dreadful malady."

She was relieved to hear the name of Lady Withers arise, slightly mollified as well to learn there was a reason why the lady had not called on her.

"I am sorry to hear it. I wondered at her not having called."

"She wondered the same thing, that you did not see fit to pay her a duty call. I trust you are enjoying your customary high good health?"

This was the first time it occurred to Barbara that a call from her might have been expected. Fannie had not mentioned it, but she was sorry she had been lax in the first obligation to arise with her new set of guardians. Before she could make any reply, he spoke on.

"I have been meaning to compliment you on the good sense you have shown in this affair, Lady Barbara. We had some fears, Agnes and myself, that you would not agree to the change of custodians. I conceived the notion—I can't imagine where the idea came from—that you would dislike to have me exercising control over you." This speech was not delivered in any accents of a compliment, but, on the contrary, there was a mocking note to it, nor was the choice of words at all diplomatic.

She regarded him with keen distaste. "It is a matter of very little interest to me who is *nominally* in control of my welfare. At my age, you know, it is no more than a formality."

"You are no longer young, certainly," he agreed, with an appraising scrutiny of her face, "but according to the terms of the legal agreement, I am in complete control of your doings. I do not mean to treat the matter so lightly as your last guardian did."

"I will give you very little trouble. Just have my cheques mailed to me quarterly on time, and we shall rub along tolerably well."

"I have been meaning to speak to you about your allowance," he said at once, taking up a seat across from her and examining his nails with interest. Then he polished them against his lapel and yawned behind raised fingers. "These late nights are the very devil, are they not? I see you too are showing the effects of them. When did you grow those circles under your eyes, Lady Barbara?"

"At the same time as I grew my wrinkles and gray hair. A dozen or so years ago. What is it you meant to say about my allowance?" She straightened her shoulders and lifted her chin in a fit of pique, for she knew very well she had been having too many late nights, and their effect was beginning to show. Still, the light was behind her, and she could not believe she was so hagged as to make that remark apt.

"You're overdrawn. There won't be any allowance this quarter," he answered blandly.

"*No* allowance? Don't be absurd. I am only overdrawn a few hundred pounds. How should I jog along on *no money?*"

"Actually, you are overdrawn several hundreds—well into the next quarter's installment as well. That phaeton, I fancy, is the culprit, and the team that draws it. No, on second thought, you could not have paid much for that pair of lame screws I see in the park."

The team spoken of were not to her taste. Too leather-mouthed for a lady to control with any ease. Gentz had purchased them for her, and paid a handsome price too, but she said none of this. "I am paying for the phaeton by installments, Clivedon, and the grays were selected and paid for by myself."

"I have paid off the full price of the phaeton. I dislike to see you run into debt."

"You did *what?*" she asked, jumping to her feet.

"Paid for the phaeton. It is quite a common custom to pay for one's purchases. I can't think why you are excited about it."

"I didn't intend paying *cash*. Oh, what a mess you've made of things already. You must give me an advance from the next quarter's money, then. I need a new ball gown this very week."

"There will be no advances, Lady Barbara. You must learn to cut your coat to fit the cloth, like everyone else."

She inhaled a deep breath and resumed her seat. Her credit was good; she wouldn't make a fuss about this. As he had charge of her monies, she must humor him. He spoke on. "I have taken the liberty, as well, of sending a note around to the more stylish *modistes* that I do not wish them to extend you credit," he added.

"You take a great deal of liberty, sir!" she answered hotly.

"I mean to employ the full prerogative of guiding my charge, Lady Barbara," he answered with a smile.

"And I wish you will stop calling me Lady Barbara every minute. Call me Babe. Everyone does."

"It is a sad comment on your dignity that you allow everyone to be so free with you. I will expect more discretion, now that your behavior will reflect somewhat on myself."

Her dark eyes narrowed dangerously, and she was aware of a rising heat in her blood. "Don't think to exercise this prerogative you speak of as though I were a child, sir. I am very much accustomed to being my own mistress. I will behave *exactly* as I always have, and you may go to the devil."

"Eventually, no doubt, but in the interim I shall attempt to keep you from doing likewise." He arose languidly and looked at her, in a fairly disinterested way.

"Are you ready to leave? I'll take you to Lady Graham now."

"Lady Graham?" she asked. "I don't want to visit that old Tartar. Take me to your sister, at once."

"My sister? But surely I mentioned Boo has thrown out a few spots. Nickie as well, I think, which leads me to suspect a contagious disease. Measles very likely. You will be staying with Lady Graham."

"Clivedon! You can't be serious. I will not stay with her. She is a positive ogre. I'll go to Lady Withers. I have had the measles. I don't mind that."

"*I* mind for you. Measles can be caught more than once, and you would not like to be ill at the height of the Season."

"I'd rather catch smallpox that go to that mausoleum in Mecklenberg Square. Why, she lives away out at the edge of Somers Town, miles from anywhere."

"There has been an excellent new road put in. You'll see four or five stages a day pass by, to relieve the quiet. Till you are back in looks, Lady Barbara, I want you to lessen the pace of your socializing. It is a shame to see you run to seed at a relatively young age." He turned and strolled at a slow pace towards the door. She remained where she stood. "Come along," he invited.

"I am not going to Lady Graham's place. I refuse to be fobbed off in this manner."

He smiled at her fondly, as though she were an unruly child. "Oh, I have not the least intention of fobbing you off. I mean to take a very active concern for your well-being. You will find me tediously interested in all your doings. I have arranged outings for you both this afternoon and this evening."

She listened to this and found it gratifying. She still disliked both the location and character of her new keeper, but if Clivedon meant to dance attendance on her, it would be supportable. Rather a feather in her cap, to have him running at her heels.

"Are you quite sure Lady Angela will approve of that?" she asked with a pert smile.

"I have not discussed the matter with her," he replied, smiling as he ushered her out the door and led her to his carriage.

He was amusing all during the longish drive to Mecklenberg Square, talking of social doings. As he left her with Lady Graham, he mentioned that he would see her very soon. She assumed he meant that same afternoon, and wondered that he did not stay to luncheon, as the drive home and back again was long enough to occasion some inconvenience.

Four

Luncheon found Lady Barbara sitting across the table from a pair of ladies who strangely resembled Chinese mandarins. Age had yellowed their skin and slanted their eyes down at the outer edges to give them doleful expressions. Lady Graham was the chief mandarin, an overbearing dame with gray hair and wearing the last pair of tiered sleeves in London. The lace from these ancient relics was entrusted to no hands but her own, where it received twice weekly a washing in cream. It was the major physical act she she performed during the normal course of her days, but she had girded herself for more strenuous pursuits to amuse her guest. Her sister was slightly less ancient and a good deal less overbearing. In fact, she was a slave in all but name to the elder.

"You look peaked, Lady Barbara," Lady Graham accused. "Have you been ill?"

"No, not at all."

"You are too thin. All skin and bone, like Mabel." A glare was leveled on Mabel, who was indeed much less well fleshed than her corpulent sister. "Here, have a dish of this soft pudding. It will help pad you out. Ladies want padding; it pleases the gentlemen. And you will want nourishment for your outing this afternoon too. It is very wearing, racketing into town. We like our privacy here very well, but of course they stuck in a metaled road as soon as ever we got here."

Barbara accepted a heaping load of soft pudding, which she tasted before concealing it behind a bowl of fruit.

"Have you ever been to Bullock's Museum?" was the next speech.

"I can't say that I have."

"Good. You will like to see Napoleon's carriage. It is on view there. One ought to take some interest in history, and I daresay that Corsican upstart will be remembered a few years. "

"We must go some time," Barbara answered politely, smiling to herself at the drabness of the outing.

"We go this afternoon," she was told.

Mabel peeped up as though she would like to say a word, but she was ordered to eat her soft pudding, and did it obediently.

"Clivedon plans to return this afternoon," Barbara mentioned.

"Clivedon? Nonsense. He is off to a weekend party at Haddon's place in Kent, with Lady Angela. He left from here. There will be a match, mark my words."

"He said . . ." Yet he had not actually said *he* would accompany her on the outing, merely that he had arranged one. An angry feeling began sprouting in her bosom, of having been outwitted by him.

"It was his suggestion you would like to see it. And this evening we go to a concert of antique music. They are resuscitating the Elizabethan madrigal this month," Lady Graham told her, with a satisfied nod of her head. "I don't usually racket around so much, but to hear the madrigals is worth any exertion. It will be interesting for you. It will not be a late night at all; you will get plenty of sleep, as Clivedon suggested."

"Clivedon suggested it, did he?" she asked, her voice strangely tense.

"Certainly he did. You should call him Lord Clivedon, by the by. Brassy manners will not do on Mecklenberg Square. You want to show him proper respect. I was surprised to hear such good sense from him. I was afraid he would expect me to drag you off to drums and gay revels, but he knew better. Clivedon is a little loose in his own amusements, there is no denying. But then, men are more free than ladies; always have been and always will be. Eat your crust, Mabel," she added, sparing an eye for her other charge. "It will curl your hair." This caused the old witch to emit a nasty laugh.

Feeling sorry for the sister, Barbara mentioned the annoyance of straight hair.

Lady Graham frowned at her having uttered a word on her own initiative, and again took over the conversation. "Sunday of course we shall do no more than go to church, but Monday I mean to take you to Burlington House to see the Elgin Marbles."

"I have seen the Elgin Marbles, Lady Graham," Barbara said in a firm voice.

"I saw them as well, when Elgin had them at his own place in Park Street, but they are much better displayed now, I hear. That great sculptured slab from the Temple of Nike was off in a corner where the work could not be appreciated. Take your sketch pad along, Lady Barbara. It will be an educational afternoon, to appreciate the Hellenic touch in sculpture."

Barbara said nothing. By Monday, she trusted, Clivedon would be home from the party, and if he thought she was to spend the Season in this manner, he would have something to learn. She went to Bullock's Museum to view Napoleon's carriage that afternoon, and in the evening she dozed through a very inferior rendition of Elizabethan madrigals. The audience was composed of ladies and gentlemen who looked nearly as old as the music. She doubted half of them were awake to hear it. Heads nodded on shoulders, and the snores were louder than the lyre. Both Lady Graham and Miss Mabel sat at attention, their noses quivering with the unwonted excitement. As Barbara was tired, she tolerated the dull evening without uttering a single word of complaint, though she was slow to rise to appreciation on the scale of her hostess. Church was attended on Sunday morning. Not the chapel royal, but a little out-of-the-way building in Somers Town, the building smelling of new bricks and mortar and the sermon of brimstone. The black jackets of the men and black bombazine gowns of the ladies both smelled of camphor. Lady Barbara realized she had fallen amongst Dissenters, and racked it up in her account against her foe.

Lady Graham did not approve of any frivolity such as museums and music on the Sabbath. There were Bible readings after each of the three meals, and there was a "period of contemplation" from two to four, for the meals, of course, were served at country hours. The guest spent not a moment contemplating the hereafter, the subject suggested by her hostess. She contemplated instead revenge on her guardian. After her quiet weekend, she was well rested up to take him on. It was only the anticipation of it the next day that kept her from coming to cuffs with the chief mandarin when she scolded Miss Mabel for dropping a spot of gravy on the tablecloth, as though she were a child. She would not satisfy him to have Lady Graham report any misconduct on her part. She volunteered to play a few hymns on the old clavichord in the corner that evening, but the idea was vetoed. Music should not intrude on the Sabbath, except possibly in a church, and even there, it was suggested, it had a whiff of papacy about it.

It was not yet nine when Lady Graham began to yawn into her tiered sleeves and her sister to eye the lamps, preparatory to extinguishing them. The striking of the long-case clock in the corner would be the cue to lay aside their books of sermons. Not even netting or knitting was allowed on the Sabbath. At one minute before nine, the door-knocker sounded. "Who on earth could be calling at this hour of the night?" Mabel wondered. One would think it were midnight at least.

"Clivedon, of course, ninny," her sister informed her. "No one else we know would consider a call in the middle of the night eligible. I am remarkably glad he sent you to me, Lady Barbara. I was afraid, when Lady Withers spoke to me of the plan, he meant to send you to her, and she is a sad, runabout creature. You would not want to stay with her. It would ruin your chances for a good match, meeting nothing but rakes and rattles." Barbara listened, wondering which of the few octogenarians she had been introduced to her cousin was lining up for her. "Ah, Clivedon," the dame continued, assessing her caller's bow as he came in.

"Good evening, ladies. Sorry to importune you at such a *farouche* hour. I was driving past on my way home from my visit and, as your lights were still on, I hoped I caught you before retiring."

"We were about to retire," he was told, while Barbara figured that if he was on his way home from Kent, he had not been passing by, but had come several miles out of his way.

"I shan't detain you a moment. Merely I wanted to inquire how Lady Barbara is getting on." He glanced at her, a fleeting look only, but long enough for her to glimpse the laughter in his eyes, before he turned back to the hostess. "You are to be congratulated, ma'am. She looks improved already. I can see you have followed my wishes and not let her stay up till all hours."

"I must confess we didn't get into our beds till after ten last night," Lady Graham admitted. "But we attended the late service this morning to catch up on our rest. Lady Barbara got her ten hours, and will have eleven this night."

"Excellent." He smiled, looking about for a comfortable seat and finding none. The one sofa held the mandarins, while Lady Barbara sat on a hard-backed, unpadded seat that gave a view from the window. She had been sitting there since before darkness had fallen, looking into a perfectly empty road. He took a matching chair beside her.

"I hope you enjoyed the house party at Oak Bay, Clivedon," she said. "I didn't realize, when you left us, where you were going, or I would have wished you a happy visit."

"I have already spoken to you about that, Lady Barbara," Lady Graham intervened. "About treating Lord Clivedon with respect."

"I hope I show no disrespect to apologize, ma'am," Barbara said, wondering what freakish nonsense she was to hear now.

"You called him Clivedon! Watch your manners, missie. *Lord* Clivedon is what you should call your elders."

As Clivedon showed definite signs of displeasure at this allusion to his age, Barbara was not tardy to make the desired change, and use it at every chance. But the chief mandarin had soon taken control of the conversation again. "One would be sure of a good time at Oak Bay. The Haddons are not such loose-livers as most one meets. They would not be keeping you up till all hours, and expecting you to dance and gamble. I am very happy to see you settling down with Lady Angela, Clivedon. Bring her to call on me one day."

He inclined his head in obedience, without the least intention of obliging the lady, then turned back to Barbara. "I hope you enjoyed the museum?"

"Fascinating."

"There were a great many bucks lurking about," Lady Graham told him. "I am not at all sure we ought to have gone unaccompanied, but no harm came of it. I gave them a hard stare, and they didn't pester Barbara. I kept Mabel on one side of her and myself on the other. The concert was more to our taste."

"To your taste as well, Lady Barbara?" he inquired solicitously.

"Delightful," she answered, in a pinched voice. "I quite look forward to the trip to Burlington House to see the marbles tomorrow as well. Do you come with us, Lord

Clivedon?" There was a menacing spark glowing deep in her eyes. "There is a matter I most particularly wish to discuss with you."

"What matter is that?"

With a quick look towards the ladies, she answered, "Financial. It is rather important. May I expect to see you tomorrow?"

"Ho, Clivedon will keep a sharp eye on your money, miss. Don't worry your head about that. He handles all my investments for me. An excellent manager."

"Thank you," Clivedon said modestly. "I would be delighted to see the marbles again, but unfortunately I am otherwise engaged in the afternoon. I could come in the morning for an hour. Shall we say eleven, to allow you time to get your rest? That does not conflict with your plans, Lady Graham?" he asked politely.

"We had certainly not planned *two* outings in one day. We shall be here in the morning."

"Eleven is fine with me. I look forward to it," Barbara told him, with a level eye and a certain intonation in her voice that caused him to smile.

"So do I look forward to it. I really must go now. Pray forgive the late call. Ladies." With a bow, he was off, and as the clock had struck nine during his visit, there was no delay in getting the two lamps extinguished and getting up the stairs to bed, with the aid of one candle between the three of them.

A second early night was not so easily lulled into sleep as a first. At ten, Barbara was still awake, and at eleven she was aware that she would not close an eye for several hours. She had ample time to work herself into a temper. Some traces of it were still with her when Clivedon called the next morning at eleven. But till she was in his curricle she uttered not a word the mandarins could object to.

Before she said a thing, Clivedon turned to her with a rallying smile. "Do you know, you amaze me," he said simply. "I couldn't believe my eyes, to see you sitting with a book on your knees, and not throwing it at that woman's head. I was sure I would find the bird had

31

flown the coop when I stopped last night. I had already changed my team preparatory to dashing off to find you. When you didn't even point out that Mecklenberg Square is not en route from Kent to Grosvenor Square, I was afraid they had broken your spirit. What possessed you to knuckle under so easily?"

She hardly knew what to make of this speech. "You realize full well you have placed me in an intolerable situation, in other words, and I should like to know why you have done it, Lord Clivedon."

"Lord me no lords, if you please. I will be happy to explain. When a young lady has managed to tarnish her reputation, it requires some outstanding show of virtue to recover its luster. I hope a Season with Lady Graham may prove effective, with, of course, Mabel to guard your sinister side. Sinister in the heraldic sense, that is. Your left side is all I meant. In any case, this will be either the makings or ruin of you. If you mean to abandon yourself to a life of dissipation, you might as well do it quickly and have done. While you live in limbo, your relatives all worry about you. If, on the other hand, you reform, then we shall all rejoice and trot out the fatted calf, in the usual way of greeting a reformed profligate son—or daughter. Which is it to be, Lady Barbara?"

"I am not a profligate, thank you very much for the description. Neither am I an eighty-year-old relict, to be consigned to Mecklenberg Square and Bible readings three times a day. I have borne it for forty-eight hours, which is about forty-seven and a half more than *you* could do, and my patience is at an end. I want you to send me somewhere else. *Anywhere* else. This is too much."

"I confess I chose the most upstanding of my relatives to test you. You did better than I had any reason to expect. Consider it an ordeal by fire—endure it a little longer and I shall let you go to Lady Withers. It *is* the measles after all, confirmed beyond a doubt now. Before too long it will be safe for you to go there. Agreed?"

"You cannot have been listening, Clivedon. I said my

patience is at an end *now*. I will not eat another soft pudding or another crust to curl my hair; I will not be chided like a schoolgirl, and I will not go to bed at nine o'clock. Don't think you're going to make a Miss Mabel Mouse out of *me!*"

"Dear girl, no one tries to make dross from gold."

"Compliments are cheap, and ineffective. I will not stay another day. It is up to you whether you wish to be saddled with a female of *undoubtedly* tarnished reputation, as opposed to the ambiguous patina I seem to wear at the moment. Don't think I mean to back down. I don't. I hold cards of invitation to a ball at Farrow's tonight and a rout at Lady Sefton's the next. I have been invited to a picnic at Richmond Park—"

"You are apt to miss *that* date. Richmond Park, if I recall aright, is easily forgotten by you."

"I can't imagine what you are talking about," she answered, glancing off to the left to wave at a passing acquaintance, to conceal the flush she felt creeping up her neck. Two years, and he still remembered!

She waited to hear what he would say about it, but the subject was dropped like a hot coal. "As it happens, I plan to attend Sefton's rout and the Farrows' ball myself. I shall take you."

This was the sort of time she had envisioned, and her lips turned up softly at the corners. "Will Lady Angela permit it?" she asked boldly.

"I am hardly in a position to ask her permission for anything. I trust she will not object to your coming along with us."

"I shan't mind having her along either, to keep me nice and proper. Lady Graham has a high opinion of her, I can tell you. If ever you wish to trim her into line after the wedding, send her to Lady Graham. They will deal famously."

"We do not speak of a wedding yet, and it is in any case unlikely in the extreme she would ever require trimming into line."

"No, waking up is more like it."

He got astride his high horse at this remark and asked, "What was it about your money you wished to discuss?"

"I want you to arrange funds for me. I owe Mademoiselle Celeste twenty guineas for bonnets, and as I mean to buy a new one this week as well, I ought to pay her something on my account."

"Don't worry about your accounts. I have taken care of all that. As to a new bonnet, however, that will be impossible. I have already told you I have cut off your accounts. There is nothing wrong with the bonnet you are wearing. You don't require a new one."

"Do you intend overseeing my wardrobe as well as my accounts? Next you will be selecting my gowns."

"Censoring, not selecting. I had Agnes go through your trunks before they were sent to Lady Graham's place. Those we disapprove of are not amongst your things. You didn't miss the half-dozen we considered unbecoming to an unmarried lady?"

"You went through my personal effects! Rummaged through my trunks! Upon my word—"

"No, no, you misunderstand the matter. *Agnes* did the rummaging, and selected for my perusal those gowns she thought too low-cut. Only the things you will be wearing in public. If you wish to outfit yourself in black lace in your boudoir, I haven't a word to say about it."

"My peignoirs are none of your business!"

"Yes, I have just said so."

"You shouldn't have been looking at them, then."

"I had no intention of doing so, but my sister considered it such an odd thing to find that she brought it with the gowns to show me. Hardly an object one would think to see in a maiden's closet, but in that of a light-skirt."

"You would know more about that than I. It happens the peignoir was a gift."

His hands tensed on the reins, causing the horses to jolt. "If you are accepting such gifts as that from men . . ." he said, in an awful voice, and seemed unable to go on.

34

"Frenchmen have very different ideas on what is suitable to give a niece for a gift. My great-uncle Montaigne, who is seventy-five, gave it to me in Paris."

"You would do well to be rid of it," he said, in a somewhat mollified tone.

"Perhaps Lady Graham would like it," she answered blithely. "May I know what gowns . . . Clivedon, if you have taken my new green Italian silk!"

"It was the first to go. Green never did suit those blue eyes, Barbara. And it wouldn't make a jacket for Lady Graham either."

"I mean to wear it to Sefton's rout!"

"Did you? Might I suggest the blue jaconet instead. For a rout party, a muslin will do, and it is highly garnished and low-cut enough to be obviously *not* an afternoon gown, despite its having been worn for one."

"Where are my gowns? What have you done with them? If you've burned them, I'll—I'll get an edict against you."

"You mean a warrant for my arrest, I expect. The gowns are not burned. They will do well enough for a married lady, or a confirmed profligate, as the case may be," he told her. "Where would you like to go for this drive, by the way? Bond Street?—No, it will only call to mind your lack of funds, and I am already bored with that subject. Let's make it Hyde Park."

"I don't care where you take me, so long as it isn't Burlington House."

"I wouldn't dream of stealing the thunder from Lady Graham's treat."

"You are *hateful!* You've dreamed up the dullest possible things for *me* to do, while you—"

"No waltzing or gambling at Oak Bay," he reminded her, with a fleeting smile. "Don't overestimate my weekend's gaiety."

"I bet Lady Angela gave you a hand with my timetable."

"I take the entire credit for myself. No, to be fair, the concert of ancient music was not my idea. I had suggested

35

the lecture of the Philosophical Society, but your hostess felt there would be unsavory literary types lurking there. Never mind, you will have a chance to waltz tonight and complain to all your beaux what a tyrant I am."

It was all that kept her from doing something utterly foolish. She looked forward to going to parties with Clivedon—it would set her higher than she had recently been perching, and she was curious too to see how he behaved with Lady Angela.

"Getting over your sulks?" he asked. "Come, this is your last chance till tonight for any decent conversation or show of temper. Better take advantage of me. *It* is what I meant to say."

"It's impossible to talk to you."

"How do you know? You never tried. Oh, you've flirted with me in the past and lectured me in the present, but we have never talked. Now, as your guardian, I should like to know a little more about you. What is it you enjoy to do? What sort of people and music and books do you like?"

"I like to waltz, to go to parties and be gay. I like amusing, lively people and music and books. Who does not?"

"I see." His answer was light, like her own, almost offhand, but she sensed she had wasted an opportunity to know him better. It was not often she was invited to partake of rational conversation. She was angry with herself suddenly, to have been so flippant. She didn't like those things she mentioned, not to any great extent. She liked the country better than the city, liked riding better than dancing, she preferred good conversation to gossip, too. Most of all, she would like to feel she belonged somewhere, that there was a spot in the world where she was more than a bothersome guest. She wanted someone to love, and to love her, but she could hardly say so to a near-stranger, and a hateful, heartless stranger at that.

"You enjoy travel, I think," he mentioned, but in a halfhearted, make-talk sort of way.

"I do not much like it," some perversity caused her to say.

"You do a fair bit of it."

"When the people you are staying with travel, you have to either go with them or cause a great bother, trying to find someone else to billet yourself on. There is no saying either that you won't end up at Mecklenberg Square," she added tartly.

"Where would you prefer to end up?"

"At home. At Drumbeig. But it is too far away, and there is no one to take me."

"Did Fannie never take you home?"

"No, not once," she answered, feeling very sorry for herself, and letting some trace of it creep into her voice.

"What is it like, Drumbeig?" he asked, with enough interest that she answered in considerable detail.

"It's beautiful—away north in the Cotswold Hills, in Oxfordshire. Excellent riding of course, rough and rugged terrain." She spoke on at length, mentioning her friends there, and as he posed a few thoughtful questions, she was soon relating to him episodes from her very childhood.

"I have a hunting box not too far away from your place," he mentioned. "It is beautiful countryside. Was there no one you might have stayed at home with after your father's death?"

"It was nearly time for me to be presented—everyone said I should be, and as father was—was seeing rather a lot of Fannie at the time, he left me in her charge."

"How old were you when you went to Fannie?"

"Seventeen. I was presented at seventeen. Fannie thought it old enough. I was at Devonshire House a year before that, when my father was still alive, but ill. He had to be near the best physicians. Dr. Ward had him in his private sanatorium, and he wanted me to be close enough to visit him often. I stayed half a year there after his death, and half a year with Fannie before I made my come-out. She said it would help me forget him, going to parties and balls."

"Did it?"

"I didn't try to forget him. My happiest memories are of my father. I was very young when my mother died. I have nearly forgotten her, though Papa used to say I was very like her. No, I do not want to forget the best friend I ever had. I am sorry his memory is growing dim in my mind. I have no picture of him in London. Sometimes I can hardly remember how he looked."

"I must apologize for leading you into this conversation. It can hardly be amusing for you, and you have told me that is what you like, amusing talk and people."

"If you feel a fit of apology descending on your shoulders, apologize for where you have sent me to live. I didn't mean to bore you with my autobiography."

"It was not at all boring."

There was less talk on the return trip. Each was sunk in his own ruminations, Barbara of her past, Clivedon trying to remember her then. Seventeen was a young age for a country girl to have been thrown to the London wolves. An impressionable age too, just at the edge of womanhood. He had only the haziest memory of her at that time. Young enough himself that he was interested not in girls but very dashing older ladies. He recalled a few amusing incidents, but perfectly harmless. Galloping instead of trotting in the parks, being a little rowdy and countrified at polite do's. He felt a strong and utterly futile wish that he had known her better then. Or even two years ago, before she had fallen in with the Continental set. It was only recently she had become the infamous Babe Manfred. If there was any good fiber left in her, she'd straighten out. He didn't think the twig was so inalterably bent that it was impossible.

In the afternoon she went dutifully to examine once again the Elgin Marbles, and agreed verbally with the mandarins that it had been a wise purchase, while mentally balking at the high price paid for these smashed relics of antiquity. Yet there was a strangely compelling beauty in the carvings. A peaceful order that was sadly lacking in her own disordered life. It was restful to see

38

those shepherds and athletes caught in their prime, beautiful and immutable forever in marble. Never to grow old and have circles under their eyes. Never to be running into scrapes. How peaceful it would be to be a statue, she thought.

Five

Barbara was not at all fagged when the hour for the Farrows' ball rolled around. She thumbed through those gowns that still remained to her, selecting a deep blue that matched her eyes and set off her pale coloring. Harper did her hair up high on her head, held in place with a pair of sapphire-tipped pins she had had made to her own design at Rundell and Bridges. She was happy Lady Withers had not considered this gown too risqué. It was one of her favorites. Lady Graham, when she beheld her first sight of it, was not of the same mind.

"You're surely not taking Barbara into company half naked!" she exclaimed, horrified with bare shoulders and no sleeves.

"It is the style this year, Cousin," he explained with a bemused smile, finding no fault in it.

"You men are all alike, always in favor of any style that shows you parts of a lady's body you shouldn't see."

"Barbara has a shawl. Better put it over your shoulders," he advised her, with a shared look that did not augur his expecting her to keep it there long.

"A French style, I daresay," the old dame scolded, while Mabel risked a little smile of approval. Recalling her guest's mixed parentage, Lady Graham went on to mitigate her insult. "Not that I mean to say the Frenchies are *all* bad. They are very wise about money. Tight as drums, or so I have heard. Not so bad as the Austrians, with that wicked waltz they have invented. Ladies and gentlemen holding onto each other in public. You won't let Lady Barbara *waltz,* Clivedon?"

"Certainly not!" he answered at once, feigning great shock. When he saw the young lady's lips open to object, he rapidly spoke on. "Nor shall I waltz myself."

Lady Graham shook her head in approval. "And I want her home early, mind."

"Don't wait up for her, ma'am. I wouldn't dream of keeping you up past midnight, and these do's often go on till one, you know."

He had no notion of leaving a minute before two, and neither had his companion. "Just leave the door on the latch. Harper will be up," Barbara mentioned.

"The butler will be up. I couldn't sleep with the door on the latch without Smudge up to guard us. One o'clock, eh? That is very late. Too late for me," Lady Graham decreed.

They escaped into the night. "This is hardly worth the trip, if we are not to waltz and be home at one o'clock," Barbara offered.

"I didn't want to shock the old girl. Better cover up those naked shoulders," he joked, as they settled into the carriage.

"Deceitful creature! To hear her praise you . . ."

"And *you!*" he informed her, lifting a finger. "She was kind enough to tell me you were not nearly as wild as she had been led to expect."

"I wonder who gave her that reading of my character. It wouldn't do to suggest it was yourself."

" 'A trifle headstrong' is the phrase I used, but then, she knows you are not completely English." They chatted with no altercation till they reached the city.

"Where does Lady Angela live?" Barbara asked. "We are to pick her up, you said."

"No, no, she does not come with us. She goes with her mother. We'll see her there."

Barbara thought that if *she* were Clivedon's girl friend, she would have something to say about this arrangement. Lady Angela, she assumed, was built of sterner, or more polite, stuff than herself.

No time was wasted to find Angela once they had been announced. He walked directly to her side. "You are acquainted with my cousin, Lady Barbara, I think?" he asked her.

The two girls had met casually several times over the years, for they had both been on the town for some time. Though they were each daughters of an earl, each youngish and attractive, they had never been more than nodding acquaintances. Angela was not precisely a prude. She was fashionable, and a good horsewoman, but she held herself rather high. She had never been to a masquerade, and had no desire to attend one. Almack's was her preferred spot for socializing, and while it was very prestigious socially, it had a reputation for dullness. "We have met," Angela allowed, and offered her hand with a smile that was polite without showing the least warmth.

A quick appraisal of toilettes took place between the two, with Barbara wishing she had worn white—so well it looked against Angela's dark coloring. But it made herself look like a ghost. Angela thought it was time she abandoned white and broke into some livelier hues. She was sick to death of white.

Clivedon's duty was to stand up with one of them and find an escort for the other. His preference, which he had soon translated into a duty, was to partner the lady he had escorted to the ball, but Lady Angela had put a hand on his arm in a very possessive manner, and disengaging himself proved difficult. The whole happened so quickly it was no more than a fleeting thought. A young gentleman hurried forward to make his bows to them while they were still saying good evening to each other. He was Lord

Ellingwood, a cousin of Angela's and considered one of her court, though he did not, in fact, care any more for her than she cared for him. They were of the same age, and thus the lady found him a child and he thought of her as an older woman. It was in Barbara's direction that he was smiling shyly. Being somewhat a backward fellow, he was strongly attracted to comets, the more dashing the better. He was not ill-favored. He was tall and well enough built, with a passingly handsome face that one was inclined to forget as soon as he left the vicinity. Of much more importance than all this, he was a baron and he was in possession of a good fortune that was likely to become better when his two aunts departed the world. He asked for permission to accompany Lady Barbara for the opening minuet. With no visible disappointment, she accepted.

She found him remarkably dull, but her disappointment faded when she saw Colonel Gentz across the room. She had not the least suspicion he would be here, and for a few weeks he had been her closest companion. She wanted to regale him with the tales of her recent trials. She had thought he would be at Burrell's with Fannie and Bagstorff, and even if he remained behind, she would not have expected to meet him at such a proper do as this. But she was happy to see him walking towards her at a brisk pace as soon as the dance was over.

"Babe!" he said, taking her hand and squeezing it. "Where the devil have you been hiding yourself all weekend? I went around to Withers', but learned you were not there as Fannie thought. Lady Withers mentioned someone called Graham, but couldn't give me the address."

Babe rapidly concluded that the address had been withheld on purpose, and considered giving it to him. No, Lady Graham would dislike this foreigner, and one's hostess must be taken into consideration. "I am living in the wilds. You would need an Indian guide to find me," she laughed, trying to dismiss it. He pestered her a few more times, but found out no more than that she was somewhere north of the city. Ellingwood, forgotten, bowed himself away. When the next set began, she stood up with Gentz, with some little premonition that Clivedon would not like it. She realized her feeling had been correct when she saw him glaring at her from the side of the room and taking a close look at the colonel. The use of an army rank was a holdover from the Napoleonic wars. Gentz was now a civilian, outfitted in a black jacket like everyone else on this night. He was an older gentleman, in his mid-thirties like Clivedon, but seemed older. It was perhaps his Continental manners that lent him a slightly raffish air. They were elegant, almost excessively so when he dealt with ladies, and his dealings were mostly with ladies. His smile was just a shade too wide, his ease too pronounced, as though to proclaim he was not inferior to anyone. But he was tall and handsome, an amusing flirt. She enjoyed her dance with him but did not regret its termination either.

"When shall I see you again, Babe?" he asked. "I am *desolate* away from you. You know I only turned down the Burrells' invitation to be with you. When may I see you?"

"Do you go to Sefton's rout tomorrow night?" she asked.

"I'll try if I can wangle an *entrée* from someone. Maybe the fellow who got me a ticket for tonight's do can arrange it. You can't imagine how busy I have been, trying to find you, and worse, *get* to you."

That this should have been a trial told her clearly enough he was not entirely welcome in polite Society, and she regretted her former closeness with him. He grabbed her hand and kissed it violently, then darted away before any definite meeting was arranged.

Looking around to see what might have sent him off in such haste, she saw Clivedon advancing towards her, walking quickly. "Who let that mugger in? It's to get you away from the likes of him I sent you to Cousin Graham."

"There's nothing wrong with Theodor," she defended.

"That commoner in gentleman's clothing!"

44

"He is an officer, and, one assumes, a gentleman."

"He's a fortune hunter."

"He's not likely to weasel any money out of me at a *ball!*" she laughed. "Unless he has mastered the art of extracting blood from a stone, he isn't likely to get any from *me* anywhere else either."

"I hope you didn't ask him to call on you."

"I value my head more highly! La Graham does not care for foreigners—and a waltzing Austrian at that! *Tch-tch,* she'd send us both to church to be sprinkled with ashes. I suppose you are wondering who you can find to partner me for the next dance. Don't take your duty so hard, Clivedon. I see Welby there alone in the corner, playing with his watch. I'll go to him."

"It is no doubt that quarter-strain of French that urges you to be chasing after men, when you should better wait for them to come to you."

"*Sans doute* it is my blood's age, not nationality, that makes me so eager. I am no longer a deb who must sit batting her fan in a corner till she is asked to dance. We ape-leaders set out with our ropes and trap what we want. Ten to one someone will stop me before I get to Welby," she added, with a toss of her head to smile at a passing friend. Sir Lyle Covington immediately drew up beside her.

"Busy next dance, Babe?" he asked.

"*Lady Barbara* is engaged to me for the next dance," Clivedon answered, with a repressive emphasis on her title and name.

"Save me the next one, Babe," Covington said, unrepressed, and walked on.

"Pity we hadn't placed a wager on my finding a partner. I could use the blunt."

"*Money* is the more common and ladylike term for the commodity."

"I wouldn't like to be *common*," she answered, assuming a prissy face and placing her fingertips daintily on his arm.

"Or ladylike," he added.

"Now be fair! Has any lady this evening taken your arm so elegantly as I do, as though I can hardly bear to touch you? You have had a full half hour of ladylike attention from your other companion. Variety is the spice of life, Clivedon. Let me spice up your evening with some of my indecorous chit-chat. Balfour has just slipped out the door with Mrs. Harkness, and I am dying to see whether they left or sneaked upstairs. He *does,* you know. Fannie tells me he was caught practically in the act at Brockley Hall last month."

"Barbara! I wish you would think before you speak!" he said loudly, with a fearful glance around to see if she had been overheard.

"I *did* think. I was going to say caught with his pants down, but was afraid you might not like it, it is so graphically accurate. A little ambiguity in such cases is more delicate. Old York is well into his cups tonight," she added, with a careless glance across the room.

"The music is better than usual," he said, trying to divert her mind.

"Is it? I hadn't noticed."

"You said you liked lively music."

"I usually do, but I was standing up with young Ellingwood, you know, and he has three or four left feet, poor boy. I had to concentrate on outmaneuvring them all."

"He is five-and-twenty years old. Hardly a *boy.* Now, *he* is the sort I wouldn't mind to see calling on you. A nice, decent fellow. Well to grass, too."

She peered up at him from the corner of her eyes, to see if he was smiling. He wasn't, though he watched her with interest to read her reaction to his suggestion. What he noticed instead was how dark a blue her eyes were, and how long the sweep of her lashes. Soon he noticed a slow smile peep out on her lips, tilting them up at the corners, and without realizing it, a smile alit on his own lips.

"I *knew* you were teasing me," she said, in her low drawling accents.

"I was not! Twenty-five is plenty old enough for you, old lady, so long as the man is good and sensible."

46

"If he is *too* good and sensible, the age is irrelevant. He will not do."

His plans for her reformation were to lead the way to propriety by avoiding her old haunts and old friends and seeing her marry a gentleman who would continue the job. This would require a man of strong character and resolution. He came to see that the man must have as well a heart of stone, or she'd only deprave him. The expression on her face was a combination of mischief and laughter that struck him as very wicked and very French.

"Clivedon, let's sneak out into the garden and blow a cloud," she said, in a low, conspiratorial whisper.

"I beg your pardon?" he asked, stunned.

"I said let's sneak into the garden and blow a cloud. Smoke a *cigar*."

"You're a lady!" he exclaimed, in horror. "Do you mean to say you *smoke*, on top of everything else?"

"On top of what else? Good gracious, I don't duel or box or visit the men's clubs. One would take me for a hoyden."

"You *are* a hoyden!" he told her, in a louder voice than he intended using.

"Shh—you don't have to announce it so loudly. I didn't ask you to slip off to an hotel for the night, after all," she added, deciding to be offended with him.

To his infinite relief, the music began, and to his equally infinite dismay, it was a country dance, which romps he found sadly lacking in dignity. There was little dignity in either the dance or conversation that ensued for the next while, but there was much laughter and high spirits. At its end, Barbara was handed over to Sir Lyle Covington by Clivedon, with a worried glance after them to see they didn't go out to the garden to smoke a cigar.

He returned to Lady Angela. "You look worried, Larry," she said. "Is it your cousin that causes it?"

"Yes," he answered unhesitatingly.

"She is shockingly fast. Standing up with that horrid Gentz person. I don't know why you allow it."

He wondered how he might prevent it. "I wonder at

47

her sticking this long with Lady Graham," Angela spoke on. "She's past reforming, that one. She'll elope with Gentz one of these fine days, but at least you will have the satisfaction of knowing you tried to help her. No one can say it is your fault. You did your best for her."

"I wonder if I did. Maybe Lady Graham was a mistake. She sails a little tighter ship than I realized, and I knew she was no sybarite."

"A willful, headstrong girl like that, you mustn't give her an inch or she'll take a mile. If Lady Graham can't control her, no one can. I suppose she's pestering you to move her elsewhere, is she?"

"She is not happy there."

"Time will tell. I see Cousin Ellingwood is mooning after her like a puppy. I must hint him away from her. She'll eat him alive."

Clivedon had been thinking quite seriously of making an offer to Lady Angela. It was past time he married someone, and she was pretty, accomplished, a pleasant girl, he had always thought. He felt an unaccustomed dash of annoyance with her tonight. Looking at her closely, he thought her lips sat at a sullen angle. Her eyes didn't sparkle, and she hadn't said an interesting or amusing word all evening. "Shall we have our second dance now, or save it for later?" she asked him with a complacent smile.

The situation between them was growing to the point where he must either have her or start backing off. He knew in that instant he meant to back off. He had very nearly said, "Let's have our second and get it over with." Good God, what would she have thought if he had blurted it out? "Let us save it for later," he said, with a very polite smile.

When next they did stand up, she noticed no coolness in him. "Larry, I have been thinking if I couldn't help you with Lady Barbara. Go out with her one afternoon to give your poor cousins a rest. And in my position, you know, no censure will attach to being seen with her."

"I can't imagine why it should. You are social equals,

48

and should get along well." He knew this last for an idiocy, but was so angry with her tone he hardly knew what he said, but only knew he wanted to set her down.

"Where is she? Ah—she is with Ellingwood again," she said, looking across the floor. "Pity. I'll hint him away from her."

"If you wish to help her, Angela, that is hardly the way to set about it."

"Oh, but . . . Of course. Quite right," she said with a prim little smile that hid her anger. "I shall call on her tomorrow and drive out with her. Would that please you?"

"If it pleases you," he answered. Kindness, he knew, had nothing to do with it. She did it to ensnare himself, but he had sprung free of her trap, and felt lighter in spirit than he had all spring.

Six

The outing of the two young ladies together was not a great success. Lady Angela had a patronizing air about her that set Barbara's teeth on edge before ever they left Mecklenberg Square. The note sent over in the morning said she would call and take Lady Barbara out for a drive. It had not asked her if she would like to go, but told her she would. As Lady Graham had been threatening a trip to Exeter Exchange to see the lions and tigers, it was a relief to escape, but really, a tenth visit to other parts of the Tower was hardly more exciting. Lady Angela had her own team and sporting carriage, and considered hrself a notable whip. Being two years older than Barbara, she undertook to instruct her in the proper manner of handling the ribbons, and in a few other matters non-equine as well.

"Do you really think that bonnet . . ." she began, but stopped when she received a certain flash from her guest's eyes.

As sure as Barbara waved at a friend, Angela would mention something derogatory about the person. She was trying, in her way, to help Clivedon, but there was no tact or subtlety in her methods.

"I thought you might enjoy to see the mint," she explained, as she headed east.

"I wonder where you got that idea," was the frigid reply, and they had not yet been out a quarter of an hour.

"Just two ladies alone, we cannot very well go shopping, and in any case . . ."

"Yes? You were going to say something else?"

"Nothing."

"Clivedon has spoken to you about me, I take it? Has explained that I have temporarily outrun the grocer?"

"He mentioned something of the sort," Angela admitted.

"I see. Well, do you know, I'm afraid I might be tempted to walk away with a handful of samples if we go to the mint. Let us just drive through the park instead. It's free, so far as I can remember."

"If you like."

"If you are afraid of the traffic, I will be happy to handle the ribbons for you," Barbara suggested, in a spirit of pure mischief.

Lady Angela smiled with great condescension and said that would not be at all necessary, or wise. "You have had a few accidents with your own new team, I understand?" she said.

"Yes, for no matter how well one drives herself, there are always others on the road who drive less wisely, and cause accidents."

At four o'clock, they drew up to the barrier in the park, where it was the custom for the fashionable to stop and gossip and flirt. It was not many minutes before Colonel Gentz approached them.

"Babe, what a pleasant surprise." Even as he spoke, his black eyes slid to Angela, raking her admiringly and boldly.

Barbara made them acquainted, feeling annoyed that this most rackety of her suitors should have accosted her at this time. Her companion made it perfectly clear she did not wish to be on terms with the colonel. She quickly hailed up more genteel friends and, turning her back on Gentz, spoke only to the others. Gentz shrugged his shoulders and laughed.

"What are you doing with these poker-backed people?" he asked Babe.

"Suffering in silence," she replied, angry with the top-lofty tone of her companion. Lady Angela need not have made it *quite* so obvious what she thought.

"I had no luck getting a ticket for Sefton's do. When can I see you, Babe?" he asked.

This annoyed her too. "I don't know. We'll meet here and there, I suppose. And *don't* pretend you are languishing for me either."

"Where's your own carriage? We could meet here tomorrow if you drove out."

"I've been meaning to ask Clivedon where my horses and carriage are. I will need them."

"I'll be here every day, waiting for you at four. Come if you can."

"I will," she answered, but had very little thought that it would be possible.

They chatted for a few minutes. Then Gentz, realizing he was not wanted, took his leave.

"What a *strange* man," Angela said, discovering her right side again as soon as he was gone. "Some sort of a foreigner, isn't he?"

"Yes, an Austrian."

"Shocking manners, trying to flirt with me when I hardly know him."

"As to manners, we all slip up on occasion. Turning one's back on others is also considered rude."

"Shall we go?" Angela asked in a pinched voice. She saw she was having no luck in handling the hoyden. Lord knows she had tried, as she explained to Clivedon that same evening at Sefton's rout. "But she was shockingly tiresome. Would do nothing but go to the park and gossip with that old *roué*, Gentz."

"Was he there?" Clivedon asked angrily.

"She ignored everyone else the moment he arrived. I

think she had arranged to meet him. Really she wouldn't *hear* of going anywhere else. I tried to listen in on what he said, and I believe they were making another assignation for tomorrow. He said something to the effect that he'd be waiting for her."

"I'm glad you told me. I think it's time I put a stop to Colonel Gentz's wooing."

He did not stand up with Barbara that evening, but as they drove home, tired and both feeling rather cross for some reason, he said, "You neglected to mention meeting Gentz this afternoon."

"Your friend was less reticent, I see. I was sure I could count on her to do it. Did you set her to *spy* on me, Clivedon?"

"Certainly not. The drive was her own idea."

"I trust she will not be persuaded into another such poor idea."

"I didn't suggest it."

"Don't bother pretending you haven't been complaining to her about me! She let slip my little shortage of funds."

He mentally cursed Lady Angela's lack of tact, but aloud he said, "It was kind of her to take you out. Appearing in public with such people will be good for your reputation."

"It is very bad for my spirits! It is clear you have her in your pocket, and I trust you will whisper in her big ears that I have a carriage of my own, and can drive it better than she does, too. And that reminds me, where are my prads?"

"Your *team* is stabled at Lady Withers' place, along with your carriage."

"I want them sent to Mecklenberg square at once."

"That is impossible, I'm afraid."

"There is a huge stable there, holding nothing but a pair of tired jades. You are just being stubborn. They're *my* horses, and my carriage, all paid for now, thanks to you, and I want them."

"You had better speak politely if you hope to see them this Season," he answered in an imperious tone.

"How dare you treat me as though I were a child? Lady Angela, that paragon of prudery, drives her own carriage, so you can hardly call it fast behavior. What is the excuse for denying me them?"

"A sense of duty to the public. Three accidents so far this Season, isn't it?"

"If those nags are not at Mecklenberg Square tomorrow morning, Clivedon . . ."

"Yes? What dire threat do you dangle over my head? If your team and carriage are not there, and they won't be, you will sit home till I decide to call for you, or until Lady Graham takes you out." Yet he did feel rather foolish, depriving her of this perfectly acceptable sport. The high spirits of her team were an excuse; he feared she would take off if she had her own carriage.

"You refuse utterly to discuss it, then?" she asked, her voice nearly quaking with anger.

This was too volatile a temper to leave her in overnight. He sought to soften it. "Any lady may lead a gentleman, if she knows how to set about it. *I* will not be led by your locking horns with me," he suggested helpfully, and waited several seconds for a reply. When none came, he went on, "Well, and are you not interested to hear how I might be managed more effectively? Try a little tact, Lady Barbara."

"You are not seven years old, or twenty-seven, to be led by me."

"I am thirty-four actually, if you are interested."

"I'm not, but at thirty-four I cannot believe you will be misled by insincere smiles and an appearance of servility."

"Nothing is more repugnant than servility and deception. I suggest we form a truce. You are no longer a youngster yourself, but fast advancing out of your youth." She glared at him with snapping eyes. Even in the darkness of the carriage he could see a sparkle. "More lenience than could safely be granted a green debutante is perhaps owing to you. I concede Cousin Graham was a mistake."

54

"One of the Creator's graver mistakes, in my opinion. I daresay even He has a bad day from time to time."

In the concealing shadows, he made no effort to hide his smile. "With occasionally a superb day to make up for it. That is intended as a compliment to yourself, by the by."

"I was sure you referred to the creation of Lord Clivedon."

"Not a bad day either, but I withhold the word *superb* for His female works."

"Are you hinting that I am now to be released from Mecklenberg Prison?" she asked, unimpressed with these few efforts at gallantry.

"In a few days, yes."

"Do you mean it? Clivedon, this is not a trick, like your arranging those odious outings to museums? Oh, I wish I could see your face, then I'd know if you're serious. It's so demmed dark in here."

"*Very* dark," he emended.

"You didn't used to be so stuffy a few years ago. You weren't forever pinching at me then."

"I was not your guardian then. In my new position, I feel a moral duty to—"

"Fiddlesticks! It is not immoral to say *prads*, or *demmed*. I wonder what can account for these *angelic* heights your propriety is reaching."

"You accredit the improvement to the wrong source."

"It is no credit at all. I consider it a distinct liability. You are becoming a governess as well as a guardian. How very boring for you."

"You are too hard on yourself. You are a wretched nuisance; you were never a bore."

"It is very odd I'm not, for I am so often bored myself."

"When can you possibly find time to be bored?" he asked.

"It hits me at odd moments, right in the middle of balls or routs even. Like tonight, when Camfreys started telling me about his demmed—*very* superior hunter, which is a spavin-backed old jade, as everyone knows. I so wished to sneak out for a cigar."

"Did you do it?" he asked warily.

"No, I didn't think my governess would like it."

"But you have done so, in the past?"

"A few times, with Gentz."

"You shouldn't," he said, more mildly than she expected. "Bad *ton*. If anyone should see you . . ."

"Don't take me for a greenhead. I'd never get caught."

There was a longish and uncomfortable silence. "I don't sneak out for any *other* reason, and I know perfectly well that's what you're wondering, sitting there silent as a mouse, isn't it?" she asked angrily.

"It occurred to me."

"I knew, when you started to puff up like that—"

"I am not puffing up, and if I were," he said, unpuffing his chest, "you couldn't see it in the dark."

"I can feel it from here. You always used to take a big breath and hold it. Well, maybe I imagined it, but I was right."

"I don't recall holding my breath in the past."

"You nearly turned purple the time . . ." She stopped suddenly. "Oh, it doesn't matter. That is all in the past."

"Which time was that?"

"The time I was having a champagne-drinking contest with Lord Cherney. Gracious, and we only had *one* bottle between us. I could hold more than three glasses then, and a good deal more than that now."

"You have a good memory, Barbara. Odd you have forgotten Richmond Park."

She could see nothing in the dark, and was grateful she too was not on view, for she had a strong impression she was blushing.

"My good memory has not forgotten one thing. Am I to get my team back tomorrow?"

"Oh no. It is a truce, not total surrender. You will have to try more tact than bragging about your drinking. And smoking," he added in an ironic voice.

Seven

Lady Barbara got her team the next day, by the quite simple expedient of asking Lady Graham if she objected to having them in her stable, as Clivedon thought she would.

"I have no objection in the least. Where did he get such a notion? Mind, you must not drive out alone, Barbara. I shall send a groom with you, for I am too old to sit up on a high seat, and Mabel would certainly fall off. She has no balance or coordination. She never could walk across the street without bumping into someone. I used to drive a gig myself when I was young. Exercise would do you a world of good. Certainly you must have your rig sent around."

When Lady Withers received the note from Lady Graham, she complied at once, without a thought that Clivedon would dislike it. That same afternoon the blue phaeton was dashing into town, with a groom in ancient gray livery sitting behind to lend the driver cachet and an unaccustomed air of respectability. She drove down Bond Street at a careful pace to avoid any accident, while she looked about for friends or a guardian. When Lord Ellingwood waved, she pulled up beside him for a chat, for she felt just a little fear that Clivedon would take revenge on her, and wanted to appease him in advance.

"Can I take you for a spin, sir, or are you afraid I'll land you in a ditch?" she asked.

"It would not be too high a price to pay for the honor," he replied, feeling himself very chivalrous.

"Will it be the park, or the Chelsea Road?" she asked.

"Let us go to the park," he answered promptly. It was not often Ellingwood had such a dashing companion to show off to the town, and he wished to make the most of it.

Colonel Gentz had slipped out of her mind entirely, but he was there at his post, hoping for a glimpse of her, and was the first to accost her at the barrier. "Babe—good of you to come. You got your prads back, I see. Good show." They chatted for a few moments, and while still she leaned over talking to him, Clivedon reared up behind her carriage, in his own curricle, harnessed tandem.

It was sheer vexation that lent the rosy hue to her cheeks as she made them known to each other, and that caused her to babble a host of irrelevancies. Vexation had the opposite effect on Clivedon. He was next to mute with anger, but he managed to get out a few commands.

"Ellingwood, take that rig to my stables, if you please. Lady Barbara is coming with me."

"I have permission to keep my phaeton at Lady Graham's," she replied, with a bold tilt of her chin.

"Lady Graham is not your guardian, ma'am. She is only your chaperone. *I* say what you are to have, and I say the phaeton goes to my place. I will take you home. Come along."

Gentz looked on with the keenest interest. The embarrassing scene caused a smile to light on his face, and he observed Barbara eagerly to see what she would do. She thought there was a challenge in his look, an urging to come to cuffs with her guardian.

"Now!" Clivedon rapped out. His tone was glacial, but

she discerned fire beneath the ice. The next step, she feared, would be for him to remove her by force, and to forestall this degrading step, she spoke to Ellingwood.

"Would you mind terribly? Such an imposition, but you see this Gothic guardian of mine is an utter dictator. If I refuse to humor him, he'll send me to my room for the night with bread and water, and I wouldn't like to miss the play at Drury Lane. Shall I see you there?"

"I hope so indeed," Ellingwood answered, while Gentz took note of the fact as well. It was Gentz who helped her down from the phaeton, swinging her lightly in his arms, and Gentz again who aided her into the other curricle.

"Thank you, Theo," she said, embarrassed, annoyed, and also a little fearful.

"Always a pleasure, Babe," he replied, and lifted a hand to salute her as she was driven off.

"I hope you're satisfied, making a fool of me in front of my friends!" she said to Clivedon as soon as they began moving.

"You do a pretty good job of that by yourself. I have spoken to you before about Gentz. I now tell you categorically, you are not to speak to him again. If you so much as *look* at him, steps will be taken to remove you from the city."

"It is hard not to speak to one's friends when they are met."

"Yes, particularly when they are met by prearrangement."

"It was not arranged in advance."

"I have reason to know otherwise."

"You have been gossiping with Lady Angela again, I see. I marvel you two lovebirds can find nothing more interesting to discuss than *me*. I know well enough where you received this misinformation."

"The information proved accurate enough."

"I didn't *plan* to meet him there. I only meant to drive out the Chelsea Road. It was Ellingwood who suggested the park."

"He would not be hard to lead into suggesting your own wishes."

"I suppose you mean to use this as an excuse to forbid me my carriage."

"You have heard where the carriage is going. You may be sure no note from Lady Graham will see it removed to Mecklenberg Square. I use it as well as a reason to cancel this evening's play, as you were at pains to let Gentz know where he might find you."

"That's not why I said it! I was only trying to lend a semblance of normality to the very embarrassing scene you created."

"The scene was not of my making."

"Don't think you're going to run my life, Clivedon. I shall see whom I want. I shall go where I want, and I'd like to see you stop me."

"Keep your eyes open. You'll see it right enough."

At Lady Graham's, he told the dame that Lady Barbara was feeling unwell after a little accident in the park, which had caused the sending of her carriage to a wheeler. He said as well that her guest had decided to remain home this evening, to recuperate her nerves.

"She does look flushed," Mabel ventured, with a worried glance to her sister.

"Flushed? She is pale as a ghost. Certainly she shall have a lie-down," the chief mandarin decreed.

"A little broth and some bread and butter later on," Clivedon added.

Lady Barbara stood mute, but directed such a penetrating stare on Clivedon, from a pair of eyes blazing with fury, that he felt a little trepidation. What if all this suppressed indignation should discover an outlet? Before the other ladies, he could say very little, however. "As you enjoy driving in the park so much, I shall call on you tomorrow," he said. "A pity you must miss the play tonight, but there will be other plays. I shall bring you an account of it tomorrow."

To these overtures she did no more than look, unsmiling.

"She's had a shock. Best let her get to bed," Lady Graham said.

She was taken at once to her room, while her chaperone asked a dozen questions about the accident, and commiserated with her on the misfortune of a broken wheel. No one knew how to make a wheel or anything else nowadays. It was all due to moral laxity, and would not be changed till the world got religion. Any answers received were quite at random. There was only one thought in Barbara's head. She must attend the play at Drury Lane that night, by hook or by crook, and she wished, as well, to do it in Colonel Gentz's company. She would show that man once and for all who was in charge.

She had no ally in her plan. Even Harper would not assist her. They were not close enough for that. She must evade the ladies, and get from the edge of Somers Town to the heart of the city, without a carriage and without much money. How was it to be done? Her first move must be to allay suspicion. She would ask for a little laudanum to allow her a good night's sleep. She would close her door carefully, make her own toilette—unfortunately not so daring a gown as she would like to wear, thanks to Clivedon's interference—and she would get a note to Gentz. How she regretted not having given him her direction. She had several hours in which to make and revise her plans, but during that time, no idea occurred to her how to get a note to Gentz. At five o'clock, she saw the stage from Islington to London bowling past, and looked at it with rising interest. There would be another at seven. She would take it, and hire a cab from the hostelry to go to Gentz. No—impossible to call at a gentleman's home unescorted. She'd go to Fannie's. There was still a small staff on, and she had a key if they were not there.

She followed her plan, finding less difficulty than she had feared. Lady Graham, as it happened, approved of laudanum, and had a bottle on hand to treat an ailing tooth of Mabel's. This medication was poured into the pitcher by the bed and the toilette was begun. The hair was a long and laborious job, and her gown too, buttoned down the back, took an age to fasten. Getting past the saloon, with the ladies sitting before the grate, was the most dangerous step. It too was overcome, by remembering a side door, away from the butler. She ran a few hundred yards down the road, to prevent waiting for her ride right in front of Lady Graham's house. She felt startlingly out of place on the common stage, wearing an evening outfit, but though the passengers stared as hard as they could, they none of them said anything. She got a cab to Fannie's, and was admitted without using her own key. The small staff were not so surprised to see her as servants in a well-ordered house would be. Certainly it did not occur to any of them to notify her guardian. She had the footboy take a note around to Gentz, and sat awaiting his arrival.

Within an hour he came, smiling his approval. "Excellent, Babe! You can't keep a good girl down, eh?"

She took his arm at once to go to his carriage, and outlined her adventure as they drove along. "The *pièce de résistance* will be when I waltz into Drury Lane on your arm," she told him, with a triumphant smile.

"That's a bit heavy for me, my girl. I'll end up in the Court of Twelve Paces with Clivedon. Charming as you are, I'm not ready to die for you. We'll go to the Pantheon instead."

"No! It is for the pleasure of seeing his face when I enter that I have gone to all this bother."

"Have you considered what he will do in retribution?"

"What more *can* he do? He has me locked up in a prison, with my carriage taken away. He can only send me home, and I wouldn't mind that."

"He can do plenty to *me*."

"Pooh—he won't challenge you to a duel. Are you afraid of him, Theo?" she asked.

"Not in the least, but what is my reward for bringing him down on my head?"

"Am I not reward enough?"

"You would be, but one evening of your company is

hardly sufficient. Marry me—that would be more than enough reward."

"I may have to," she laughed recklessly, for she was beginning to wonder just what Clivedon *would* do.

"You make it sound like a penance," Gentz said, feigning offence.

"You would suit me better than some I can think of," she rallied, but said no more, in case he should begin to take her seriously.

The delays involved at every step of her flight insured a tardy entrance to the theater, which was exactly what she wanted. It was no surrepticious sneaking in, unnoticed in the confusion, that she had in her mind, but a noisy entrance to create the maximum of disturbance and gain the most attention. The curtain was about to arise. That hush of anticipation that precedes the commencement of the drama had fallen over the hall when Theo held the door of his box for her. The rest of his party was already there, a minor Russian diplomat and a female of doubtful background. Both were older, somewhat tawdry persons, not even friends of Fannie, and completely unknown to Barbara. She scarcely glanced at them. Her mind was on Clivedon and her eyes on his box, whose location she knew well. In common with several other heads, his was turned to view her entrance. She walked to the front of Gentz's box and remained standing a moment, to insure being seen, waving and nodding to a few friends, before turning to recognize Clivedon. His expression was hard to read, several yards away, but she could sense the tenseness of his posture. She raised a gloved hand and waved to him. He nodded his head almost imperceptibly, then turned away. She saw he was with his sister and her husband and another lady, not Angela. Someone asked at the last minute to replace herself, then.

She had been expecting an immediate and violent reaction from him. She thought he would jump up at once and come to her, make a clamor, and drag her home. He sat immobile, gazing at the stage as the curtains drew open, with every appearance of interest in the play, while his blood thudded angrily in his ears and he considered what he should do.

Whatever he did would be done in private, for making her once again the center of attention was not his wish. She had already been seen with Gentz, so the best course was to seem to be aware of her coming. No one would believe it, sitting with that motley crew of foreign nobodies. Agnes leaned over and poked his ribs. "Larry, what are you going to do?" she whispered.

"I am going to enjoy the play, and suggest you do the same," he told her, in a damping tone.

All through the first act, Barbara kept darting peeps towards her guardian's box, wondering if he had not seen her, and knowing full well he had. She was first deflated, then curious, and finally uneasy in the extreme. The first intermission seemed a very long wait, but at last it came, and she tensed herself for his visit, certain he would come to her. He left his box. When Gentz arose to do likewise, she told him she would stay behind, and was unhappy when he elected to stay with her. She waited, but when the door opened, it was only Lady Withers and her husband who came in and took up the seats vacated by the Russian and his friend. They were coolly polite, so distant that one wondered they should have bothered coming at all. They remained till the intermission was over, saying nothing about Clivedon, nor did Barbara.

When Agnes returned to her own box, she said to her brother, "I have done as you suggested and *tried* to lend her an air of respectability, but pray don't ask me to repeat the performance at the next break, for I couldn't think of a single word to say."

At the recommencement of the play, Barbara again risked a glance at Clivedon. He did not so much as turn his head towards her. What was going on? She could not believe he was going to *ignore* her move. Her nerves stretched taut as she fidgeted in her seat, having a perfectly miserable evening. She was grateful it was not a comedy being performed, for to have to try to laugh at such a time would have been impossible. The frown she wore was in keeping with the general mood in the theater, but its cause was unique to herself. At the second intermission, she could remain cooped up no longer. She took Gentz's arm to go into the lobby for a walk, and saw Clivedon standing with a large group of the very tip of society, chatting unconcernedly. Lady Angela, she noticed, was of the party. And still no attention was paid to herself. The uncertainty mounted, till she could stand it no longer. She started walking towards the group, Gentz clearly unwilling and trying to hold back, so that she was required to take his arm most forcefully, while her own insides were quaking. As she got up to the large party, she looked to the left, as though she had just that moment spotted Clivedon.

"Good evening, Lady Barbara," he said over his shoulder, in a polite tone. "Enjoying the play?"

"Very much, thank you," she answered with a challenging smile. "No doubt you are surprised to see me here."

"Not at all," he answered, and turned his head away.

"I made sure you would be surprised, as you *ordered* me to stay at home!" she said in a loud, sharp tone. There was an uncomfortable silence over the group, as the well-bred collectively wondered how they should pretend not to have understood her.

"Come along, Babe," Gentz said, urging her past.

"No! I want to hear what my guardian has to say," she answered, with a bold, questioning look at him.

"Your guardian will deal with you later," was all he said, still in a pleasant tone, though there was an edge creeping on to it. The black eye he turned on Gentz was less pleasant still.

"You see, you have been frightened for nothing, Theo," she said, with a mocking smile at her alleged protector.

"I was not frightened!" Gentz felt compelled to announce.

"Lady Barbara's guardian will deal with *you* later as

65

well, Colonel," the guardian said, in a low tone that sounded absolutely menacing.

Even the well-bred gave up any pretense of doing anything but listening and staring, their faces full of greedy curiosity.

Barbara began to perceive she had misread the seeming indifference that had greeted her earlier. She was struck with a sudden fear that even a duel was possible, for she had never seen Clivedon so quietly furious. His anger in the park was nothing to this. He looked exactly like the tigers at the Exchange, ready to pounce. "Clivedon!" she said in alarm, "it was not Theo's fault. It was my idea to come."

"Later!" he said, in a voice so charged with fury that it had an electrical quality to it.

"Indeed it is not his fault!" she repeated, more loudly, and more frightened.

"There is no fault in it," Theo said hastily.

Angela fixed her face into a proper pose and spoke up. "When a lady disobeys her guardian, most people would consider it a grave fault," she informed Colonel Gentz. Looking to Clivedon for approval of her championship, she was stunned to see the way he looked at her. "Well, certainly she should do as you say, unless . . ." But she could find in neither heart nor head any excuse for Babe.

"Lord Clivedon recognizes that *I* have some influence with the lady as well," Gentz said, and knew he had erred, though he was in fact trying to smooth the matter over. "That is . . . as . . ." There was a dreadful hush, while he stumbled to a halt.

"Oh, do be quiet, Theo," Barbara said, then laughed nervously.

"You were saying?" Clivedon asked him.

"As Babe's fiancé, my wishes are to be considered as well," Theo answered back.

"Fiancé! I knew it!" Angela declared.

"A joke," Clivedon told her, but neither his face nor tone was at all facetious. "You have not forgotten Lady

66

Withers' party after the play, Lady Barbara? I shall take you," he added.

Never was anyone so happy to hear the box boys announce the return to the play as Lord Clivedon was that night, unless it should be Barbara.

She turned and walked away, her knees like jelly. "Theo, what possessed you to say such a thing!"

"I know when I see murder in a man's eyes. He plans to kill me. He can hardly call out his own charge's fiancé. We are engaged, milady, at least until I get safely out of London. I'm off to Burrell's tonight."

"You can't abandon me! Oh, Theo, he will kill me instead! I know he will. I'm sorry I ever came."

"I wanted to go to the Pantheon instead. *You* are the one insisted we come here. I'll be lucky to get home in one piece. Don't tell him you don't plan to marry me till I am out of here."

"The thing to do is to leave at once and go to Burrell's, both of us."

"Suit yourself. I wouldn't mind leaving now, but I'll take you *home*. You are very lovely, *ma mie,* but you are not worth my life."

They had reached their box, but instead of entering, they went around the corner towards the stairs, to see Clivedon standing at the top with his arms folded, and a look on his face that invited trouble.

"Leaving, Colonel Gentz?" he asked. "What an excellent idea. I would do the same if I were in your boots, and I wouldn't stop running till I got out of town. Won't you join my party, Lady Barbara? There are six seats, and only four of us attended, so you won't have the pleasure of sitting on anyone's knee or the edge of the balcony railing, but with luck you will find some other means of making a show of yourself."

Gentz nipped off down the stairs, while Clivedon took Lady Barbara's elbow in a grip that left two bruises, as he led her to his box. "Can you behave yourself for thirty minutes, or is that beyond you?" he asked in a voice of mock solicitude.

"Clivedon . . ."

"Does Lady Graham know you are gone?"

"No, I sneaked out."

"Go into my box. I'll join you as soon as I have sent her a message. And you had better be there when I return."

As he wrote his note outside the door and dispatched it with a page, she hadn't much choice in the matter.

Eight

The continuing of the play, and perhaps Lady Withers' tact, which found her cousin a seat between herself and the wall, prevented any embarrassing questions till the play was finished. Before leaving, Clivedon found a moment's privacy to speak to his sister.

"I'll take the hoyden home in my carriage. She's apt to hit you and Joe on the head and nip off on you. Take Miss Millington with you, will you? I want to find out what Babe's been up to exactly, and rehearse her for your party. I don't have to tell *you* what to say."

It was not till they all left that Lady Barbara received a few congratulations from passers-by in the lobby. How had the story spread so quickly? But then, Babe's doings were always one of the major subjects of gossip.

As she walked quickly to the door, with Clivedon's arm firmly holding her arm, Lady Angela called to her. "Congratulations, Lady Barbara, on your engagement. Now I expect you will go to Austria with your cousin and her new groom. Is it to be a double wedding?"

Barbara was reduced to near incoherence. All through

the last act she had been asking herself why she had done it, why she had come to this play, why she had sought Gentz's escort, why *he* had proclaimed himself her fiancé, and most ominously of all, what would Clivedon do? That his retribution would be severe she knew very well. He sat like a stone Jehovah throughout the play, not looking at her, but with anger oozing from his silent form, settling about her like a fog, almost palpable in its intensity. Blinking at Angela, she answered, "No. Oh no."

"That was a joke, of course," Clivedon answered for her, very firmly.

"A joke? Why, it is the *on-dit* of the evening. I have heard it discussed a dozen times since leaving my box," Angela answered. Then she walked along by Clivedon, saying in a low voice, "What a scandal! It would be best to give a show of indifference. I warned you how it would be. Is there anything I can do to help?"

"If you can think of anything to quell the scandal, you are more ingenious than I," he replied, hastening his steps, till Angela fell back to rejoin her own party.

His carriage was waiting. He saw his charge in and took a seat opposite, while she sat holding on to the edge of the banquette, waiting for his attack. He was too upset to oblige her. "We'll speak later. You are to behave at the party as though nothing has happened. Don't apologize to anyone. Lady Graham knew you were going, gave her permission. We must hope folks are simple-minded enough to believe that. If this engagement is mentioned, you laugh. It is a joke. You understand?"

"Yes."

For half a block they went on in silence. "Clivedon?" she said in a hesitant voice.

"Yes?"

"Why don't you say something."

"We'll talk later."

"I don't want to wait. I want to get it over with now. Shout at me."

"I don't want you to arrive with red eyes."

"I'm sorry I did it," she offered.

"A little late for regrets."

"What are you going to do?"

"I am going to discuss it later. Be quiet."

She sunk into silence. She had done much worse than this in her life, and never felt the least compunction. But then others had not treated her stunts so seriously, made them a matter of disgrace.

If the play had been bad, and it had been perfectly horrid, the party was infinitely worse. There were the curious eyes prying, not the laughing eyes of Fannie's friends, but the censorious gaze of people from a different milieu. There were the sly questions, and there was Lady Withers, trying to smooth the waters and keep guests at bay, while keeping up some appearance of mingling. All her reserves of tact were called upon. Worst of all, there was Clivedon being so polite and solicitous, with always that menacing light in his eyes, that glare that ordered her to smile and talk, while her head reeled with what was yet to come. It seemed to go on for hours. There was turtle soup, the first of the season, always looked forward to with pleasure, but giving less pleasure than soft pudding tonight. Her head was throbbing long before it was over. The only relief was that Lady Angela was not there. It was odd she was not, as Lady Withers had mentioned she was invited. What had kept her away? When she mentioned it to Clivedon, he answered in his most cutting voice, "She is a little particular in whom she associates with. Need I say more?"

This was more than enough to pull Barbara out of her dumps. Don't apologize, he had said, and she had seen its inefficacy already in trying once to apologize to him. She hadn't done anything that awful that she would cringe and beg for mercy. No, and she would never have done anything at all if he had not treated her so abominably. Her spirits were higher than they had been all evening when finally she confronted Clivedon across the saloon, empty now but for themselves.

"Congratulations on a fine evening's performance," he began, on a sardonic note.

"Thank you, sir. It is but the first of many performances that will ensue between us if you insist on treating me as you have done."

"I tend to treat people pretty well as they deserve. I have not seen such a childish display of bad manners as you put on this evening for some time. If you had followed my lead at the theater and let on I knew you were coming, nothing would have been thought of it but that I was a little lax in what company I allowed you to keep. It was your flaunting in everyone's face that you were disobeying my orders, and that announcement from Gentz! Was that your idea?"

"No. I was surprised at his saying it. I rather think it was *your* friend's interference that gave rise to it. Odd she should have been so busy, as she is known to be very particular whom she deals with."

"You're quite sure you didn't plant the idea in his head?"

"Oh, the idea has been there an age, but I have not encouraged it."

"It seems to me that with any real conviction you might have removed it before now."

"He was only afraid you'd call him out, and thought propriety might deter you, if he were thought to be my fiancé. He is well aware how high you hold yourself, you see."

"Simpleton! That's not why he said it. He thinks to force my hand by that announcement."

Barbara had not set out to conciliate him, and was very surprised to see he had calmed down considerably. His next speech was hardly angry-sounding. "I think we smoothed it over as well as could be done, calling it a joke. Though, according to Angela, there was plenty of tattle. Hardly the first time you've managed to make yourself the center of vulgar attention."

"No, and not likely the last either," she answered very pertly. "What are your plans for me?"

"It *will* be the last, if you know what is good for you." A hurried discussion with his sister had decided him to remove her from Lady Graham to Agnes at once. The former dame was too old, too strict, and antique in her activities to hope to appeal to Barbara, and her home too was proving an inconvenient distance from them. He did not wish to seem to be giving in to her, certainly not rewarding her for her trick, but as he had previously mentioned the change, he hoped to imply he was only executing his own plans.

"I have asked Lady Graham to send your things here. You are too great a burden to foist on one of her years. My sister will keep you for the time being. And I will just drop the hint, she is not at all happy to do it. If you cause her the *least* bother, you will be sent packing."

"Who will be stuck with me next?" she asked.

"Running out of places where you are welcome, are you? Just as well you realize it. The next step will be for you to set up in a rented house with a hired companion. You may imagine what that will do to your reputation. You haven't been welcome at Almack's for several Seasons, milady. If you wish to continue visiting *any* respectable establishments, you had better change your tune."

"I could go to Almack's if I wanted to. I still pay my ten guineas a year. I stay away through choice, as it is so monstrously dull." Her name was still on the lists of the prestigious and highly respectable club, but she had been treated with such frosty civility at her last visit that she knew she was not far from being asked to resign. What was it had happened? Ah—she had sneaked a couple of fellows in the back door after eleven o'clock. That was her great crime. The doors closed at eleven, and King George himself might knock in vain after that hour.

"They are kind enough to take your money, in other words, as long as they don't have to take *you* along with it. If you are seen again in public with the likes of Gentz and that pair of libertines he had along tonight, you may expect to receive a cancellation of your membership in the mail."

"I didn't know who he would invite."

"A petty clerk who owes every tradesman in the city,

73

and a lightskirt more often seen on the stage than in the audience. Who did you expect he would ask? Princess Esterhazy?"

"Oh no, hardly one of the patronesses of Almack's, though, as one of his countrywomen, she was kind enough to stand up with him at an embassy party not too long ago."

"You may be damned sure she wouldn't do it at a more public reception."

"*Very* sure, Clivedon. No vulgarity, if you please. Lady Angela would despise it. And lay it at my door too. I am already in such disgrace with her that I shan't sleep a wink for worrying about it."

"I wonder you *can* sleep. If you had any conscience, you couldn't. You may imagine what Lady Graham has suffered this night because of you. You have caused my sister and myself great embarrassment, and tomorrow the streets will be buzzing with news of your engagement to a gazetted fortune-hunter. You are not his first choice either. He's already left one victim high and dry in Austria. I wonder if *that* is why he doesn't return. He seems mighty shy of a duel. But then, being pointed out as a jilt will hardly be a new experience for you. Pleasant dreams, Lady Barbara," he said, and arose to stride from the room.

She sat looking at the empty doorway, then arose and went out after him. A servant showed her to her room, where Lady Withers had laid out one of her own nightdresses for her. She had kept up a brave front, but was assailed with doubts as she got into bed. She had never been made to feel so guilty before, at any of her scrapes. Fannie would have laughed at tonight as well, but she saw that amidst people of Clivedon's sort, it was taken more seriously.

She knew Fannie's circle was not the highest circle. Some of her friends were hardly accepted at all in real Society. It had been otherwise before her connection with Bagstorff, but lately they had both been omitted from parties they had expected to be asked to. The new set, while amusing, were not the set she would hope to make a permanent alliance with. When she married, as she hoped soon to do, it would be one from the better society she sought. The fact was, when she received any offers, they did not come from the higher society. They came from the likes of Gentz. She had about run out of respectable friends, and made some resolution to improve. It would not be easy when she already knew Lady Withers didn't want her, accepted her under duress from Clivedon very likely, but she would try.

The morrow loomed unpleasantly. She would have to go and apologize to Lady Graham, and have a bell peeled over her for half an hour. What on earth could she say to excuse herself? Clivedon had spoken earlier of taking her to the park, but of course that outing would be canceled. She was angry that her carriage and team were still denied her, that her gowns had been taken away, and that she had no money, but she would *try* to be polite to everyone. And if she failed, she would go home to Drumbeig. It was of home that she dreamed when at last she slept.

Nine

Barbara was cross and irritable in the morning, with a combination of poor sleep and the visit to Lady Graham hanging over her head, but she adopted a polite tone as she sat down across from Lady Withers in the breakfast parlor. She apologized very civilly, then said, "I wish to visit Lady Graham this morning, ma'am. Will it be possible for me to use your carriage, or do you plan to use it yourself?"

"Visit Lady Graham? What on earth for?" Agnes asked, with a dreadful premonition that a trick was behind the request. That the dashing Babe should actually be going to apologize to anyone was hard to believe.

"To thank her for her kindness in having had me, and to beg her forgiveness for last night," she answered.

"I see," she said weakly. The obvious course was to accompany Barbara on this visit, yet she was strangely loath to pass so much as half an hour with the Tartar in the wilds of Somers Town. Larry was coming by; she would palm the unpleasant duty off on him. The wary face her

76

guest wore at this suggestion confirmed her suspicions as to the visit being no more than a ruse to get out.

When her brother came by, Agnes met him alone and voiced her fears. "It is undoubtedly a dash to Gentz that is in the back of her mind."

"He's left town. I called on him last night to hint him away, and he'd left for Burrell's, they tell me at his place."

"I don't suppose she knows that. If she finds it out, she'll be off after him."

"She's going to take close watching. I'll look after the visit today, in any case. She'll find herself stuck with carrying out her pious little sentiment of begging forgiveness. She'll be lucky if Graham doesn't take a stick to her back."

Babe was considered a very accomplished actress when she exhibited none of the vexation expected of her at Clivedon's escort to see Lady Graham. She did not harass him for the return of her phaeton or any money, nor do a thing but sit as silent as a jug all the way north, dreading the ordeal. The dame was very much on her high ropes, but after a lengthy, lively, and thoroughly enjoyable tirade, during which her erstwhile guest was suitably humble, even at one point hard pressed to blink away a tear, the Tartar accepted her hand. The whole world was rotten, she allowed, and this lady likely no worse than the rest, if the truth were known. At least she had the manners to come and apologize and the breeding to do it at once, as she ought. Miss Mabel whispered aside that she would miss her very much, and to remember to eat her crusts for the hair. Weak with relief that it was over, Barbara relaxed into some quiet conversation on the way home.

She was curious to learn whether she was a prisoner or a guest at Cavendish Square, and worded this question somewhat more adroitly.

"You may have callers and go out," he allowed, "but for the present, we would prefer you not see your foreign friends till this affair blows over. Agnes will determine who is to be allowed to see you, and she or myself will escort you when you wish to go out."

"I am putting you to a great deal of trouble."

"Not at all," he answered in a voice not quite sincere.

She was heartened to learn that she was not in such deep disgrace as she feared. She even had some hopes that she would see her phaeton again, if she towed the line. She was determined to do it. Their kindness was a better influence than harsh treatment. Eager to be liked, to make friends, she firmed her resolve to be an unexceptionable guest.

"You are quiet today," Clivedon mentioned after they had gone a block without any talk. "One of your fits of boredom fallen on you?"

"No, it is impossible to be bored today. Merely I am flattened with relief, to have the visit over. I worried for hours about it last night."

He could see she had lost sleep over something, and wondered if she had actually intended all along to do no more than see Lady Graham. She did not seem to be fidgety, as though she were forming alternative plans. "You have not forgotten we are to have a ride this afternoon?" he reminded her.

"Do you still mean to do it? I thought after last night . . ."

"Certainly I do. I am looking forward to a reward after this morning's visit. If *you* have changed your mind, you ought really to have let me know. Folks *do* appreciate being informed when an engagement is to be canceled."

She suspected a reference to Richmond Park in this speech, but decided not to recognize it. "You can tell me about the play, as you said you would. I didn't hear a word of it, I was so worried you'd kill me."

"Do I strike you as being so lethal?"

"More wrathful, especially when you kept putting it off. I own I feared the worst, to see you ignoring me at the theater and enjoying the play as though nothing had happened."

"Don't expect too coherent an explanation of it," he said, allowing a small smile to lighten his features.

78

"Clivedon, were you *acting?* I would not have expected it from you. I didn't know you were so deceitful," she laughed, easily lured into her customary high spirits.

He was not inclined to depress her. "There is a good deal of deceit and hiding of our true feelings necessary in polite Society, to soften the collisions of taste and opinions. We don't always confess to disliking a lady's uglier bonnets, or to admiring her more risqué gowns either, if she is a *young* lady. I once failed to mention as well that a certain duke was using a shaved deck at a game of cards. That one piece of politeness I have often regretted. There is such a thing as carrying civility too far. In matters of mores, where manners blend into morals, there is an ambiguous gray ground that is tricky. A young lady's behavior, for instance, often falls into this questionable gray area."

"How very wise you are," she congratulated him. "I have often been bothered by that myself, though I never sorted it out so clearly in words. I have often wondered how blind one should be in such matters. I expect I have not been blind enough, and that is why I have the reputation for being horrid, because I always *can* see very well when someone is trying to lure me on to doing something I shouldn't, and take him to task for it. I suppose the polite thing would be to ignore it."

"What sorts of incidents are you speaking of?" he asked, with the liveliest interest.

"Men, what else? They are the ones who will try to lead us amok. They will often want you to slip away from a polite party, and when you call them to account, they fly up in the boughs. You stand accused of either having jilted them, or been jilted by them. Fannie says I ought to make a joke of their tricks, but it goes past joking sometimes."

"You have been poorly advised by your last chaperone," he said brusquely. "In future I would like to be told if anyone makes such a suggestion to you."

Their promising chat soon disintegrated into a lecture, and the comfortable familiarity was all gone from it, as he hinted that a lady who behaved herself was not likely to receive the offers she spoke of. But she said not a word about Lady Angela, for she was quite determined to improve.

Fresh trials awaited Babe when they reached Cavendish Square. Lady Withers attended them, sitting amidst a welter of newspapers that strewed the sofa and spilled over to the floor, while she rooted through them in a state of distraction. "Larry! The worst thing! Barbara is truly engaged!" she exclaimed in a dying voice, with an offended glance to her guest. She shoved a paper into his hands, and he glanced at it briefly, his lips compressing into a line.

"This is your doings?" he asked Barbara.

"What are you talking about?" She grabbed the paper from him, to read in black and white that Lord Clivedon was pleased to announce the betrothal of his ward, Lady Barbara Manfred, to Colonel Gentz. "Clivedon—what does it mean?" she asked, round-eyed. "Who can have done this?"

"*You* didn't drop this announcement off on your way to the play last night?"

"Good God, no! And neither did Theo. Oh who can have done it?"

"It uses *your* name, Larry," Agnes pointed out. "It must be Gentz."

"No wonder he darted off to Burrell's!"

"I am sure Theo didn't do it," Barbara insisted. "He planned to leave at once. He only said it because he was afraid you meant to call him out, Clivedon."

"You are naïve. That was not his reason. He's barking up the wrong tree if he thinks . . . I'll go down to see him immediately, as soon as I have written a retraction to the *Morning Observer*."

"It's in the *Morning Herald* as well," Agnes warned. "I haven't found it in any others."

"Please do it." Barbara said at once to Clivedon. "I don't want to have to *marry* him."

"Pity you hadn't told him so!" he answered, his voice rising.

"I never said I would! Never had the least intention of it."

"Just when we thought we had managed to make a joke of it," Agnes lamented. "This coming on top of last night . . . I think Barbara must be taken to the country, Larry."

"No, it will only serve to confirm the rumor if we hustle her out of town to hide her shame. Best to print the retraction, and assume an air of injured dignity at *someone's* poor taste. If it was Gentz, I'll strangle him." He turned at once to leave the room, and was stopped at the door by Lady Angela, who entered holding in her hands two newspapers.

"I see you have already read it," she said, smiling. "I think we managed this pretty well. When you told me last night to do what I could to stop the scandal, Clivedon, I hit on the idea of getting the advertisement into the papers at once, that everyone might see this match had your approval. So odd for it to come unexpectedly from Gentz, in such a scrambling way, but this will show you were aware of it beforehand, had already sent the notices in, and it will look less shabby. It will be in the *Gazette* this afternoon as well. I went straight home after the play and wrote up three announcements, and had them taken around to the paper offices last night. It is why I missed your lovely party, Lady Withers."

There was a stunned silence. "You are amazed at my foresight, I see," she laughed merrily.

"I am amazed at your insolent interference," Clivedon replied, glaring.

"Interference? Why, you told me to do what I could! Lady Barbara's name is already in sufficient shade that a marriage without your sanction would finish her. She can hardly jilt the man, after he announced in public they were engaged. It is best to put a decent wrapping on it. Smile and pretend we are satsified. I daresay she and Gentz will rub along well enough."

"She is not marrying Gentz!" Clivedon said. "We spent the night convincing everyone it was an ill-advised joke."

"It was ill-advised for him to say he was her fiancé if

she doesn't plan to marry him. *She* didn't deny it. Certainly it was not seen as a joke by anyone *I* spoke to last night."

"You were busy circulating the story, in other words," Clivedon rounded on her. "You will have this morning's gossip cut out as well, explaining how you took upon yourself to make this announcement, without so much as *consulting* me."

"You told me to do what I could! It was an excellent idea. Mama and Aunt Cleo were in complete agreement with me. When you have reconsidered the matter more coolly, you will see it is for the best. Lady Barbara has been meeting him quite publicly at the park every day. It will be no surprise to anyone that she will marry him. Indeed, it will look extremely odd if she does not now."

"As to that, everyone is accustomed to oddness from Barbara," Agnes said wearily. "Perhaps it *is* for the best, Larry . . ."

"No, please! You *must* do something," Barbara implored, with a desperate glance to Clivedon.

"I suppose even Barbara will recover from *one* broken engagement," Clivedon said, then strode from the room to write up three retractions.

Angela trailed after him. "I am sorry if I did something you dislike, Larry. I meant it for the best."

"No doubt," he said curtly over his shoulder as his pen scratched quickly across the sheet.

"If there is anything I can do to lend a hand in the predicament . . ."

"No, I wouldn't want you lending any more hands."

"You may be sure *I* will not cut her. *I* shall behave as though nothing has happened. Mama will dislike it, but I shan't cut her only for this."

"Generous of you, considering it is yourself who put her in this fix."

"The announcement didn't come from me initially. I would just make sure she doesn't intend to slip off behind your back and marry him before I took that note around to the papers. You will look extremely foolish if that were to happen."

"Thank you for the suggestion. I shall bear it in mind."

"With a girl like that, you know . . ."

"Don't you have some calls to make now, Lady Angela?"

"Yes, I must run along. Sorry if I caused any bother."

"Not at all," he said, on a note of heavy sarcasm, and she left.

"I'll be back shortly," Clivedon said to his sister before leaving. "With luck I'll get the retraction instead of another announcement into the afternoon papers. If anyone calls, admit them and explain that this announcement did not come from us."

"I can't believe Angela would take so much on herself. But she meant well, of course."

"Very likely. It saves me the nuisance of pelting down to Burrell's to give Gentz a thrashing at least. I shall be on hand to smooth things over this afternoon."

"So unpleasant. I hadn't thought having Barbara would be *quiet*, but I didn't expect so much activity so soon."

"You should have!" he replied, and laughed. "We both should have. But really I think the worst is over, with Gentz out of the way. She is not completely lost to all sense of propriety, you know. We had a little talk this morning about men and morals. And Fannie—the trollop."

"Her going to apologize to Lady Graham was better than I expected of her. I wouldn't have had the bottom for it myself."

"Whatever else one may say of Babe, I never heard her accused of a lack of pluck. We'll squeak through, old girl." He tapped her chin with his letters, and left, smiling, which struck Lady Withers as an insensitive attitude to adopt to all their troubles.

Ten

It was a tight squeak, but over a few days the rumors of Lady Barbara's engagement were dead. She did not hide her head at home, but went on very proper excursions with either her chaperone or her guardian, sometimes both. With such companions, the engagement was no more than mentioned. It was only Fannie's old friends who teased her about it. "You sly rascal, Babe," they would roast her, "giving Gentz his *congé*. Some other fellow in your eye, eh?" But her old friends were finding access to her less easy. She was "out" when they called at Cavendish Square, and they were not met at the dignified do's she attended in the evenings. It was only in the park or at the theater that they accosted her. Lady Angela made good her threat and came to honor Lady Barbara with another spin in the park.

"Get that creature out of here," was Clivedon's order, and she was not allowed into the saloon. Barbara was relieved to be rid of the girl, but she noticed too that Clivedon could be remarkably ruthless when he took someone in dislike.

"She didn't mean any harm," Barbara offered.

"You are generous. Excessively so," he told her.

A week after the affair, Clivedon decided she had reformed sufficiently to be let out in her phaeton. To insure she did not take up any seedy foreign friends with her, he occupied the passenger's seat himself.

"Let us see how you handle the ribbons," he said. "I seem to remember seeing you bolt down Oxford Street out of control last month."

"They are not so biddable a team as I would like," she admitted. "I had them of Bradbury, and I *think* he was happy to be rid of them."

"Don't tell me this is the leather-mouthed set of grays Bradbury has been trying to be rid of forever! Barbara, I didn't take you for such a greenhead. What did you pay for them?"

"Four hundred."

"He offered them to me at three. He saw you coming."

They were a flashy team, high-steppers, and not noticeably bad-natured, but difficult for a lady to control. "We'll avoid heavy traffic today," he told her. "If you can learn to handle them on the quiet roads, you may try them in the city later."

"I have driven them in the city before."

"I know. I happen to be acquainted with *one* of the gentlemen who had the poor luck to be sideswiped by you."

"It was as much his fault as mine. He wouldn't give way to let me pass."

"And you couldn't hold them back. I see how it was."

As this was exactly how it had been, she ignored the comment and concentrated all her efforts to keeping them back to a trot, till they were on the Chelsea Road. They went along with no mishap for a few miles, which emboldened her to let them out. An easy canter soon stepped up to an outright gallop, at which time Clivedon suggested she rein in. "I'm trying to," she said, becoming frightened.

"Pull harder. Watch out for that gig pulling out ahead, there to your left."

She had already seen it, and was yanking desperately at the reins, which had the unwanted effect of inciting her team to greater speed. It was apparent to Clivedon as quickly as to herself that she had lost any semblance of control over them. They were flying down the road at a breakneck speed. It was less clear to the driver of the gig, who felt he had the right of way, and pulled into the main road before them, expecting her to hold back. Clivedon lurched wildly against her, in an effort to get the reins out of her fingers. She very nearly fell off the seat of her high-perch carriage, only managing to hang on by her fingertips. The added confusion of trying to lend her a hand left Clivedon only half his attention for controlling the team. The right rein fell from him entirely, and the unchecked horse galloped smartly into the ditch, pulling its mate with it, barely avoiding an accident with the rear end of the gig. The driver of the other vehicle looked over his shoulder, but, seeing the occupants to be unharmed, he proceeded on his way, with no more than a breath of relief and a quiet imprecation on the manners of the smarts and swells, who thought they owned the road.

There was a tense moment while they both waited for the sickening snap of broken wood or the creak of leather giving way, the whinnying of a horse in agony, or the shooting of a pain in their own bodies. They experienced only one of these omens of disaster. There was a shattering sound as the front axle snapped. Their own physical reaction was no more than a heart pumping tumultuously, and a sudden lurch as the carriage tipped. The runaway horses had pulled the carriage's front end off the built-up portion of the road, to tip at a precarious angle towards the ditch, with the axle broken, while one wheel spun futilely in the air, a foot off the ground below.

With Clivedon's arm still steadying her, Barbara wilted in shock and fright against his shoulder, shivering. He put his other arm around her, badly shaken himself. "Are you all right?" he asked.

Her head sank on his chest to gain her breath. In a moment she looked up, laughing nervously. "I couldn't have made a much worse mess than this by myself. Thank you for your help. We'd better unhitch this demmed team. I hope their knees aren't broken."

He half expected tears or hysteria, and was surprised to see her laughing. He was able to relax then himself. "It would save hauling them to auction. Sure you're all right?"

She tried her neck with a jerk of her head to left and right, flexed her elbows and knees, and proclaimed herself unharmed. "Better dismount carefully or we'll tip this whole rig into the ditch," he cautioned. He hopped down and steadied it while she descended. Together they hurried to the team to calm the nags and unhitch them.

"We're in for a walk," he informed her. "This front axle is snapped clean through where it hit the road-edge. The prads seem unharmed, but very nervous. Better stand back, Babe."

"Be careful, Clivedon," she warned. "Silver bites."

"Which one . . . ouch!" He leapt forward as the biter got her teeth into his forearm.

"Oh, did she hurt you? Horses bite so demmed *hard*."

"It was nine-tenths sleeve she got ahold of." Still, he was wincing with the one-tenth of the bite that was not sleeve, but his own flesh.

"What shall we do with my phaeton? Can we go away and leave it here?"

"We'll have to walk onto the nearest coaching house and have them come back for it. It's nearly off the road, and highly visible. You're sure you're not hurt?"

"Only my pride," she admitted.

"Let it be a lesson to you," he said, as they began to trudge down the road, leading the team.

"You may be sure I'll never ride with *you* again. Once bitten, twice shy."

"Surely that should be *my* line. I hate a horse that bites. What I referred to, of course, was my wisdom in not letting you career through town with this pair. We'll see if we can palm them off on some strong-armed gent at Tatt's, and get you something tamer. What possessed you to think you could handle them? You selected them yourself, you said. Didn't you try them before buying?"

"I didn't exactly choose this particular pair," she said, glowering at them. "I said I wanted grays, and a friend chose them for me."

"Gentz?"

"Yes."

"You were seeing a good bit of him, I take it?"

"He is Count Bagstorff's best friend, you see, and naturally he came to Fannie's with the count all the time, so I was frequently in his company, but it was not a—a romance. More of a flirtation, you could call it. We neither of us meant anything. He was very gallant and let on he was madly in love with me, but he didn't mean it."

"How do you sort out the phonies?"

"It's easy to tell when a man is shamming it. He thinks only of himself, and it comes out in little ways. He *says* all sorts of chivalrous nonsense, but doesn't go an inch out of his way to really please you. Talk is cheap."

"It seems to me you dragged Gentz several miles out of his way last week, hauling him up to Mecklenberg Square. How did you get a note to him, incidentally? I can't believe Lady Graham's servants would be so obliging."

"I didn't write him from there. I met him at Fannie's—sent a note from there."

He came to a dead halt in the middle of the road. "Am I to understand you met him *all alone* at Fannie's house? How did you get there?"

"On the stage, and in a hired cab from the stop. But we were not all alone. There were a few servants there. She hasn't completely closed up the house."

"Have you *no sense?* Meeting the likes of Gentz off in a deserted house!"

"It wasn't deserted."

"It easily could have been. Servants don't stick around twenty-four hours a day when they know their mistress is out of town. Don't you *realize* the danger!"

"But they *were* there."

"You didn't know they would be."

"I wouldn't have met him inside if they hadn't been. I would have waited for him outside, at the door."

"And changed your gown in the same place. Nice."

"Oh, no, I wore my evening gown on the stage."

"You're insane."

"Unconventional, not foolish, and not a complete flat either. I have been around for a few years, and know better than to meet a man of Gentz's kidney in a vacant house."

"You have no more sense than a child. It's that damned Fannie . . . It's a miracle you've kept out of real trouble for so long."

"If I were not used to a *little* trouble, you'd have me fainting away on you this minute, and I don't suppose you'd care for that. Lucky I am so used to accidents. I don't see any place to stop. I more usually smash up in the city. Maybe we should have gone in the other direction. There was an inn we passed not long before the accident."

"There's a place up ahead—the Gray Goose, it's called. It can't be much farther."

They trudged on doggedly, occasionally being passed by a carriage, but no one offered to stop and help them. The Gray Goose, spoken of as a little way forward, seemed to move along with them. Clivedon was certain it would be lurking around every bend in the road, but they had walked two miles before they reached it, tired, dusty and thirsty. They hired a room and called for wine and, while refreshing themselves, Clivedon arranged for the removal of the phaeton from the road. When he tried to hire a carriage to get home, there was none available.

"I'll have to send someone into town to have my own sent out," he informed her. "I'll send Agnes a note as well, to explain what happened. It will take a couple of hours. We might as well relax. Maybe we can get some cards to pass the time. I won't suggest a *walk*."

"I'll suggest a straitjacket if you do!"

"Cards it is."

"Good! This is my chance to make some money from you, to tide me over till the next quarter," she said happily. "Let us call for more wine and enjoy ourselves in the interval."

One bottle of wine had miraculously disappeared in

89

the quarter of an hour in which the difficulty was being straightened out. When the servant came, Barbara suggested champagne would be a nice change.

Feeling somewhat culpable in the fracas, Clivedon nodded his agreement to this. Champagne was brought, along with a well-used deck of cards, which she took up. They flew through her fingers as if by magic, while she shuffled and split like a Captain Sharp. "Before you suggest silver loo or all fours, let me inform you it is piquet we are to play," she told him. "Five shillings a point, and a guinea a rubber, to make it interesting?" she asked.

"That is likely to put you rather deeply in my debt before the two hours are up. Then, too, there is the matter of your being without funds," he mentioned, smiling at her expertise.

"You, as my accountant, must know my credit is excellent, as I am never allowed to use it. Naturally I shall pay you interest, in the *un*likely event of my losing."

"Naturally, at ten percent, but it is the custom to pay one's gambling debts without delay."

"That comes as news to me. I am sure a hundred people at least owe me gambling debts which they do not hasten to discharge."

"An Austrian custom, no doubt."

"Also a French and Russian custom. One not unknown to John Bull as well, I might add."

"You refer to the John Bulls who frequent Mrs. Duncan's den, perhaps? Bad *ton*, Lady Barbara, and bad business too."

"I only went once. How did you know it?"

"You know who my spy is."

"She wasn't there. Ah—Ellingwood! She got it out of him. He was there."

"Trampling on you with all those left feet, was he?"

"No, he was losing his shirt at the faro table. I bet he didn't tell her *that*."

They played as they chatted. He was surprised at her clever calculation of the odds. She played well, and quickly, having an uncanny knack for the right discharge
90

and guessing, or knowing, what cards he held. "That is your point," he was soon obliged to acknowledge.

"Also my quint, I think?" she asked, laying out five hearts.

"You are lucky."

"Luckier before you moved in your chair, hiding the reflection in the mirror behind you," she said, laughing. "*You* to be taken in by that old stunt. I gave you more credit for bronze, Clivedon."

"I didn't look for a Greek's tricks from a lady."

"That depends on the lady. And besides, I didn't have to tell you."

He was down at the end of the first rubber, and realized he was not playing with an amateur. With more attention, he took the next one, but it was not easy. Luck as well had something to do with it. He had been dealt a good hand.

"Good gracious! We've drunk up the whole bottle of champagne!" she announced at the end of the second rubber.

"What time is it getting to be? My carriage should be here by now."

He went to the proprietor, but it had not yet arrived, and he returned to play another around and order another bottle of champagne.

"I'm a little hungry after that long walk," she told him. "Could we not have some sandwiches at least, Clivedon? The customary fare of we who don't want our play interrupted. What a clever old gentleman he was, Sandwich, to have invented them."

As they were drinking a good deal of wine, he thought it not a bad idea to eat something. Sandwiches were brought in, and they settled down in good earnest for another hand. The proprietor was soon there to announce the arrival of the carriage, but as they were midway through the set, they neither of them paid him much heed. They played on. As Babe drank, her discards became somewhat erratic.

"Damme! I discarded my club-guard, and there you

steal my pique. I made sure I would pick up a king or queen."

"I didn't look for such carelessness from Captain Sharp. The wine is going to your head. Have some more."

"That is my rubber," he soon said.

"I'll take the next one."

"My carriage has been waiting half an hour. We'd better go. That is two out of three for me. You owe me one guinea and five shillings, lady."

"You're not going to cry craven on me and *quit!* Paltry behavior, not to give me a chance to make it up."

"It is getting rather late."

"Fiddlesticks! Your sister knows of our accident and won't worry about us. Let us order a new deck. This one sticks to my fingers. I'll think it a low trick if you don't give me a chance to even the score."

As Clivedon had not the least inclination to quit, but only suggested it from a sense of duty, he was not difficult to persuade to continue. The next rubber went well for Barbara, and she was crowing to him that after a *little* too much wine, another glass had the unaccountable effect of clearing her head. "Which has disappointed more than one gentleman," she added unwisely.

He looked up quickly, ready to lecture.

"Gambling partner, I mean, of course."

"Nothing but a cigar will clear mine," he replied.

"Well, for goodness' sake, why didn't you *say* so? Have one. Go ahead. It won't bother me. I like it. I'll have a few puffs myself, if you'll let me."

"I don't carry any with me."

"Stoopid! The servant will get you one," she laughed.

A cigar was brought, while they continued playing steadily, with a good deal of inconsequential chatter. The excitement of the accident, the unusualness of playing cards with a lady cardsharp, and perhaps the wine as well robbed the afternoon of any aura of reality for Clivedon. It was like a few hours out of the world, where convention was irrelevant. When she asked to be allowed a few puffs, he handed the cigar over without even finding it very odd, though he smiled to see her puff daintily, with short, light puffs. When there was a knock at the door, he called, "Come in," without even looking up, but only a glance to see the wine was gone.

"Bring us some coffee, if you please," he called over his shoulder. "We've had more than enough wine."

The stricken face of his partner caused him to look to the door, with still no horror that it might be anyone other than their servant. There, framed in the arch, stood Sir Edward and Lady Dailey, toplofty friends from the city, relatives to Agnes's husband, and famous in a small way for being interfering gossipmongers.

"Oh my God!" he said, dropping his hand of cards onto the table, with a wildly staring eye to Barbara, who appeared to be turning bright red. While he watched, she exhaled, and smoke puffed from her lips, while she quickly batted it away with her fingers.

Then she smiled nervously and curtsied, saying "How do you do?" in a strange, high voice.

"Clivedon! What the deuce is going on here?" Sir Edward demanded, shocked to the roots of his white hair.

While he demanded, his wife's eyes slewed around the room, taking in the empty wine bottles, the ashtray, the two decks of cards, and the crumb-laden plate, indicating a prolonged gambling session. Lastly she looked to the culprits, who did not realize till they looked guiltily at each other what an appearance they presented. Clivedon's hair was tousled from having run his fingers through it, and his cravate hung loose, jerked out of its knot an hour ago for greater comfort. Barbara was equally disheveled, her gown dusty from the walk and her hair mussed, with a few fine strands pulled loose to fall around her ears.

Lady Dailey's silence was of the ominous sort. She was rehearsing what she would say as soon as she got back to town.

"There was an accident!" Clivedon said, in a choked voice.

"That is why I stopped," Sir Edward replied.

"Good thing we did, too!" his spouse declared indignantly, finding speech at last.

Clivedon glared at her, and his shoulders straightened defiantly.

"I saw Lady Barbara's phaeton being dragged into the wheeler's down the road and heard she was here. I thought she might need a lift to town, but I see she is in no hurry to be rescued," Sir Edward said, in meaningful accents. Lady Dailey nodded her head in emphatic agreement.

Barbara felt once again the sting of hot water. She cast a mute eye on her protector, astonished to see his anger melting into a glow of mischief. He was nearly smiling. "No, no hurry at all, thanks just the same," he said. "As you see, we have been passing the afternoon pleasantly while awaiting my own carriage. It has just arrived, they tell me, and we shall be on our way."

"Is that a cigar you are holding, Lady Barbara?" the wife demanded.

"Yes," she answered, dazed.

"I never heard of a lady putting a cigar in her mouth."

"I never heard of one putting it anywhere else," Clivedon pointed out.

She quickly handed it to him. "She was holding it for me while I added up our score," Clivedon continued. "But if it offends you, Lady Dailey, I shall put it out at once. Or were you about to leave?" he suggested pleasantly.

This clearly formed no part of her plans. He butted it, and turned back to Barbara. "Well, do you know, we are even-steven? Two rubbers each. We'll finish it off this evening, shall we? Sudden death. We really must be getting on. Very kind of you to stop by, Lady Dailey, Sir Edward. Thanks awfully, but we don't require a lift to town."

As he spoke, he took the lady's arm and steered her to the door. She went, speechless, with just one last roving look over her shoulder to make sure she hadn't missed any orgiastic detail.

Clivedon closed the door and leaned on it, casting a long, unreadable look on his companion, while she wondered whether she was in for a scold or, with luck, some intimation that he too was at fault this time. "Let *that* be a lesson to me," was all he said, then he smiled, shaking his head, and walked to the table to look at her hand.

"Go and comb your hair. We're getting out of here before they have half the town landing in to see the debauch. I give you that rubber, by the by. You were in a fair way to taking it. Had the king, eh? I thought so. *Next time*, however . . ."

"But aren't you *angry?*" she asked.

"Angry? Why should I be? We did nothing wrong. I personally have not so enjoyed myself for weeks, and don't intend to let the pleasure be robbed from the day by a pair of clapper-jaws like the Daileys. But mind, I don't want you to make a habit of leading me astray, Babe," he added, with a quizzing smile.

Eleven

Clivedon was at pains to describe the afternoon in his own terms to his sister before she should hear the other versions that were bound to be circulating around town. "It was unfortunate, but you could hardly be expected to sit idle for several hours. Surely there is nothing wrong in having a glass of wine and a hand of cards," she answered reasonably. "I am surprised you should have been smoking in a lady's presence, Larry, but if Barbara did not object, I don't see why Lady Dailey should."

"Barbara didn't object. In fact, she was—holding my cigar for me when they arrived."

Agnes laughed. "What of that? They cannot think she was puffing a cheroot, I suppose! But really, their talk is always colored out of all recognition. No one will think anything of it."

"If the lady were anyone but Barbara, no one would. That's the devil with having a bit of a reputation. Every little thing she does is magnified to seem like a crime."

"At least it was you she was with. Had it been friend

Gentz, that would be a different matter. The world will not suspect there was more to it than an accident and a game of cards, when Clivedon was her companion."

Clivedon did receive a few jibes. He found a surprised stare pretty effective in setting down the impertinent. Lady Barbara was offered a few cigars, but never when she was with her guardian, and she did not see fit to tell him of it. Camfreys insisted he would arrange to have a cigar named in her honor, and in the old days it would very likely have been done, but when the suggestion met with horror, he made a joke of it and forgot it. The affair did not become serious enough to interfere with a more important step in Babe's reformation that Clivedon was working on. Before she was totally respectable, she had to appear at Almack's and be seen to be not only permitted but welcome in that social holy of holies. His own and Lady Withers' influence with the patronesses was to be the lever to raise Barbara to these heights. She was still a member at least, which had happily surprised him. Lady Jersey and Lady Cowper were invited to tea at Cavendish Square, where Barbara sat in her most demure gown, between her respectable relations. Another set of patronesses received a visit to their box at Covent Garden, and not less than four of them had the unexpected pleasure of standing up with Clivedon at balls that week. "We haven't seen you at Almack's lately, Clivedon," Lady Jersey reminded him on this occasion.

"I plan to attend Thursday," he told her. "Now that I am Lady Barbara's guardian, I must escort her to such places," he explained, not allowing any trace of strain to creep into his words.

"To be sure," the lady replied, astonished. "Lady Barbara is going to come back to us, is she? So long as *you* bring her, it will be all right," she allowed.

This was by no means a welcome, but he had at least given warning that she would attend, to divert the impact of her arrival. When the two entered the door on Thursday evening, they were accompanied by Lord and Lady Withers. Before they were three steps inside the hall,

97

Lady Angela, never giving up the chase, dashed towards them, with her mother and Aunt Chloe in tow. Ellingwood too stepped forward with the greatest alacrity to claim a dance.

There were plenty of interested looks at the dasher, but this was only to be expected. There were, as well, enough distinguished friends to give an appearance of a welcome reception, and Clivedon and Agnes were on the alert to see that no gentlemen but acknowledged prudes got near her, at least for the first while. By then the excitement of this rare bird's presence had worn off, and the whole party, including herself, relaxed.

There was another person present who claimed quite as much attention as the infamous Babe. This was Lord Romeo Rutledge, the younger son of the Duke of Stapford. He had been in Greece and Italy for the past fifteen years, in an effort to strengthen a pair of weak lungs that had affected him since childhood, and was just lately returned. He had left a sickly boy of ten, white-faced, hollow-eyed and studious. He returned still a trifle on the slim side, but with his eyes restored to a youthful luster, his hair bleached golden by the Adriatic sun, his soul full of the glory of Greece and the splendor of Rome, and his mouth full of the literature of each. He was a dreamer, an idealist, an artist, and an outstanding Adonis. He was also single and a pretty eligible catch, for though but a younger son, he was of noble blood, and it was not supposed that old Stapford would leave even a younger son quite penniless.

Lord Romeo had been in the country already for six months, but till the present had got no farther than Taunton. In that most unlikely of spots, he had discovered a serving wench of classical beauty, whom he had been painting and pestering, till her father, a publican, had taken the idea of sending her away to the country to be rid of the moonling. Lord Romeo then packed up his pigments and meandered on to London to seek another model. The ladies were all eager to meet him, but could not but be disconcerted to be told, with an innocent, searching smile, that their nose was too big, or their eyes too close together. There was no polite preamble to his verdicts. He came, he looked, he decreed. He cared not whether the body before his eyes was that of a princess, a duchess, or an upstairs maid. If physical perfection fell short of the Greek ideal, he had no use for the woman.

He had been staring at the doorway, alert for a model, for half an hour before Lady Barbara entered. His eyes widened upon observing her. For the occasion, her long blond hair was dressed *à la Grecque,* framing her classic face. Her white gown was draped in a vaguely Grecian line, and had as an edging a Greek key pattern done in gold. To match this, she wore gold-strapped sandals on her feet. From head to toe, she was designed to please him. Lord Romeo thought he was having a vision, after the manner of a desert traveler thirsting after water. He could not quite credit that Aphrodite or Venus had been reincarnated in the nineteenth century.

He walked with a palpitating heart to a good vantage point and stood stock-still, staring at her. He watched transfixed as she stood up to dance with a mere mortal, then, reassured that she was real flesh and blood, he got hold of a score pad and pen from the cards room and sat to sketch her. His hand trembled, but he knew it was not the makeshift nature of his drawing equipment that was at fault. Just so must the hand of Praxiteles have shaken when he modeled his Aphrodite of Cnidus. He was too distraught to do the goddess justice. He sat another quarter of an hour gazing at her, while several persons stared at him, nonplussed at his foolishness.

When he saw the vision being walked to the edge of the dance floor, he arose, trancelike, and wafted towards her. He came to stand face to face with her, not so much taller than herself, for he was of small but perfectly proportioned stature. He looked into her eyes for about fifty seconds longer than was seemly, then spoke. "I am Romeo of Athens." His voice was low-pitched, well-modulated, a soothing voice. He did not bow, scrape a leg, or offer a hand, but just stood, gazing.

"I thought he was from Verona," she replied, intrigued at his odd behavior and not unaware of his beauty either.

His face softened into a very sweet smile. "You have a sense of humor too. You are perfect. I shall paint you, Golden Aphrodite."

The coming together of the two most interesting persons at the assembly drew considerable attention. As a little crowd seemed to be drawing close around them, Clivedon hastened his steps in the same direction. Like everyone else, he had been informed of the young man's peculiar habits, and was sorry to see anyone of questionable behavior near his charge. But at least he was a gentleman, one of whom no worse was said but that he was odd. He watched, alert to intervene, and waited.

Barbara had heard about the artist as well by this time, and decided to be rid of him by a gentle teasing. "What color do you mean to paint me, sir?" she asked.

"Silver and gold, like a moonbeam, is the effect I shall strive for. Hair gold as sun-kissed wheat, skin luminous as an opening rose, cherry-ripe lips, corn-flower eyes and . . ." He raised his hands like a priest making a sacrificial offering. "That neck defies comparison."

"I see," she said, blushing in confusion at this outpouring. "What shall you do after it is done? Eat it, or put it in a vase to water it?"

"After I am done, I shall marry you, Zeus permitting," was his simple answer, accompanied by a bow of superb grace.

Clivedon concluded this came close enough to scandal that he stepped forward to rescue her. "Lady Barbara, have you met Lord Romeo?" he asked. He had not done so himself, and felt rather foolish.

"Not exactly," she admitted, seeing Clivedon was displeased.

"Allow me to make you known to him. The Duke of Stapford's younger son. Lord Romeo, this is my ward, Lady Barbara Manfred." He hastily considered introducing himself as well, and was about to do so when Romeo spoke.

100

"What a delightful irony! I adore it. But I would have recognized Aphrodite; I have known her before, in many guises. Come, my sweet Barbarian, we shall move together." Without more speech, and without so much as a glance at Clivedon, Romeo took her hand and walked to the very center of the floor, where no sets were yet forming. Horrified as to what might ensue, Clivedon grabbed the closest lady, who was Lady Angela, and walked swiftly after them, to try to give an air of standing idly waiting for the music.

"You are just returned from Greece, I understand?" he mentioned.

"Via Taunton," Lord Romeo told him, sparing a quick look. He then cast a glance at Angela and shook his head sadly. "You should go to Greece to improve your complexion, ma'am," he told her, with a face perfectly innocent of malice.

She said nothing, but looked to her partner, bewildered. The distracted lord could think of nothing more to the point than performing another introduction, which he did, and again silence descended.

"How did you like Greece, Lord Romeo?" Barbara asked, with a helpless look at the others.

"The Grecian women are not so beautiful as they were in days of yore. The features are coarsened by the invasions from the north. When we go there, we shall breed a new race in the Hellenic mold."

Stunned, she said nothing for a moment. Her partner seemed to prefer silence. At length she asked, "Have you seen the Elgin Marbles yet? Perhaps you would be interested in them."

"Lord Elgin should be drawn and quartered for having removed them," he told her in a soft, silken voice. "Gold does not confer the right to rob a people of its cultural heritage. There is a good deal of resentment in Greece over it."

"I don't fancy they resented the thirty-five thousand pounds paid for them," Clivedon said.

"I shall not go to see them, as an act of disapproval,"

101

the soft voice spoke on. "I don't need cold marble. You will be my inspiration," he said to Barbara.

Three of the four were vastly relieved when two more couples joined them. Lord Romeo ignored the newcomers, which was better than he might have done. One of the ladies had a figure not even an Englishman would find attractive, and which a lover of the Hellenic ideal was bound to denigrate.

Lord Romeo was sufficiently in the world to realize that motion was expected from him on a dance floor, and was graceful enough in his movements that he did not look quite absurd, though his steps were at odds with those of his partner and everyone else in his set. His mincings and gyrations, quite lovely as a solo performance, occupied him enough that he uttered no more outrages till the dance was over. At its end, Clivedon took Lady Barbara's arm and began to lead her off.

Lord Romeo was hard at his heels. "Did I understand you to say you are the lady's guardian, sir?" he asked.

"That's right."

"I must marry her. When Olympus decrees, man obeys."

Clivedon cleared his throat impatiently. "We'll speak of this another time, if you please."

"Where may I call on you, and when?"

"We'll be in touch," was the only answer he received.

"My goodness, what a *strange* young man," Barbara exclaimed.

"He is a knock-in-the-cradle," Lady Angela assured her at once, for she was on Clivedon's other arm.

"Queer as Dick's hatband," he agreed.

Peering over her shoulder, Barbara saw that he still stood in the center of the floor, gazing after her, besotted. "I wouldn't encourage him if I were you," Angela suggested.

"I'm not! I was afraid he meant to follow me, but I see Lady Drummond-Burrell has taken his arm to lead him off. I hope he is not going to prove a nuisance."

"You are an optimist," her guardian stated, with an awful foreboding that the majority of the nuisance would fall on his own shoulders.

The greatest, really the only flaw of the evening was that Lord Romeo continued making an ass of himself, staring at Barbara and refusing to stand up with anyone else, but this could not be attributed to any encouragement on her part, and she escaped censure. It was the strange young artist that was discussed that night. Princess Lieven was charmed with him for telling her she was so ugly she achieved a strange sort of inverted beauty. She was equally charmed with his verdicts on her friends and enemies. She was delighted to inform Sally Jersey that Romeo thought she must have been quite tolerable twenty years ago, and her hair was still not utterly contemptible. Everyone had to meet him and express amusement at his sayings, and repeat them themselves to show how little they minded. He was proclaimed an Original and adopted on the spot by Society.

Before Clivedon's party left, Romeo had discovered not only where he might present his offer to Lord Clivedon next day, but where he should find his model as well.

"I will come to you at Cavendish Square tomorrow morning," he told her as she tried to edge out the door on her guardian's far side.

"Oh," was all she could think of to say, yet she was not depressed to have attached Society's new darling.

"Lady Barbara is busy tomorrow morning," Clivedon told him in a dismissing way.

"Please, the Fates have not given me a patient soul," Romeo explained to the hiding lady. "May I come in the afternoon—at three?"

With a strong wish to get out the door, Clivedon nodded his approval to Barbara.

"All right," she answered.

"Till then, my soul is in your keeping," he told her, with a perfectly serious face. Then he lifted her gloved hand, slowly unfastened the wrist snap, placed a kiss on her inner wrist, and stepped back with a bow for her to leave.

"The boy is mad," Lady Withers declared as they got beyond his hearing.

"Yes, but he's awfully sweet, isn't he?" Lady Barbara replied, with a peep over her shoulder. Her guardian and chaperone exchanged a crestfallen look and hastened her steps towards the carriage.

Twelve

Lord Romeo may have been insane; several people thought so, but he had enough wits about him to know what he wanted, and enough tenacity of purpose to pursue his goal doggedly. With a morning to be got in before he could go to his lady, he made use of it by calling on her guardian. In his hands he bore a slim leather case, which Clivedon presumed to be a sort of folio of his smaller art works. With some curiosity and more annoyance, he had the fellow shown in. "I have come to ask your permission to court Lady Barbara," Romeo told him, with no time wasted on banalities.

"Have a seat," Clivedon invited. The graceful form folded itself onto a chair.

At this point, the visitor's eyes alit on a Grecian vase that stood on top of a bookcase in Clivedon's study. "Ah, you have got one of Spiro's forgeries," he said, arising to examine the piece. "He does a good imitation of Clitias, especially the black figures on the exterior, but the handles give him away. He doesn't take time to form his handles properly, Spiro. They are invariably crude, and poorly joined too. Yes, you see they do not hold at all," he continued, pulling off the right handle and returning Clivedon's vase to him in two pieces.

Having paid several hundred pounds for this trifle, the owner was not best pleased to be either proven a dupe or possibly to have had a genuine masterpiece vandalized.

"Thank you," he said in a voice laden with irony, laying the pieces aside.

"You're welcome," Lord Romeo answered in quite a different spirit, and resumed his seat.

"So you are come to sue for Lady Barbara's hand," Clivedon said, his eyes narrowing and a steely glint creeping into them. "She is quite an heiress, you realize. She is expected to make a good match."

Lord Romeo smiled, an Attic smile, and nodded his shapely head in agreement. "I am the best match she could make," was his simple answer.

"That is your opinion," Clivedon pointed out, finding it strangely impossible to gauge the young man. "What is your financial position?"

"I do not concern myself with money—my exact position I cannot tell you, but I know the Gods smiled on me. I have wealth as well as talents and beauty."

"What sum do you speak of?"

"My man of business has drawn all that up for me. It is in here. Isn't this an exquisite bag? It is made of goatskin, lined with pink silk." He opened it and, instead of drawing out the papers, ran his fingers over the watered silk, while Clivedon threw up his eyes in impatience. "Here it is for you to look over," he said at length. "If it is not enough, pray tell me, and I shall get more."

His host regarded him, wondering whether to laugh or call for a guard from Bedlam. "Fine. Just leave it with me, and I'll be in touch with you. Where are you putting up, Lord Romeo?"

"You'll take good care of Paros? My leather case. Paros was my favorite goat, from the island of the same name. You were asking—ah yes, where do I stay. I am at my father's home, in Belgrave Square. I see you are surprised I could tolerate it. I am stronger than I look, but it

106

grieves me daily, I confess. It is very ugly, monumentally so. I disapprove of every piece of stone in it, but it is my duty to spend some time with my family."

"I hadn't heard your family were in town."

"They are not. I commune with their spirits."

"I see." What Clivedon was rapidly coming to see was that he dealt with a beautiful moron. Still, the boy was Stapford's son. The home he abhorred was considered by the rest of the country to be one of the city's finest, and until he got a look inside Paros, he would not turn him off.

"Are you finished with me now, sir?"

The speech was unpleasantly cringing, but there was no tone of self-abasement, nor any look of it. The beautiful face across from him was remote, with a soft smile curving the corners of the lips.

"I guess that's about all for now. I'll call on you after I've looked over these papers."

"I could put you in touch with a real Clitias vase, if you are interested," the boy said next.

"What would it cost me?"

"Cost? I have no idea. A great deal, probably. A price cannot be put on beauty. It would help to detract attention from the rest of this appalling room." The blue eyes roamed slowly around a chamber the owner had spent considerable time and money on making elegant.

"Kind of you."

"Merely an effort to ingratiate myself with Lady Barbara's guardian, to see him in improved surroundings. My soul thrives on beauty. Your entranceway as well, if you will pardon my saying so, Sir, is barbaric. The pillars neither Doric nor Corinthian, but a poor pastiche, and the entablature . . . Shall I design a replacement for you, Lord Clydesdale?"

"The name is Clivedon," the host said in a tight voice, "and I am satisfied with my entablature."

"Clivedon? I must try to remember that. I have no memory for English names, they are all so ugly. My own included. I refer to the family name, for Fate was present

107

at my christening and gave me a civilized first name, though it is no Grecian. Well, may I leave, then?"

"That would be nice."

"Yes. I have been dreading this visit as well, and found it almost worse than my imaginings. Good day, sir."

Lord Romeo sauntered from the room, stopping after four paces to frown in sorrow at an Adams doorway that did not agree with him. Clivedon sat on, looking at the empty doorway for two minutes after he was gone, then opened the case and pulled out an orderly set of papers. He was now convinced Romeo was a fool, but his father or someone had seen to it that his business affairs were handled in a wise way. The lad possessed not only an estate in Hampshire, but another spread in Essex, and considerable monies in the funds. A regular nabob, in fact, which might possibly account for Society's amused toleration of the boy. With his excellent family connections and no real shame attaching to his name, it was hard to turn him off. He hoped Lady Barbara would have the sense to do it.

Lord Romeo spent the remainder of the morning walking about London, shaking his head at various architectural atrocities. Wren's dome at Saint Paul's he found a vastly inferior imitation of Saint Peter's in Rome, a pretentious little toy. Carlton House he assumed to be a freakish joke, and the Gothic spires of Westminister Abbey he consigned to immediate demolition. Indeed, there was scarcely a building in the whole city to give him the least pleasure. The Earl of Burlington's Piccadilly mansion found a little favor with him, a doorway on Great Ormond Street had a decent pair of pillars, and Saint Thomas's Hospital, from a distance, had enough purity of line to appeal mildly to him. For the rest, neither a dome nor an arch of any sort was permissible. The Greeks had not discovered the arch. A lintel supported by a line of columns was the Greek way, and the botched Palladian buildings that flourished in the city were all abominations. No wonder Englishmen all looked pale and sullen, he thought. This environment would be enough to do it.

He forgot to take any lunch, but remembered to begin

wending his way towards Cavendish Square early enough to be there a little before the appointed hour. The ladies awaited him.

He stopped in the doorway to look at them. "Who has done this to you?" he asked angrily, in a tone at odds with most of his speech.

Barbara looked at a very pretty mulled muslin gown, quite in the highest kick of fashion. "What?" she asked, astonished.

"Where is your *peplos?* The outfit you wore last night. What are you doing in that disgusting *thing?* And your hair is all wrong." He paced quickly towards her. "Who is responsible for this?" he demanded of Lady Withers.

"Pray have a seat, Lord Romeo," the hostess replied, alarmed but still polite.

He sat down, but could not long remain seated in his state of agitation. His eyes flew to Barbara, disliking the plait of braids around her head, the gown that did not drape, and when he saw a pair of blue kid slippers on her feet, he was up.

"This is all wrong. This is not how I want to paint you. You must wear the *peplos* and sandals you had on last night. I shall arrange your hair. Those locks must fall forward wantonly, to make Olympus tremble. Lady Weather—do you have a decent room in your house to use for a background? Or a garden not disfigured by inferior statuary?"

The easiest remark, indeed the only one that occurred to the dame, was to correct him on her name. "I am Lady Withers, not Weather."

"Withers? I knew there was a horse in the family somewhere. That is why I called your brother Clydesdale."

Lady Barbara regarded him closely and concluded he was being purposely rude. "Do sit down and stop making such a cake of yourself," she said quite sharply. "If you wish to paint me, you will behave, Lord Romeo."

He sat, meek as a lamb, and began gazing at her, finding the face, despite its coils, as perfect as ever. "Now," she went on, pleased with his docility, "I see you don't mean to waste time on being polite, and as you are eager

109

to find a background for the painting, let us decide on one." She turned to Lady Withers. "Perhaps the morning parlor, in front of that pretty fanlit window."

"I don't paint windows," Lord Romeo said at once. "And I most particularly dislike fanlights."

She raised one supercilious brow. "The study then, in front of the Adams fireplace."

"Adams has a deal to account for, destroying the saloons of half the homes in England with those atrocities. No, I see we will require an outdoor setting. You have let Adams loose in this house." He glanced disdainfully at walls where Adams had defiled the surface with his designs. "I shall catch the play of the sun on your golden hair. Deathless Aphrodite, on your rich-wrought throne. There is a rather good doorway in Great Ormond Street—"

"Don't be an idiot," she said baldly. "You must do it here, if I decide to let you do it at all."

"Really, Lady Barbara is very busy," her chaperone took it up at once.

"She must make time," was the artist's reply. "The glorious gifts of the gods are not to be cast aside. Let me see this house."

He arose and went into the hallway, frowning at a very nice curved staircase, peering into a small private parlor with a shiver of revulsion. "I have seen enough. More than enough. Take me outside," he demanded.

At her wits' end, Lady Withers took him into a tiny garden, where two rosebushes in a shaded corner straggled vainly towards the sun, a few yards away.

"How ugly England is," Lord Romeo said, looking at the roses with a sympathetic nod. "I know just how you feel, roses. But the far corner gets a drop of light. I shall bring a caryatid with me to put in that corner. It is done in the middle classical period, stiff and uncompromising. Similar to those adorning the Porch of the Maidens of the Erectheum. My plan is to do Lady Barbara in the late classical style, with more naturalism, and perhaps undraped to show the beauty of her body, her gentle foot trampling a hyacinth."

110

"I beg your pardon?" Lady Withers gasped, unsure she had heard him aright.

"What of the *peplos?*" Barbara asked, curious but not totally shocked, as she assumed he was out to shock them.

"I have reconsidered. We shall discard the *peplos*, to heighten the contrast between periods."

"We shall discard the whole project, if this is the way you mean to carry on," she told him, with a flashing eye.

He was struck most forcibly at the beauty in her eye, and smiled with simple pleasure. "For such a woman, we will long suffer woes," he said, to no one in particular.

"Well, sir, have you no more to say than that?" she pressed him.

"You are very ignorant," he admitted sadly. "The body is not something to be ashamed of and to keep hidden. With a form such as yours, you should be proud to reveal it to the world. It is prudish England and her false modesty that perpetuate this folly of painting women in clothing. And such ugly clothing too. The female form is the most beautiful structure in the world. From that flowing bosom, all allurements flow—love, desire, blandishing persuasion, to stir mankind."

"I think you had better leave," Lady Withers decided.

"That is poetry, ma'am, not, alas, my own. My talents lie in another direction. Painting is poetry without words, and poetry painting that speaks. You have the Anglo *géne* at discussing the body and sexuality. But till we are married, I shall content myself to paint my Lady Barbarian draped, if you insist. I shall have my caryatid brought here, and tomorrow at three I shall come with my equipment, and my talent. I want you wearing the *peplos* you wore last night, my dear," he said to Barbara. "I shall arrange your hair. We'll begin the preliminary sketch tomorrow—that face, sweetly speaking, softly laughing." Then he looked around the garden. "Shall we go inside and eat? I don't believe I have thought to eat yet today."

"It's past three o'clock!" Lady Withers reminded, while reminding herself luncheon was past, tea several hours away. "You cannot mean you have not taken anything yet?"

"I may have had a nectarine. I like nectarines. Do you have any?"

"I'm afraid I haven't," she confessed.

"Bread and cheese will do, and a bottle of ouzo."

"What is that—ouzo?" the hostess enquired, giving herself over to confusion.

"A liqueur from Greece, flavored with anise. It tastes very bad, but it makes me drunk quickly—Homerically drunk. It is divine. I have come to adore it."

Lady Withers took her charge's hand and dashed quickly into the house to order bread, cheese, and tea. This meager repast was in the process of being consumed when Clivedon was announced. "You have decided to take the Clitias vase," Romeo greeted him. "I am monstrously glad."

"My mind is not quite made up."

"Would you like some cheese?" Romeo offered. "It is extremely bland and quite stale. I blush to offer it, and of course tea does not go at all—"

"Thank you, no," Clivedon replied, with a look at his sister, who looked back in helpless dismay.

Soon the unwanted guest arose. "Thank you very much for your efforts at hospitality, ma'am. I shall return tomorrow at three." Then he turned to Barbara. "Where are we going this evening, my dear?" he asked her in a caressing tone.

"Lady Barbara is attending a ball at Lord Winchelsea's house," Clivedon told him.

"Winchelsea? What names you people dream up. How is one expected to remember Winchelsea? Very likely I have been invited. I shall ask my valet. He handles my correspondence for me," Lord Romeo said, in a vague way. "But in any case, I shall see you there."

"You can't go without an invitation," Barbara reminded him.

"I go everywhere without invitations. I shall be there. Don't wear anything ugly," he pleaded, then left.

"Larry, the boy is impossible," his sister wailed.

"As close to mad as makes no difference," Larry allowed. "But I don't think there's any vice in him."

"No vice! You are far out in your opinion. He wants to paint Barbara nude, in Great Ormond Street, and if he is not dead drunk on ouzo we may count ourselves fortunate."

These statements had to be explained in considerable detail. As it seemed likely to take several minutes, Clivedon suggested Barbara get her bonnet to go out for a spin. When she was gone, he turned to his sister. "Yes, he is damned odd, but well-born, and *very* well to grass."

"How well?" The sum mentioned was sufficiently large to mitigate Lord Romeo's behavior and even to call to mind to Lady Withers that he really was excessively handsome.

"She shan't marry him, of course, but there can be no harm in letting him paint her here, well-chaperoned and well-gowned. It will keep her out of other mischief. She will soon tire of him," Clivedon thought.

"Yes, I was fagged to death myself after ten minutes of his company, and she handles him remarkably well. Calls him to account as though he were a stripling."

"He *is* a stripling."

"They grow very handsome striplings in Greece," his sister said, smiling in a bemused way.

"Very short ones as well. I confess I am interested to see how he paints. He talks a high set of standards, but I expect he'll give us no more than a cartoon likeness, exquisitely mounted in goatskin."

Thirteen

Lord Romeo was at the Winchelsea ball, whether by invitation or otherwise was not ascertained. When he created such a stir, there was certainly no thought of hinting him away in any case. Lord Romeo was rapidly becoming one of the Season's top beaux. He spent a good deal of his time dangling after his model, but found opportunity as well to point out to his hostess that a *chiton* would be kinder to her overly full figure than a clinging silk gown, and to his host that he would be happy to redesign his entranceway. No one took offense at any of his speeches, for they were delivered always with the native innocence and goodwill of a child. Lord Liverpool was obliged to refuse him a sitting, due to the pressures of political work.

"What a pity. Such exquisite ugliness ought to be captured for posterity. I perform particularly well with the two extremes of perfect beauty and perfect ugliness, unalloyed with any charm or taste or accomplishments. Perhaps Lady Castlereagh . . ." Romeo turned his appraising eye on another candidate well-qualified to sit.

When he stood up with Lady Barbara, they formed a

very pretty picture, the young, slight, fair couple, moving gracefully together. "We must look charming together," he thought. "I wish I could see us."

The next morning an enormous carved statue of a woman arrived at the doorway of Cavendish Square on a cart, and was hauled by eight men into the garden, where it was placed against a fence in the corner. Lady Barbara and Lady Withers went out to examine it and puzzle over how Romeo had got it back from Greece. It was heavy enough to sink a ship.

At three the artist arrived to find his model outfitted in the mode demanded by her chore. He nodded his approval and said, "Now all we need is a brush to do something with your hair."

Harper had been at pains to arrange her hair *à la Grecque,* and the lady herself was not of a mind to have it disarranged, but Romeo was adamant. She was set down in a chair, the pins pulled out, and he lifted it through his fingers, all under the startled eyes of Lady Withers, who felt she ought to object, yet knew not quite how to set about it with this strangely willful young man. Soon he had it as he wanted, in a looser style than Harper devised, with a few stray tendrils allowed to escape. "I strive for a naturalistic effect," he explained, "to contrast with the middle-classic form of the caryatid. The folds of the gown too I shall treat more softly. Those of the statue, you will notice, resemble the fluting of a column in their severity. I want a more rounded form, to suggest the curve of bosoms and thigh." One white hand reached out towards the part of the anatomy first suggested, to rearrange a fold, and Barbara gave it a sharp slap.

"You'll keep your hands to yourself, sir, if you mean to complete this job."

He smiled sweetly and accepted the stricture poetically. At least the ladies had come to assume his higher flights of absurdity were borrowed from his favorite poets. "My tongue falls silent, and a delicate flame courses through my skin at your touch," he told her. Then he turned to the chaperone. "She is cruel to me, is she not, Lady— Withers, right? I am coming along with my names, you

115

see." Agnes found herself flushing with pleasure that her name had been recalled after no more than four meetings. Really, the boy had a charming smile.

"That is a marvelous gown you are wearing today, Lady Withers," he continued. "The deep rose is a highly felicitous hue to emphasize the maturity of your years." The conclusion dampened her pleasure somewhat, but the remark was intended as a compliment, and found some favor. "Like a rose just before decay sets in. That is the glorious moment—or a peach the instant before it falls. Marvelous."

That decay was so close at hand was hardly a thought to cheer, yet Lady Withers smiled slightly.

"Shall we go into the garden before this hair tumbles down completely?" Barbara asked.

Agnes did not mean to devote her hours exclusively to playing watchdog, by any means. She had a dozen servants who could fill the job easily enough, but for the first day she would go along, to see how Lord Romeo behaved. He was solicitous to find her a chair in the sun, which inconvenience she overcame by calling for a parasol to keep the rays from darkening her face.

"I shall be brown as a milkmaid before this painting is done," Barbara complained. She was not allowed any shade at all.

"No, you peaches-and-cream girls do not darken," he told her. "The pink of your cheeks will become slightly more pronounced. It will prove flattering." He had already set up his easel and was sketching with swift strokes, all the while chatting in his soft, almost crooning voice about his travels abroad. He spoke of the ordered and serene beauty of Greek art, of sun-drenched skies arcing above classical ruins of antiquity, of orchards eons old where he walked, musing on the philosophy of Pericles and Demosthenes. He also spoke quite outrageously of the social customs of the era, finding slavery to have been unfortunately necessary and prostitution raised to a religious function, in some manner that remained obscure to the ladies.

"Prostitutes are not quite so acceptable in Greece today," he mentioned sadly. "How are they looked upon in English society, Lady Withers?"

There was some insidious quality in his manner that made the question seem not salacious or even ill-bred. In a philosophical mood, she found herself looking for the truthful answer. "Why, they are more or less accepted in theory, but kept behind the scenes in fact. They are not invited to one's home, of course, or to polite parties. They attend the theater and have their own do's. The gentlemen attend, but ladies do not."

"There is a prostitutes' do called the Cyprians' Ball held each season, I understand," he went on. "I must go, to see what the English ladies of pleasure look like, and how they perform. Someone pointed one out to me yesterday, and I was surprised at her plainness. She must be skilled at her trade to have acquired such a high reputation. She was pale as grass and ill-formed, yet I found myself strangely attracted to her."

Lady Withers looked at him and delivered no stricture. At the end of an hour he laid down his pencil. "I have finished the sketch. Would you like to see it, ladies?"

They were both eager to do so, and rushed to his easel. "It's beautiful!" Barbara exclaimed. "I am not so pretty as that."

"I have not begun to capture the essence of your beauty. Still, I have gathered some of the joys which bright dawn scattered, I think. In oils it will look much better. Half your beauty is in the coloring. There are practically no Greek paintings extant, you know. I must devise my own technique, working from what few relics remain—a painted bowl or vase, a few panels. You see what I am about, contrasting the two classical styles?"

Looking at his depiction of the caryatid, Barbara got a glimmering of his intention, but the more loving care had been rendered to her own likeness. An expression rested on the portrait's face that was not her own. There was a peace, tranquility, serenity in it, yet with no loss of animation. The eyes seemed almost alive, and the mouth looked ready to smile. "How peaceful I look," she said.

"I am painting you as you will look after we are better

117

acquainted, when I have made you more familiar with the Greek philosophy. It is the expression found on the best sculpture in Greece, comprising, in my view, simple elegance, intelligence, satisfaction. Leonardo captured something of it in the *Mona Lisa*. She has an Attic smile, though her nose is appalling. You, Lady Barbarian, have not yet achieved that state of Attic bliss. When you do, we shall change your name. You are a trifle restless yet, but you will get over it. Are my nectarines ready, Lady Withers, or must I have that dreadful cheese again? I hope not."

She had had no luck in procuring nectarines, but sent her servants for what fruit she had. He was served a pineapple and oranges instead. The fig on the plate, he informed her, should have remained on the bough another month. The pineapple he found interesting, the orange very sour, "but I shall finish this one, as I would not like to hurt your feelings," he explained to her.

There soon developed a routine to the family's dealings with Lord Romeo. He came each afternoon to paint, and he met them in the evenings at various social functions. Crowds continued to flock around him to hear themselves insulted. Only the Prince of Wales, with great tact, stayed away. He was pronounced on all the same by the undiplomatic arbiter of beauty, who found him to resemble an aging Adonis who had fallen into a vat of Portland cement and had come out deformed and enlarged, to harden into creaking immobility. Once the dreadful verdict was out, Prinney relented and had him to Carlton House to hear all his expensive treasures ridiculed. It was assumed there would be a commission to do a little redesigning after this visit, but Lord Romeo's suggestion that the whole be blown up and the job started again from scratch was too expensive, even for the most expensive monarch in Europe.

Lady Withers found herself daily drawn to the yard to watch him work and to listen to him, and perhaps too to gaze at his astonishing beauty. In any case, Clivedon took pleasure in teasing her about her new flirt and warning Barbara she had better look lively, or she'd lose him.

Clivedon seemed content with the painting sessions, although he personally never attended them, and heard of them only second-hand. He might have felt a few qualms had he bothered auditing them, for Romeo's monologues were very outspoken indeed.

When the ladies told him what was spoken of, they grasped on some such trifle as "accidie," a matter on which Romeo had once lectured them. "It is a sort of spiritual sloth or listlessness," Agnes outlined to her brother. "It is very widespread in London, he tells us."

"He has certainly escaped the taint. He was rifling Petersham's collection of snuffboxes at Harrington House yesterday morning, and has ordered the owner to be rid of a round hundred of them. He is helping him make up the even three hundred and sixty-five, for Petersham likes a different one for every day of the year. He has—Romeo, that is—forbidden any colors but green, yellow, and pink for spring, for March, April, and May respectively. They now require another dozen pink. He is redesigning the stairway at Burlington House, on his own authority, and speaks of taking the dome off Saint Paul's. I quite blush at my own comparative inactivity. I wish he would give us a more comfortable seat in the House, but he doesn't concern himself with that."

"You may joke," Agnes defended her protégé, "but he is fanatically interested in artistic things and knows a great deal. I own he draws me on to become interested myself."

"It is the artist that interests you, sis."

With a little blush, she arose quickly to speak to cook about trying for some sweeter oranges and riper figs. Romeo had not liked the last pineapple either.

Clivedon turned a dark eye on Barbara. "And is it of 'accidie' the artist speaks to you as well?"

"Amongst other things. We discuss poetry and philosophy and history."

"That would have the charm of novelty, at least, for you."

"I read things! I am not as ignorant as you think. Romeo lent me a book of poetry by someone called Shelley
119

that is very interesting. A thing called *Alastor* I am reading. Are you familiar with Shelley?"

"Not personally, but I am familiar with his writings. And reputation," he added in a certain voice.

"You are implying something horrid. What is it?"

"I have nothing against his poetry but do not recommend his philosophy. He is a revolutionary, an atheist, anti-monarch, anti-government, anti-religion, and possibly anti-money. I am not sure of the last item."

"Money? What is that? I seem to remember the word from my past."

"It is the stuff you used to carry in your reticule to gamble with."

"Ah yes, it seems my Harper mentioned it to me last night. She has the odd notion I ought to pay her her wages."

"What, are you actually completely out?"

"Certainly not. I have three shillings and twopence, which I am saving against an emergency."

"You might have told me! I didn't mean to put you in such a position as that."

"I am in a worse fix than that. I have a bill from the wheeler who repaired my phaeton, and am beginning to receive rather inferior service from the servants here at your sister's house too, who *do* expect a little *pourboire* from time to time."

"I'll arrange some funds for you at once. How much do you require?"

"Whatever you can find it in your hard accountant's heart to forward me. Ten guineas would not go amiss. Make it fifteen if you can."

He pulled out his money pouch and counted some bills into her hands. "Now, here is progress!" she exclaimed. "I expect I may even see that pair of nags to go with my carriage one of these days. What is the delay? Is Tatt's gone out of business, or is Romeo only letting them sell horses that come up to his ideal of equine beauty?"

"It is myself who is hard to please, in this case. I am working on a deal, and expect to have something by the week's end."

"Next thing I know, I'll be sitting down to the fatted calf."

"We are pleased with your progress," he allowed with a bow. "Yes, I think as soon as you send this pseudo-Greek packing, we shall anoint you with your own ball. Or are you considering having him?"

"To marry, you mean?"

"I trust he will not suggest any other sort of alliance."

"Well, he is fascinating certainly . . ."

"In what way?" Clivedon asked, looking at her closely.

"He is absorbed in something outside of himself, and that is always interesting. He speaks knowledgeably about Greece, but then, I haven't known him long. He hasn't started repeating himself yet. He is bound to eventually. Anyone so single-minded must e'er long, and I am not *quite* sure he won't become a bore after another week."

He shook his head and smiled at her, fondly. "How very astute you are under those sun-kissed tresses. Where did I, and the rest of the Town, get the idea you were a featherhead?"

"From my former behavior, very likely. But Romeo is teaching me serenity. *Mens sana in corpore sano* is his rule. He hasn't quite grapsed the *mens sana* himself, you are thinking, but Agnes and I are working to lead him down from Olympus."

"You three wise philosophers discuss other items than love, do you?" he asked.

"We never discuss love. Romeo doesn't believe in the existence of the heart. It is the soul that interests him. The *psychë* he tells me it is called."

"Still, I expect Romeo's *psychë* serves pretty much the function of the heart in the non-Greek amongst us."

"I don't ever recall hearing him use the word love. He talks a lot of beauty, and is interested in the body."

"The naked body for choice, Agnes tells me."

"Yes, he is quite shocking, except that somehow it doesn't *seem* shocking in him, he is so outspoken and unashamed about it. I've never met anyone else like him," she added, smiling in a dreamy way.

"An innocent, in fact."

"Yes, he is a rather dissipated Innocent. It is his having been raised away from home, amidst foreigners. And he was treated quite like a God by them, you know, which is bound to have given him a very good idea of himself."

"Something has certainly done so." Again she smiled softly, and Clivedon suddenly changed the subject. "Ellingwood was asking for you today at Tatt's. You might let him call, against the day Romeo begins repeating himself."

"Ellingwood? He often calls. I've met a hundred Ellingwoods in my life. He is not very interesting."

"He's a good chap."

"I didn't mean to disparage him. He is very nice, but so utterly predictable, whereas Romeo . . . When Ellingwood is a little older and begins thinking for himself, he might prove more engaging. At the moment, he only says what he hears everyone say."

"He is the same age as Romeo."

"No, he is several hundred years younger," she answered, with an enigmatic smile that worried her guardian considerably.

The next day, Lord Clivedon was on hand for the painting session. He stood at Romeo's shoulder, looking at the work, surprised that it was so well done. He expressed polite appreciation to the creator.

"It does not begin to do her justice. Still, a small victory has shifted to me," Romeo allowed. "Of course, all those clothes hamper me. If she would undrape, I could do a proper job."

Aware of this streak of folly on the artist's part, Clivedon expressed no great surprise, but only said, "That is impossible."

"Barbara has convinced me I must wait till we are married," he said with resignation.

"I never said I would marry you, Romeo," she reminded him, for the conversation was carried on in normal tones, audible to them all.

"You must," she was told, with no emphasis or worry or anger. Romeo continued working, his concentration soon deafening him to any speech. At the end of an hour he set aside his brushes. "It is done," he announced. This was an invitation for the three to gather around the portrait to admire it.

"Exquisite!" Lady Withers sighed.

"It flatters me immensely," Barbara declared.

"I did not capture the mood of your toes," Romeo confessed. "It was the lack of a hyacinth. Those pretty little toes, like curled rosebuds wanting to unfurl. I think you might have removed your sandals at least, but I know you are too modest."

Noticing that Clivedon was biting back a smile and staring at her toes, Barbara said, "I am not that modest. I would have taken off my sandals." Extraordinary the lack of understanding of these matters that cropped out in Romeo at times. He saw no difference between a sandal and a gown.

Romeo subjected her to one of his lingering gazes, then shook his head. "No, I shan't change it. I am becoming infected by this pernicious English Philistinism, and find I do not want the world to see your bare toes. We must go to Greece very soon, my dear, before my *psychë* is irrevocably warped. It grows stunted and deformed in this hostile climate of England. In Greece, under the shadow of the Acropolis, I shall paint you as you should be painted. I cannot do it here, after all."

"I wish you will not speak as though it is all set we are to get married. I haven't the slightest notion of ever moving to Greece, I can tell you."

"We will go on our wedding trip, and you will beg me to let you stay," he answered, slipping off his smock and laying it aside. "There you will blossom into mature womanhood, leaving behind this restless quality that displeases me. Your opposition is against the immortal gods, and will not long endure. See how even the cold English sun has brightened your cheeks."

"Barbara is looking remarkably healthy these days," Lady Withers pointed out to her brother.

"What do you mean to do with the painting?" Clivedon asked.

"I shall keep it till I have created another. There is no fullness of admiring Aphrodite. When I am at home alone, it will warm me. Where do we go this evening, my dear?" he asked Barbara. The do was mentioned, and he nodded, then asked for his lunch.

"I'm afraid Romeo doesn't eat properly," Agnes worried, after he was gone. "You must see he does so after you are married, Barbara."

"Cousin, pray don't speak as though it is all settled! I don't plan to marry him—that is—it is not settled at all. Certainly I don't want to live in Greece."

"The sun and climate would be good for you," her hostess mentioned.

"Don't be so foolish!" Clivedon said angrily. Then he began looking around the room. "Where is the picture? He didn't take it with him. I suppose it's being sent home by Zeus on a thunderbolt."

Agnes gave him a withering stare and mentioned that Mercury, she believed, was the messenger of the gods.

"Immortal gods! It's his own puny hide is all he thinks of. To hear him speak as though he were on a first-name basis with Zeus! A little Romeo goes a long way in my books."

"The picture is in the study," Agnes said.

"I'm going to have another look at it. He is a little better than I thought." When he returned he said, "I wouldn't mind buying it, if he decides not to take it to Greece with him."

"He wouldn't sell it," Agnes said. "He is not a professional, commercial artist, but an amateur in the true sense of the word, a lover of painting. He would be offended if you suggested it. What do you want with Barbara's picture?"

"To keep you warm at night, Clivedon?" Barbara asked, laughing.

"As an investment. Romeo has left behind no other painting, so far as I know, and it might be worth something in the future."

"Perhaps I will think about going to Greece with him," Barbara announced suddenly in a piqued voice, then continued talking up the place till Clivedon arose abruptly and took his leave.

Fourteen

Nothing was seen of Romeo for four days after the completion of the portrait. The caryatid mysteriously disappeared from the yard, the picture was picked up by a footman, but the artist did not call, nor did he appear at any evening functions. Oranges and pineapples wilted into decay at Cavendish square, and Lady Withers too was on the decline. Lady Barbara was half disappointed and half relieved. But on the fourth night he showed up at Covent Garden, all alone, and made a bee line for Clivedon's box at the first intermission.

"Evening star—a delight to behold you," he greeted her, dropping a kiss on her inner wrist. It was his preferred spot for kissing ladies, after the lips. "My ears hum, a tremble seizes me, I am near to death," he went on, in his gentle voice.

"Nearer than you know," Clivedon informed him, less gently.

"Brazen-voiced Stentor," Romeo greeted him, bowing, then turned to include Lady Withers and her spouse, the latter whom he did not recognize, nor find either handsome or ugly enough to interest him. "I am angry with you, milady," he chided Lady Withers, "for letting my Barbarian out in those hideous braids. They offend every delicate sense." He returned his scrutiny to Barbara. "But even in that grotesque gown and with your hair in coils, you are ravishing, Aphrodite."

"Thank you, I think," she answered. "Have you been ill, Romeo?"

"Dare I hope you have missed me?"

"Of course we have."

"Good. I have been neither ill nor idle. I have been visited by the inspiration of giving Pater a gift."

"Is your father in town?"

"No, it is to be a surprise for him. I am redoing the façade of Stapford House. It is half a gift for myself as well. It bruises my *psychë* to have to enter that vicious portal. I swear my soul shrinks within this mortal frame at every entry. I wanted to put in a colonnade, with a little atrium, you know, thirty or forty feet wide, but the municipal people are being very obstinate about its projecting into the street, and I refuse to make it *meager*. Skimpiness is anathema to me. So I am only tearing down the door and pediment and pillars, and having new ones erected to my own design. And of course the dome must go."

"Romeo—I don't think you should give your father such a gift as that!" she declared, horrified.

"He will love it. And it won't cost him more than three or four thousand pounds."

"I thought it was to be *your* gift."

"I am designing it free. There won't be another like it outside of Greece."

"Oh—to be sure," she answered weakly, and cast a worried eye to Clivedon, who hunched his shoulders in amusement.

"But enough talk of Pater. Have you missed me, Divine One? I burn to kiss you."

"No, please don't be impossible. Everyone is looking at us."

"Why should they not? Beauty is to be observed and

126

appreciated." He raised her hand and kissed it, muttering of a palpitating heart and warm, vibrant marble. Then he began working his way up her arm towards the inside of her elbow. She snatched her arm away hastily. "It was a mistake to stay away from you for so long. I have lost control," he explained.

"If you don't stop being so silly, you must leave at once," she said with a blush.

"What an excellent idea. Let me get you a glass of wine, Romeo. Come along," Clivedon said, and hauled him from the box.

"The destroying wrath has o'ertaken me," Romeo explained over his shoulder as he was dragged out.

When Clivedon returned, he was alone. "Of all the animals, the boy is the most unmanageable, if I may steal a Grecian epigram from Adonis."

"Clivedon—don't you think you should warn Stapford of the gift preparing for him?"

"You may be sure I will. I wish he'd come and take that boy home. And lock him up."

"Where is he?"

"He was complimenting three aging countesses on their resemblance to the Grecae when I left him. From their smiles, they cannot know the resemblance has to do with their sharing one eye and one tooth. Never mind, you have nothing to fear in them, Aphrodite. He will meet you at Swanson's water party tomorrow afternoon. At least I trust his tangent regarding Poseidon and Bacchus referred to that. He wants you to wear something called a *pepper*, I think it was, and to have those golden snakes taken from your hair. The pepper sounds a scanty covering, but about the snakes, I am inclined to agree with him."

"You said . . ."

"Hush, the play is beginning." She was forced to smolder in silence, while recalling very well that Clivedon had lately complimented her on her plaited braids.

Romeo did not accompany them home, but went to Clivedon's carriage and waved Barbara a kiss "in front of the whole world," as Clivedon said in a disgusted voice.

But he was not completely out of humor. During Romeo's short period of defection, Ellingwood had come into favor, and it was Ellingwood who was to accompany Lady Barbara to the Swansons' water party. Lady Withers did not attend, and as it was a group of younger people, Barbara assumed Clivedon too would be away. It was a good reflection on her reformation that she felt not one jot of relief that she was to escape her two mentors for a whole afternoon. Rather, she felt it wouldn't have hurt Clivedon to accompany her, as she saw less of him lately.

She wore neither *peplos* nor braids, but a very dashing sprigged muslin of a rose shade, and had her hair arranged low on her head to allow a wide-brimmed bergère hat to rest on top of it and shade her face. Ellingwood told her she looked dashed pretty, and Romeo, when he saw her, said, "You did it on purpose to pay me back for saying I wanted to kiss you last night. But I forgive you. Perfection is allowed to err. And I still want to kiss you."

Ellingwood was all at a loss at to how he should defend the lady from such an outrage. "See here, my good chap," he said, adopting a lofty tone.

"Never mind, Charles," Barbara told him, and, putting an arm through the extended arms of her two escorts, she went to join the party.

Some of the gentlemen were wearing bathing costumes and swimming in a pond, where they complained about the lack of depth. Others rowed ladies about in flat-bottomed miniature barges, and some groups just sat at the water's edge around tables, looking at the goings-on. There was some disheartened music wafting towards them, barely audible, from a deck behind the house. The body of water which Mrs. Swanson referred to as a man-made lake was in fact a pond of small dimensions. Romeo and Barbara first sat at one of the tables, with of course Ellingwood a jealous third, but they were not long happy with so little sport. As soon as Barbara expressed the slightest interest in going on the water, Ellingwood set off to find a free boat. There was none available, and he returned to tell her they would have Davey's as soon as he was finished with it.

"When Lady Barbara wishes to go on the water, she shall not wait," Romeo informed Ellingwood. He first began examining the small wooden table at which they sat, but even his active imagination could not imagine it to be pond-worthy. He began poking amongst bullrushes till he found a precarious raft, to which he then led her. Ellingwood was along, and with one glance at it, he said, "I can't allow Barbara to go out on that. It's not safe."

Barbara felt her spleen rise, to be told that Ellingwood was in a position to be allowing her not to do anything. Romeo was unperturbed, except to say, "I crossed the Hellespont on a smaller one. Come along, my dear."

"No, she's not going," Ellingwood insisted. "I am her escort, and I cannot allow it." He had received some instructions from Lady Withers.

He understood his twofold duties to be to protect her actual physical safety as well as her reputation, but hardly knew which was the more important. When Barbara boldy asked him, "How do you mean to prevent it?" his priorities sorted themselves out. He was clearly not expected to make a row in public. He did nothing but watch in frustration as she was helped onto the raft by Romeo, who accomplished the affair with great grace, considering the uncertain footing beneath him. With a pole, the pair advanced across the pond, which was not at all deep. The only danger was of collision with one of the three other vessels afloat on the water, but still Ellingwood was unhappy, and as soon as possible coerced a friend to give up his boat. He climbed in and skimmed alongside the raft.

"This will be safer, Barbara. Climb in here with me," he urged.

"Don't be foolish, Charles. Sit down before you topple over and get soaked," she answered sharply.

"I really must insist," he declared, and reached across the water to take her hand, to assist her into the safer boat. Romeo took his pole and gave the barge a shove off, away from their raft. The suddeness of the lurch caused Ellingwood to lose his balance. He reached for the only support available, Romeo's pole, and clung to it for half a minute, like a monkey, with two hands and two legs, in a very awkward and undignified manner, while the sickening knowledge washed over him that he was about to take an even more degrading plunge into the pond. Barbara, seeing his predicament, reached out a hand to try to steady him, and the two of them toppled over into the stagnant water with a shout and a loud splash.

Romeo stood on the edge of the raft looking after them. "Don't fear, my dear, it is not at all deep. I'll save you," he told her, in his gentle, unperturbed voice. But getting aboard either boat or raft proved more difficult than wading the ten feet to shore, and this was the option chosen by both the victims of the accident. Ellingwood spluttered and apologized, and tried to offer what aid he could to the lady, while dreadfully aware of the spectacle he presented and the muddle he had made of the affair.

Romeo reached the pond's edge before them and stood with his arms out to assist Lady Barbara onto dry land. Several others as well were on hand to render what help they could, but there was no real danger in it. There was more laughter and teasing than help. Barbara arose, dripping from head to toe, her pretty gown ruined, the thin muslin clinging to her body, while her hair trailed over her shoulders like seaweed. Romeo forgot all notion of helping her, and stood transfixed, staring. "Amphitrite!" he exclaimed, in awed accents. "Why did I not see it sooner? I must draw you thus!"

A Mr. Baxter, less artistic but more practical, removed his jacket and draped it over her shoulders, while Mrs. Swanson darted forward to rush the girl into the sanctuary of the house. Ellingwood followed quickly at their footsteps, with Romeo bringing up the rear, while the rest of the party discussed the accident.

As Barbara was got out of her soaking clothing and into a gown belonging to Miss Swanson, Romeo discovered a paper and pencil, and dashed off a rough sketch of the vision he had beheld rising from the waves. No friend to clothing on ladies, he dispensed with these objects and drew her with her hair trailing over the front of her body. He considered which of the usual poses of Amphitrite to use. He had seen her on coins riding on a seahorse or dolphin, but this interfered with the vivid memory of her emerging from the pond, and they were rejected. He drew her as he had seen her, only omitting the gown.

In a quarter of an hour she was back downstairs, dressed but with her hair still wet. "You can't go back to the party like that," Romeo told her. "Come and sit here by the window. Leave your hair loose—it will dry more quickly—and I shall finish this sketch. The face I have not done at all. I am doing you as Amphitrite."

She sat considering her predicament. This accident was bound to be much discussed, and she wondered whether Clivedon and Lady Withers would be angry with her. But an accident, after all—it could not well have been avoided. Unless she had refused to go on the raft. Yes, they would not be pleased that she had consented to go on the raft. But as she remembered Clivedon's easy acceptance of their discovery in a much worse pickle than this at the inn, she recovered her spirits and allowed Romeo to pull her hair over her shoulders and pose her at the window.

Mrs. Swanson came to look in on them. "I'm afraid you'll catch cold with your damp hair, Lady Barbara. Let me get you a blanket to put over your gown till it dries."

"I am a little chilly," she allowed.

The blanket was put around her shoulders, hanging to the floor, making her feel more comfortable. Again Romeo had to rearrange the hair. The hostess had a little inkling that the girl's new guardian might not like her to be alone with Romeo, for they were very careful of her lately. To prevent giving any offense in that direction, she asked a few of the youngsters to join the party in the small saloon. Half a dozen bucks and ladies lounged behind Romeo, snickering and laughing amongst themselves and pestering Romeo with questions, which he mostly ignored, only mentioning what goddess he was painting—"One of the Nereids."

Barbara rather wondered what had become of Ellingwood, but that unfortunate gentleman had nothing to change into. There was no son in the Swanson household, and he had the choice of donning a footman's livery or

131

waiting for a servant to fetch him dry clothing from home. He chose the latter as more in keeping with his dignity, and passed a very boring hour locked in a room, rehearsing his excuses to Lord Clivedon.

He had a chance to deliver them sooner than he thought. The instant he had got his cravate tied and gone below, he saw the tall form of Clivedon approaching the water, looking around, for himself he knew. As he walked quickly forward, he heard a saucy young lady shout, "Are you looking for Babe, Lord Clivedon? Don't worry, she is not drowned. She fell into the water, of course—what would one expect of Babe?—but she has been rescued. You will find her in the house."

"Just a little accident," Ellingwood said, hurrying forward.

"She's not hurt?" Clivedon asked.

"Not in the least."

"What happened?"

"It was that blasted Lord Romeo put her up to it. What must the pair of them do but get on an old falling-apart raft and go out on the water, and when I tried to get her into a safer boat, we fell in."

Clivedon's face was already wearing an angry expression. "Where is she? I'll take her home."

"I've just this minute got into dry clothes myself. I haven't spotted her yet—well, the girl said she's in the house, didn't she? We'll find her there."

"Managed to dunk you as well, did she?"

"It wasn't her fault."

They walked together at a brisk pace towards the house to seek out Lady Barbara. Laughter and talking soon directed them to the proper location. Clivedon felt reassured to know she was not alone with Romeo, for to have seen no sign of him sent a shot of alarm through him. He entered the door, not quite smiling but not actually angry. The first thing he saw was Barbara posing in the blanket; the second was Romeo's sketch, and simultaneously he became aware of the audience. Romeo had made good progress with the sketch. The body was all finished, in vivid detail, and he concentrated on the hair and face. Over his shoulder, the little group laughed in the manner of the righteous when titillated.

Clivedon took four long strides forward and yanked the picture from Romeo's hands to rip it in two, then in two again, and cast the pieces aside, while Ellingwood's heart sank in his breast. "The show is over, ladies and gentlemen," he said to the group. There was something in his demeanor that did not encourage them to linger. They were out the door in seconds, still whispering and giggling amongst themselves. The words "Babe" and "naturally" were heard, punctuating the laughter.

"Clivedon—what on earth is the matter?" Barbara asked, coming forward. She had expected a small scold, nothing in the nature of this towering rage. He was seething, his eyes burning mad, and the area around his mouth seemed to have turned white.

"Matter? Nothing, in *your* view, I am sure. You must be mighty pleased with your day's work, to have made yourself the center of so much ill-bred attention. Have you got anything on under that blanket?"

"What are you talking about?" she asked.

Romeo had begun picking up the pieces of his work and reassembling them. "That was a wanton piece of destruction on your part, Lord Clydesmore," he said in a carefully restrained voice. Then he added, in less-restrained accents, "Philistine!" Barbara shot a quick look at the torn picture, but saw only the head and hair streaming over her shoulder.

"It was an accident," she said, frowning at Clivedon.

"The sort of accident in which you excel. A well-planned accident, I make no doubt."

"Don't be absurd," she answered.

"Absurd? You have the bare-faced gall to . . ." He was beyond speech.

"There is nothing wrong in a young lady showing her body. You are very old-fashioned, milord," Romeo said, his voice gently reproving.

"My notions of what is proper do not extend so far back into history as your own. It will come as news to

133

you we are not living in ancient Greece, but in modern England."

With a trembling hand and some incipient idea of what had happened, Barbara lifted another piece of the torn paper from Romeo's fingers and stared at what he had drawn. "Oh," she said weakly, as it was confirmed in her mind that Clivedon thought she had posed in this manner.

"Happy with the likeness?" her guardian asked ironically.

"Not quite so good as the original, I think," she shot back. "Would you like to compare, Lord Philistine?" She put her hands on the corners of the blanket, and began to open it.

"Babe!" He made a lunge at her that nearly knocked her off her feet, while Ellingwood looked on, mesmerized.

She danced back and pulled off the blanket. "You *dare* to suggest I posed for that thing!" she said to Clivedon. "You have the damnable insolence to accuse me of that."

"I would not have suggested it," Romeo said. "It was merely the sodden gown, clinging to Barbara's bosoms, that inspired me ..."

She paid no attention to the artist; her ire was all directed against her guardian. "If I were a man, I'd call you out," she told him, her nostrils pinched.

"I will be happy to defend your honor, my dear," Romeo told her, while Ellingwood stood with his mouth clamped shut, wondering whether his presence was actually required here.

"If you weren't a damned half-witted puppy I'd put a bullet through you," Clivedon replied.

"It would do you no good to try to involve me in a shooting duel," Romeo returned. "I do not agree with guns. I would be happy to wrestle you."

"Go to hell. Put on that blanket. We're leaving," Clivedon said to Barbara, then turned back to Romeo. "I don't want to see you wagging your tail at Cavendish Square again."

"You are not going to steal Barbara from me. I know you are jealous of me. I have seen it in your eyes before now, but she is mine. Trying to keep me from her will not

134

kill our affection but encourage it." His voice was unimpassioned. Merely he was explaining the matter.

"Don't come pestering us in future. You understand? You are no longer welcome. And if you know what's good for you, you'll destroy that piece of pornography."

"You are quite mistaken in your interpretation of the piece. The female nude as executed by me is intended to stimulate aesthetic emotions, not erotic. That is an Indian fashion, which I find peculiarly repulsive. The human body is the most . . ."

While he spoke on, Clivedon put a hand on Barbara's elbow and pulled her from the room. "I'd like to know what *you* were about while all this was going on," he said over his shoulder to Ellingwood on the way out.

"It was all Ellingwood's fault, if you want to know the truth," Barbara took it up at once. "If he hadn't come lurching up against us, grabbing onto the pole, and tipped us over, this would never have happened."

"If you had any sense of decent behavior it wouldn't have happened. You don't see Miss Swanson or any of the other girls getting themselves dumped into the pond. Only *you* could create a scandal at a polite water party. We can't let you out of our sight for ten minutes. You're worse than a baby."

His carriage was brought around while they continued arguing. A brief truce was called while they made their adieux to the hostess, but the battle was resumed as soon as they were on the road.

"It's a good thing I happened to have brought my closed carriage, or you'd be riding through town like Lady Godiva, with your hair hanging over your shoulders."

"You know perfectly well this little accident was not my fault. If Romeo took advantage of me by drawing that picture *without my knowledge*, it is nothing to do with me. As to that bunch of jackals looking on for an hour and not telling me what he was doing! They would not have behaved so if it were anyone but *me*."

"That is exactly right! I'm glad you come to realize that people do not consider you to deserve the respect a lady ought. You have made yourself an object of scorn often enough that they feel free to treat you as though you were a lightskirt."

"The very way *you* treat me, in fact. It didn't occur to you that Romeo might have done that picture without my knowledge. You assumed instead that I had taken off my clothes in front of a whole bunch of people and posed for him."

"I wouldn't put it past you."

She turned her head aside and refused to speak for several minutes, while they both cooled down. At length he said, "Well, here we are with another scandal to be lived down, and your ball fast approaching. We'll be lucky if there are half a dozen people at it."

"Advertise I am to attend *au naturel*. That would draw a good crowd, don't you think?"

"It would draw the Greek, in any case. Thank God Agnes hasn't sent out the cards yet. That's one she can tear up."

"You were very hard on Romeo. You hurt his feelings."

"He has no feelings. He's a walking wad of outdated clichés. I haven't heard so much misquoted Greek since before I went to Oxford. How you cannot be bored by that egregious ass is beyond me. No idea of proper conduct—you couldn't *possibly* marry him. I realize now it is completely out of the question."

He looked at her, trying to read if she were distressed at this news, but she was wearing a face that might have been set in cement. "We can hardly avoid seeing him if we continue going out nights," he went on. "He goes everywhere, never mind whether he is invited. You'll be going out very little till our ball. We'll say you have caught a cold after your dunking."

"That will leave *you* free to attend the Cyprians' Ball tonight," she said, with a knowing look. "I expect that is what not wanting Romeo dangling after me is all about. It happens, however, that he plans to attend it himself, so your concern need not begin till tomorrow."

"My concern began an hour ago. You will not leave the house tonight. And Romeo should not have been discussing such an affair with you."

136

"*You* will attend this infamous affair too low to speak of before such innocents as myself?"

"I usually drop in. It is one of the more interesting social do's of the Season."

"What *divertissement* am *I* to be regaled with while *you* attend the more interesting amusement?"

"I suggest bed, and a book."

"Kind of you. Do you know, I have always had a great curiosity to know what goes on at the Cyprians' Ball?"

"I don't want to see your white head at it."

"If I decide to go, I will be sure to wear a wig. What color would you like to see?"

"I'm not fooling, Babe. I *forbid* you to leave the house without my permission."

She looked at him closely. His anger seemed to have dissipated. Yes, he was enjoying issuing his decrees. There seemed almost to be a challenge in the prohibition. "What will you do if I choose to disobey?"

A sardonic smile flashed out. "If you know what's good for you, you'll never find out. I don't recommend you get into any alternative mischief either."

"I haven't bothered with mere mischief since I let down my skirts and pinned up my hair."

"One trembles to think some unfortunate man will have the task of steering you through life's shoals."

"I am not a ship, to be steered into a safe harbor. *I* am the captain of this vessel."

Fifteen

Clivedon delivered his charge to Cavendish Square, sent her to her room, and explained to his sister what had happened. She threw up her hands in exasperation. "Shabby! What a sight she must have looked, dripping with brown pond water. And the sprigged muslin ruined of course. One would think Mrs. Swanson would have taken a look-in on the sketching party to see . . . But she never was quite the thing. I'm sorry I let Barbara go."

"We'll keep her in a few days to let the talk die down."

"We were to go to Stauntons' ball tonight. A great extravagant do. I particularly wanted to see how she had the place decorated, to be sure to do something different for Barbara's party. I shall be sorry to miss it. I've offered Mrs. Waring a lift too."

"You won't miss it. Why should you? Go, by all means. You are not to be punished because that heller can't be trusted for two hours."

"She has behaved fairly well till today. With her ball to look forward to, I can't believe she'll do anything foolish. She'll be safe. Still, I can't help remembering her sneaking off on Lady Graham, and traipsing into the play on Gentz's arm."

"We've seen the last of the colonel. Ellingwood certainly will not oblige her by taking her."

"Which leaves Romeo."

"I put a pretty good scare into him."

"He is a very odd fellow, certainly, but he occupies a rather special place in Society, Larry. He can get away with things others could not. His artistic genius, his having been reared abroad, and of course his fortune and his noble family . . . I'm not at all sure he should be turned off only for this. I shall speak to him, explain the situation."

"I've already explained the situation to Romeo," her brother said, "and I wish you will explain to your servants he is not to be allowed here."

Lady Withers was not quite so severe as her brother in this respect. She dropped the hint to her housekeeper that if Lord Romeo happened to come when she was out, she would appreciate the good woman's bearing the two of them company, and perhaps would just tell her when she returned what exactly had transpired.

While this was going forth belowstairs, Babe was racking her brains above to figure a way to attend the Cyprians' Ball. She hardly even wanted to go, yet to be forbidden to leave the house was a challenge she could not ignore. She must go unrecognized, of course. A young lady's attending such an affair would be scandalous, and she did not mean to be a cause of scandal again. She would conform to the outward show of Clivedon's polite circle of friends, but she fully intended throwing in his face what she had done, after it was all over and she had escaped unnoticed.

It was the matter of a disguise that occupied her once the positive decision to attend had been taken. She came to think a man's outfit was the best choice, but Lady Withers' husband was very tall, and his were the only gentleman's clothing in the house. Lady Withers and her husband were attending dinner before the ball, so Barbara had a tray in her room. Her hostess came to take a leave of her and see if she could read by her expression what was in her mind. She could read exactly nothing, and went to Staunton's with a little sense of uneasiness that dissipated as soon as she got there. At eight-thirty, Barbara sat alone, wondering if there were any wigs in the attic and wishing she had thought to look before it got dark. They would be antiquated affairs from another era—that would look odd at a modern ball. She found a mask from a masquerade party in her drawers, and a domino, but disliked to go without some concealment for her hair.

It was not yet nine o'clock when a servant came tapping at the door to inform her that Lord Romeo awaited her below. With a joyful heart, she dashed downstairs, for her most intense efforts had not produced a really good plan to overcome the host of difficulties involved in getting to the ball. She needed this ally. It was difficult, indeed impossible, to seek his help with the housekeeper sitting not a yard away, with her ears on the stretch. The talk was of the dullest. How did she feel after her fall in the pond? Not at all ill. He had not seen her at Staunton's ball and, as he knew she had been bade to dinner first, assumed she was not to attend. He must have gone—and left—very early. There was no reason for him to remain if she were not there. All this was for the third listener's benefit, for of course she knew Romeo was going to the Cyprians' Ball, but she was flattered he had looked for her first. He supposed he ought not to stay long. It might be better if he not. He arose on the spot, to her infinite disappointment. She had about three seconds in which to impart to him some intimation he was to return to some more private door than the front door. Her eyes, she knew, were full of intrigue, and she hoped he would see it. She saw, to her relief, that his were similarly alight. As he bent over to kiss her inner wrist, he slipped a note into her other hand, which went out of its own volition, so closely were their thoughts linked.

"You are my other self," he told her in a low voice, then took his leave of the housekeeper and departed. Before half a minute was up, Barbara was in her room, reading the note:

140

My dear heart: I will not be parted from you. I write this on the chance of being allowed to see you for a moment. I will be waiting in our garden. Come to me if you love me. Your own, Romeo.

The only fact of much interest to her was that he was waiting. Here was a cohort in her plan to attend the infamous ball. She picked up a pelisse, a bonnet, and slipped down the staircase, looking carefully to await her chance to dart into the study unseen and out the French doors to the garden where he had sketched her.

He was invisible in the shadows in his black outfit, but caused no more than a stifled yelp when he came forward. He drew her at once into his arms. "We will never be separated," he said in amorous accents. The secrecy, the romance of the venture, and the moonlight acted strongly on his very sensitive nature. "We are two halves, you and I, indivisible. I have my carriage waiting for you. We shall leave tonight to be married."

"Romeo, don't be foolish. I'm not eloping with you."

"You love me, or you would not be here. Clivedale will not let us meet. I refuse to leave you. This is the only way—there will be no shame attaching to it. We shall go at once to my father's place in Hampshire and be married from there."

"I don't want to be married! I want to go to the ball."

"Will your chaperone not be there, and see you?"

"No, I want to go to the Cyprians' Ball."

"I didn't know ladies of quality attended, but if you want to go, I shall take you."

"They don't attend, which is why I must go in disguise, and you must help me."

"If I cannot bend Heaven, I shall move Hell to oblige you," was his reply.

"There is no need to exert yourself so far. An outfit is all I need."

"Put on your *peplos* and sandals."

"I am not going as Aphrodite or Amphitrite. I wish to go as a man."

"Narcissus, of course!"

"It is not a costume ball," she explained with decreasing patience. "I want a jacket and trousers. Yours would not be much too large for me, I think."

"It is the wrong shape. My shoulders are much larger, and your waist smaller. Then too, it would be criminal to hide your heavenly bosoms and—"

"Never mind, Romeo. You're not going to paint me, only help me find a disguise. Do you have a wig?"

"No, I wear my own hair."

"You are enough to make me tear mine out at the roots! Don't you understand? I want to go without being recognized, for Clivedon will be there."

"I would much rather marry you. We could be halfway to the Hall by morning."

"We would be together at some inn tonight, I expect, and I have no idea of behaving so stupidly. Will you help me or not?"

"I am at your disposal. What can I do?"

"Let us get out of here for a start, before we are discovered. I think we must go to Fannie's house, and I'll change there. But what shall I wear?"

"Even if you wear my jacket and trousers, your hair must always tell the world who you are. There is no other such spun gold in this country."

She ignored the compliment, but agreed with him that her hair must be covered, and felt the charming Titian wig resting in Fannie's room was the thing to do it. Fannie had worn it to a masquerade party last year. They drove to Portland Place and, with a memory of Clivedon's anger at her meeting Gentz there, she had Romeo wait in the carriage for her, and let herself in. There were servants at home, not so surprised to see her again after her former visit to meet Gentz. The butler handed her a few letters, which she put in her reticule without reading. She made a hasty toilette, the greatest bother being to pin her own hair tightly to her head and slide on the red wig. It changed her appearance a good deal. A darkening of her brows and lashes, a spot of rouge on her cheeks, and she felt the disguise was better than she had hoped. She would hardly recognize herself. Fannie's gowns were a close enough fit to make wearing them possible, though they did not fit so well as her own. A tightening of the drawstring below the bodice on an Empress-style gown helped. Still, she feared a close observer might know her, and took up a large fan to conceal her face. On an impulse, she took up also a black feather mask, elaborate as most of Fannie's things were, including the low-cut gown of mauve lutestring she wore. It showed a good deal of her bosoms. Romeo, she feared, would be hard to control, but she threw a white shawl over the outfit and picked up her reticule to leave.

She knew her disguise to be good when her escort, lounging at the front door, said, "Good evening, ma'am. You are very beautiful. Would you be kind enough to ask within if Lady Barbara is ready to join me now? I am very tired with waiting."

"Romeo, you idiot! It's me."

"Barbara? I didn't recognize you. I don't like you so well with red hair. I hope you haven't dyed it."

"Not in half an hour. I am not so efficient, and you said I was beautiful."

"Aphrodite is always beautiful, but less beautiful without her golden hair. And I don't think I like the paint on your face. You look like a harlot. I want to take you home and make love to you. I become very excited in the company of harlots. All gentlemen do. I expect I shall enjoy the ball. I wish you weren't coming with me."

"Don't feel you have to tell me every thought that passes through your head," she said, unsettled by his plain talking, though she was becoming fairly used to it.

"I do you the honor to say what I think and feel. Hypocrisy is anathema to me. Please take off your shawl so I can see your figure."

She pulled it more tightly about her and got into the carriage. After trying several times to remove it, to kiss her, to take off her wig, and generally to talk her into eloping with him, Romeo was given to understand that he was doing no more than going to a ball, where he would behave himself if he knew what was good for him.

"I wanted to make an alliance with one of the harlots tonight," he told her. "I do not speak of a prolonged ar-

143

rangement, you understand. Only till we are married. I haven't had an affair since I left Taunton several weeks ago. I am becoming very nervous and irritable. You must forgive me. I mean to be as faithful as I can after we are married, only I am not much good at fidelity."

A few examples of his attempts at it, and his subsequent failures, made up his conversation till they reached the Argyle rooms on Regent's Street, where the ball was in progress. It was no longer early, but one unique feature of the Cyprians' Ball was the lateness of its beginning, as so many of the escorts had first to deliver their wives or fiancées elsewhere, and stay an hour to keep up appearances. It was early enough that the scene had not yet become very indecorous. She had attended less well-run polite parties. Most of the gentlemen were recognized by her, and a few of the ladies as well, by sight only. To stand and watch, it would not occur to anyone she was at a prostitutes' ball. The gowns were as fine, the jewels in as great abundance, somewhat greater perhaps, the music and refreshments similar to any *ton* party, while the rooms were elegant and well maintained. After getting the general idea of the affair, Barbara began looking around for Clivedon. She saw several faces that surprised her—husbands of *grandes dames,* and high sticklers whom she would never have expected to be in a place like this. She wondered who was escorting their wives at Staunton's do—partners there must be in short supply tonight. She smiled to see Mrs. Waring's husband, said to be "indisposed," so that his wife had cadged a drive with Lady Withers tonight.

Several heads turned to observe Romeo and herself as they entered, causing a shiver of dread to scuttle down her spine. The mask was out of place—there were no masks worn. She set it aside and raised the fan to cover all but her eyes. When the music struck up, she went with Romeo to the dance floor and took her place in a set. The gentlemen all flirted with her, and Romeo, she noticed, was enjoying himself with the harlots quite as much as if she were not present. She realized suddenly, when this caused her nothing but amusement, that she did not love

144

him in the least. He was terribly beautiful, he was interesting, he was rich, people said, but he was utterly impossible to take seriously. How could you love a man you couldn't take seriously?

No one recognized her, but when several very good friends of Fannie Atwood entered, she decided it was time to retire to a quiet corner. It was becoming late, and still Clivedon had not come. She had seen a Cyprians' Ball now, and her only other reason for being there was to vex Clivedon, so she decided to go home.

"Not just yet, my dear," Romeo told her. "There is a ravishing lady I have to meet. She does not have a lover. I want to arrange to come back to her after I take you home. You aren't angry with me, I hope? I don't love her. Merely our bodies are in harmony."

"Arrange it quickly, then," she said with annoyance.

"You *are* angry with me."

"I assure you I am not. Please hurry."

"You are perfect, you know. I never met a woman before who was not jealous. We shall deal famously. That is an heroic quality—lack of jealousy. I wish I had it, but I am very jealous of Lord Clydesmare. I hate him," he said gently.

"Do hurry, please," she repeated. He kissed her wrist and wandered off.

Watching Romeo make his assignation, Barbara's eyes were turned from the entranceway when Clivedon came in. He moved rather quickly down the far side of the room and, still watching her own escort, she saw with infinite dismay that he had led his ravishing lady to the floor for a waltz. Heavens, she'd be here all night!

It was not to be expected that a pretty damsel would be long unmolested at such a daring spot as this, and before long a young buck came up to her to request a dance. Her chagrin was great to recognize Herbie Webster, whom she knew as well as she knew anyone, and certainly he would recognize her too if she couldn't be rid of him quickly. She raised her fan against her cheek, and shook her head in a firm negative.

"Come on, then, it's no fun sitting alone, my pretty. Have a dance with me."

"No, thank you. I am waiting for someone," she said, disguising her voice.

"You'll have a long wait. Lord Romeo has replaced you, my girl. I know who you were with, and that boy will do you no good. He's a mere stripling."

"Please go away."

"Not till you've given me a dance."

Becoming desperate, she said, "Leave me at once, or I shall scream."

"That's not a good way to find yourself a rich patron, my little lightskirt."

"It's news to me if *you* have two pennies to rub together, Mr. Webster," she answered sharply.

"Oho, you know my name! Now, how does it come I don't know a pretty little piece like you?" He put his fingers to her fan to try to pull it away.

"Stop it at once," she said angrily, and struck at him with her fan.

She was more horrified than relieved to see Clivedon rear up behind Herbie Webster, very obviously coming to her aid. When had he arrived?

"Is this gentleman bothering you, ma'am?" he asked.

"Very much," she said in a voice that was not likely to betray her, it sounded so very unlike her own low tones. It was high-pitched, nervous.

"Here's a bird more to your liking—well plumed!" Webster said ironically, sneering at her. "Take care, Clivedon. The muslin company is well organized this season, and has got our fortunes all written up in a book. This one admits she's after the money."

"May I join you?" Clivedon asked, with an unconcerned look after Webster's retreating form.

She could hardly credit her awful luck. "No!" she said, still in a nervous squeak. "That is—I—thank you, but I am waiting for someone." He sat down all the same, uninvited.

"Tell me his name, and I shall send him to you," he replied, looking hard at her. She kept her fan well up and

146

her eyes cast down, only risking one peep at him. She shook her head in a firm negative in reply to his suggestion.

"This is nonsense, you know," he went on, throwing one leg over the other and leaning back in an attitude that bespoke of an intention of lingering. "You'll not be long left alone at a place like this. You're new around here, aren't you?"

She nodded and looked away, raising her fan high to hide her profile. And still that moonling of a Romeo was smiling at his friend, oblivious of the lady he had brought.

"Good God! Don't tell me it's Lord Romeo you're waiting for!" Clivedon exclaimed, following the line of her eyes.

This came too close to revealing her identity to risk another word, or another minute in his company. She arose and fled the room, with just one frightened glance over her shoulder at Clivedon. She took the idea he was laughing about something. Her plan was to leave at once and alone, in Romeo's carriage. She could send the rig back for him.

Romeo had been keeping a sort of half-eye on her while he flirted with his other lady. When he recognized the second man with her to be Clivedon, he had become angry, and when he saw her depart so precipitously he took after her, leaving a very surprised female standing alone in the middle of the dance floor. He stopped only to vent his wrath on Clivedon. "What have you said to upset her?" he demanded in an angrier tone than he generally used.

"Got yourself a new chick, Romeo?" Clivedon asked. "That exquisite taste of yours is deteriorating. I liked your other one better."

"You are incredibly stupid," Romeo told him, then fortunately left before revealing the entire devastating truth.

He caught Barbara up at the door. "What did Clysehorn say to you?" he asked solicitously.

"Nothing of the least importance. We must go at once."

"I do hate that man," Romeo said, but he was calmer

147

now, and put no particular emphasis on the words. "He'll steal Adele while I'm gone," he went on as they got into the carriage. "But I'll take you home, my dear. I wouldn't dream of abandoning you to your own devices, though you would certainly be safe enough in my carriage. It would not be the proper thing to do, and you would probably hold it against me if I did. It seems a foolish waste of time to me, but I'm not complaining."

"It certainly sounds as if you are!"

"But I'm not, my beloved. If he's stolen Adele by the time I get back, I'll challenge him to a wrestling match. I am a very good wrestler. I broke Spiro's wrist—accidentally—once in Athens. I wonder if that is why he contrives the handles of his vases so poorly."

Lady Barbara found that Clivedon's stealing of Adele offended her senses in a way that Adele's stealing Romeo had not. She was very indignant on Romeo's behalf, and urged him to return with the greatest speed.

He delivered her to the rose garden on Cavendish Square. "When shall I see you again?" he asked her.

"I'm not sure. You'd better not come back, Romeo. They will already be angry you were here tonight."

"We must make plans for our elopement," he reminded her.

"I am not eloping with you. You'd better go, or he will have stolen Adele."

"Our marriage is more important. Nothing must stand in the way of that. But really, I find myself anxious about losing Adele too. Leave it all to me. I shall make the arrangements and be in touch with you by some means. Don't doubt my ingenuity. I am very clever at arranging elopements," he assured her.

"Have you arranged many before?" she was curious enough to ask.

"No, but I have contrived dozens of illicit meetings, and the procedure is quite similar, I should think. It is the getting out of the house that is difficult. It is very exciting, fooling the oldsters, isn't it? Elopement is my very favorite way of marrying. But I refuse to go to *Scotland*, my heart. I hope you have not quite settled on Gretna Green."

She could assure him with the greatest sincerity that she had not the least interest in being married over the anvil.

"May I kiss you then, before I leave?" he asked.

With a smile between amusement and annoyance, she raised her lips and kissed his cheek. "That was not what I meant," he told her, and folded her in his arms for a much more passionate embrace, from which she had to use all her strength to extricate herself. He was a good wrestler, but Babe was not completely unversed in fighting off persistent embraces, and eventually got away from him.

"I look forward to you," he told her, with deep breaths, then added, "but I must go back to Adele now. I love you, Aphrodite."

Sixteen

Clivedon stood looking after the fleeing form of the unknown Cyprian with a frown on his face. One usually
heard rumors of a new Incognita on the scene, and he
had heard nothing of a wide-eyed redhead hitting town.
That was all he had seen, the eyes and the wig. With the
brows darkened, he had not thought for a moment he
might know the girl under another name. It was not till he
saw her looking towards Romeo that he thought much of
it, but when she arose to run off, so nervous, he looked
hard at her lithe figure, her light step, and was pretty certain he had seen it before, and often.

He went to rescue Adele from her stranding, to see
what he could find out from her. "Young Lord Romeo is
burning the candle at both ends this evening," he mentioned, smiling lightly.

"One candle and one flare," he was told by a pertly
smiling young female, whose hopes soared to have come
to Clivedon's attention.

"Who was the young candle? A new girl, isn't she?"

"Whoever she is, he's mighty shy of introducing her

around. Funny he'd bring her here then leave her and come trotting after me."

"Some of us have a little trouble resisting the irresistible," he returned gallantly.

"Not that one! He doesn't bother trying. He says and *does* whatever he wants. I never met such a queer nabs. But he's handsome as can stare. Got a real way with him. I figure I haven't seen the last of him. Said he'd be back. If it was me he'd brought in the first place, he'd hear about it. But he said the girl—*lady* he called her—was anxious to get home before somebody or other saw her. Borrowed somebody's light o' love, I daresay, unless she *was* a lady."

"Not she! I spent a few moments in her company," he said at once, then turned the conversation to other matters. Adele had only one subject on her mind, however, and had soon turned it right back to Romeo.

"He's queer in the head, not a doubt of it. Oh, are you leaving so soon?" she asked, disappointed. The waltz was just finished.

"I have just remembered a very important matter left unattended."

"What's her name?" Adele asked saucily. "You gents are kept hopping tonight, trying to be in two places at once."

Clivedon had his carriage called, and bolted at once to Cavendish Square to request an interview with Lady Barbara, though it was by this time well after eleven o'clock.

"Lady Barbara is sleeping, milord," the butler told him.

"Please awaken her. It is urgent."

Clivedon was bowed into the Crimson Saloon. He was no sooner seated than the housekeeper entered to empty her budget regarding the visit of Lord Romeo. "He arrived not long after nine, and I remained in the room with them, as her ladyship asked me to. His visit was short and proper in every detail. Very proper," she said. Like all the women in the house, she was a champion of Lord Romeo.

"Lady Withers did not leave orders to keep him out?" he asked, unhappy with this disobedience from his sister.

"No, milord, she asked me to sit with them if he came, which I did, and I just thought I'd tell you, as there was mention of an urgent matter." This last was a direct hint for information, but it went unanswered.

"Thank you," was all he said.

"Her ladyship hasn't stirred from her room since," the woman added. He nodded his head, biting back the question that bothered him. Had anyone actually looked to see if she was there? He'd know soon enough.

Lady Barbara had no sooner sneaked back to her room and pulled off the wig and mauve lutestring gown than a servant was knocking on her door with Clivedon's message. "His lordship says it's very important," the servant called in, for the door had not been opened.

"Very well. Ask him to wait," she answered in a sleepy voice, then she scrambled into a dressing gown, removed the eyebrow pencil from her brows with cream, creamed off the rouge, and hastily brushed out her hair A glance in her mirror told her she looked too excited, and too rosy from all her rubbing, to pass muster as having been disturbed from a deep sleep. It couldn't be helped. He couldn't possibly *know*. He was only suspicious. She would be on her high horse, grossly insulted at this call, and she wished her heart would stop hammering against her ribs.

She curtsied at the door of the Crimson Saloon. "What is this important matter that must get me out of my bed at close to midnight?" she asked haughtily.

"Fast footwork, Lady Barbara, if you managed to set aside your red wig and get *into* your bed in less than half an hour."

"Are you bosky, by any chance, Clivedon?" she asked with a quizzical smile, as though at a loss to understand him. "I thought you would be at that interesting do you mentioned. The Cyprians will be missing you." Especially Adele, she added to herself, with a silent gurgle.

152

"Cut line. You were there, against my orders, and I wish to hear an account of your evening's proceedings."

For half a minute she regarded him, wondering whether to admit it or brazen out her lie.

"Don't bother trying it," he advised. "I am not a complete fool. Your face is still pink from scrubbing off the rouge, and I know well enough if I sent a servant to your room, she would find the wig and low-cut gown."

"What of it?" she asked boldly, abandoning all thoughts of concealment. "No one recognized me."

"*I* recognized you, and if Webster did not, he is blind."

"He didn't!"

"You don't leave me much choice, do you? I forbade you to attend, and you disobeyed my orders. You must not accuse me of hard dealing now for doing as I see fit."

She looked at him, uneasy at the uncompromising line of his jaw, the steely edge in his voice. "What do you intend to do?"

"I cannot in conscience subject my sister to such usage as you have shown her—such absolute disregard for the feelings of a lady who has tried to befriend you."

Barbara had enjoyed life at Cavendish Square, and saw looming before her a return to Mecklenberg Square instead. "I don't want to go back to Lady Graham," she said.

"I expect the feeling is more than mutual. Do you have anywhere else to suggest?"

She racked her brain for an answer, but with Fannie away, she could not alight on anyone. The Harrows, she knew, would dislike to have her as much as she had hated being with them. She frowned into her lap, trying desperately to think of a friend or relative.

"Well? Run yourself to a standstill, have you? I mentioned the possibility at your last scrape—or was it the second-last? I think you come to realize now, too late, the wisdom of my advice. Your flaming career has ground to a halt. Nowhere to go."

"I can always go home," she answered with dignity. She was not crying, or close to it, but she was deeply upset. She would like to go to Drumbeig, but she could not go alone, and disliked to be sunk to hiring a companion, a total stranger, to go with her.

"I doubt you would long be happy in the wilds of the Cotswolds."

"You're wrong. I'd be happier there than I ever was, being billeted on people who don't want me."

"You would not be unwanted if you behaved yourself with the very least modicum of propriety."

"My lack of propriety did not disturb my other chaperones to the extent it troubles you. No one looked down their noses when I had the Czar dangling after me, or when Wellington escorted me to the ball in Paris. In fact, Fannie said it was a victory. And she would laugh at this too. I don't know why you are making such a to-do over it."

"I don't consider it a joke that you make a scandal of yourself. Carrying on with married men old enough to be your father is an odd sort of victory to crow over as well, but they were at least eminent, respectable gentlemen who would not harm you, which removed the aroma of the second-rate from it. When you sink to the likes of Gentz, and switch your stomping ground from Carlton House to the Cyprians' Ball, however, the joke turns sour. Next it will be porters and chairmen in gin alley your name is associated with. Have you no pride, no sense of what is owing your family?"

"You make it abundantly clear my so-called family have no use for me. You were kind enough to tell me before ever I came here that your sister didn't want to have me. Fannie was delighted to be rid of me as well. I shall spare you all the bother of putting up with me and go home."

"That will be my decision."

"You don't have much choice."

"I have the responsibility till your twenty-fifth birthday, and will not have it said I chucked you off to the country to be rid of you."

"You take your reputation very seriously. I see it is

your own that concerns you, after all your fine talk about *mine*. Sorry I couldn't have been a greater credit to you and attached the Prince of Wales, to remove the taint of the second-rate from my latest performance, but he is just a little passé for my taste."

"Your own youth will not much longer serve as an excuse for your behavior. You have about reached the end of your rope, milady."

"There's enough left to hang myself!" she said, and arose suddenly from her chair with a sparkle in her eyes of anger, or perhaps unshed tears.

"Babe! Don't be a fool!" he said, grabbing her wrist as she bolted past him. She was jerked around to face him. To his surprise, he saw a tear hovering at the corner of her eye, and her lips trembled. "You teeter on the razor's edge of complete ruin. If tonight's spree had been discovered, it would be enough to topple you over, once for all. Think what you are about."

All her life she had been accustomed to do as she wanted. No one had checked her. Her escapades were all good jokes, to be laughed over and discussed merrily the next morning. She saw she had skated close to the edge of disaster, and was shaken. If Lady Withers and Clivedon turned her off, where was she to go? There was nowhere left but Drumbeig, and home without parents or even a relative was hardly home. But she wouldn't beg them to have her. Not if she had to marry Lord Romeo and go to Greece.

"I only wanted to make you see the seriousness of this way of carrying on," he said, in a kinder voice. "My girl, don't you realize if Webster had recognized you, it would be the end? It would be all over town before morning. There wouldn't be a door open to you."

"He didn't know me."

"I hope you may be right. Were you talking to anyone else before I arrived?"

"Only Romeo."

"How did he come to leave you?"

155

"He wanted to make the acquaintance of one of the girls there."

"That jackanapes! Well, it seems you have once again squeaked through with your hide intact. No irreparable harm has been done."

She looked at him, hopeful, but not liking to put the question that was on her mind. "Go on up to bed. We shan't mention this to my sister," he told her. The word "shabby" was present but unspoken.

"Does that mean—am I to be allowed to stay?" she asked, rather timidly.

"Yes, if you will only please *try* to behave," he said, with a rueful smile that sent the tears spilling over her lids.

"I'm sorry," she said. "I will. Truly I will, Clivedon. I didn't mean to be so much trouble, but when you *forbade* me to go . . . well, I know perfectly well you expected to see me there, and if you hadn't been looking for me, you wouldn't have recognized me either. No one else did." She blinked away the tears and lifted her chin, in some vestigial semblance of her old self.

He found he was relieved to see her not completely abject. "Don't feel obliged to live up to everyone's worst expectations. Why should you take upon yourself to provide the town's amusement? Let them find a new whipping girl."

She thought about this for a moment, and found it good advice. Why did she behave so foolishly, but because everyone expected it of Babe? And what was in it for her? To be looked down upon and disparaged. "I wish I had known you sooner," she said, in a joking way, but there was a hint of regret too.

"You could have. I tried to get to know you once, if you recall, but couldn't get past the mask."

"You didn't try very hard."

"I'm trying harder now. You will notice with what forebearance I resist mentioning that even the mask failed to show up upon certain occasions."

"Only once!" she pointed out, then became embarrassed, as she had thus far refused to recognize any men-

156

tion of Richmond Park. He did not mention her sudden recovery of memory, but only smiled in a way that acknowledged it. She rushed on at once to change the subject. "I collect I ought to thank you for being angry with me. I mean—for your advice," she amended hastily.

"I know. I know what you mean. Barbara, about Romeo . . ."

"He came to call after your sister left, and gave me a note. I slipped out and he took me to Fannie's to get dressed, but I didn't let him come in."

"That's not what I meant. It was my hope Agnes would forbid him the house, but if you really care for him . . ." There was no longer any anger, but a quiet, searching look of the keenest interest.

"No! Don't be absurd. How could anyone love such an unlicked cub. Oh dear, that is not what I meant at all. He is more like a handsome Harlequin. Pray keep him away from me if you can, for he has taken the notion I am going to elope with him, and is deaf to all my refusals, in that peculiar way he has of hearing only what he wants to."

"And Gentz?"

"Gentz? I had nearly forgotten all about him."

"Is there anyone else?"

"Not yet, but you make me realize the advantage of a decent husband, and I mean to put the next few weeks to very good use. You will have the pleasure of attending my wedding before the summer is out, sir, and that is a promise. You see how cocksure I am of my charms. I'll find myself a companion to take me home to Drumbeig, and am convinced a husband would be more amusing than a gorgon. You and your sister will not much longer have me to put up with."

"We do not consider it an unmixed evil."

"I shall take my leave, before you fall into pretending you have *enjoyed* it, and remove any doubt that you are shamming it. Good night, and thank you."

"My pleasure. I'll come by tomorrow. While you schemed behind my back to fall into a pond and jaunter off to that disreputable do, I was busy preparing a surprise for you. A pleasant surprise, I hope."

"Oh, Clivedon! You have got my horses," she exclaimed. "Thank you."

"Baggage. Get to bed," he laughed.

Seventeen

Lady Barbara went to bed nearly at once, but she did not sleep immediately. She considered her past history with an intensity she had never accorded it before in her life. She had been a fool for six years, making a scandal of herself till her few respectable relatives and friends had nearly given up on her. No more. She was three-and-twenty years old, and long past the age when she should be married. This was her last Season. Even if Lady Withers should extend her offer to another year, she would not accept it. One could accept only so much charity from friends, and seven years on the town was too much. She'd make some match, some good respectable man, and she'd make him a good wife too. She had not a notion in her mind who the man would be, but he would be someone like Clivedon. Some effectual gentleman who took a genuine interest in her and was old enough and strong-willed enough to restrain her if she became bored and impossible. It was unfortunate she had no such flirts amongst her admirers. As Clivedon was truly trying to steer her into a safe matrimonial harbor, it was odd he had not brought any such gentlemen to her attention. Any of his own friends would do nicely, but he never took the least pains to foster an attachment in that direction. Did he think his friends would despise her as being too silly and too raffish? Very likely. And very likely he was right too. If he didn't know, who did? The touch of rakishness she had picked up over the years would not appeal to a mature sort. It was the younger bucks who were impressed by it, considered it glamorous, and not shoddy, as it was. He had seen it all along. That was why he had often mentioned Ellingwood as being suitable. No matter, a man of twenty-five would soon be mature, and as she was totally committed to behaving herself now, she could not feel she really required as firm a hand as she would have a month ago.

It was not till morning that she remembered the few letters given to her at Fannie's house and opened her reticule to have a look at them. One was from Fannie herself. She had decided to have her marriage ceremony in the country from her own little place. She would not be coming back to town at all. Nor did she suggest that Barbara go to attend the ceremony. After all those years, she was not even invited to the wedding. So much for old friends. She was no better herself. Her major emotion was relief not to have to either go or make excuses. The second letter was a bill from a jeweler that Clivedon seemed to have missed, and the third a note from Colonel Gentz, expressing surprise and delight at his engagement, which he had read of in the papers. Ass! He asked if it would be proper (and safe) for him to come to London now. This one must be answered immediately. She found a copy of the retraction of her engagement and slipped it into an envelope with a few lines explaining briefly the position. She also wrote a note to Fannie, then remembered that she must send a gift as well, if Clivedon could be persuaded to advance her some of her money. There was no resentment that she must appeal to another for her own funds. He had been right about that too. How did she manage to run through such a sum as she did? Gambling, lending to her friends, buying a good many extravagant items. She had gone on with practically no money this past month and not much missed it.

She was eager to see her new team, and eager too to begin her reformed life. Lady Withers was polite at breakfast, only saying that it might be better if Lord Romeo not be entertained in future if he called. Had Clivedon spoken to her last night then?

"Was there any talk of my dunking at the Swansons'?" Barbara asked.

"Several people asked for you. I said you stayed home to recuperate. I slipped Clivedon the word to bear me out, when he dropped in later." She mentally noted that he had gone to the Staunton ball, and not back to the Argyle Rooms. Very likely Romeo had made his assignation with Adele, then, and she would be free of him for a while.

They were still at the table when Clivedon arrived with the repaired phaeton and new team. "Get your bonnet and we'll give them a try," he told Barbara.

When she went to prepare herself, Clivedon discussed with his sister the same matter she had just talked over with Barbara. "Not too great a brouhaha. It will pass over if no new calamities arise," Lady Withers thought.

"They won't," her brother answered confidently.

"I was amazed she didn't slip off behind our backs last night, when I heard young Romeo had been here," Agnes replied innocently.

She was not enlightened on this matter by her caller. "I dropped by myself later on," he said. "We had a good talk, Agnes. Babe has had very poor advice from her former guardian. That Fannie, you know, running with a rackety crew and never trying to exercise the least restraint."

"It would not have been pleasant to be forever pinching at the girl. If they were to rub along at all, they must accept each other's ways."

"It was for the older to show some guidance. Barbara was only seventeen when she went there first. She *thanked*

161

me for lecturing her last night. I felt a perfect tyrant. Imagine, no one before ever bothered to be angry with her. I wonder she hasn't run into real trouble before this. There must be more common sense there than we ever thought."

"She is no greenhead, certainly."

"She has more than her share of town bronze now, but is still quite childishly naïve beneath it all."

"You gave her another talking-to about the water party, did you? I shouldn't harp on it, Larry. It really wasn't her fault. The thing to do is keep Romeo away from her. It was his picture that everyone spoke of—so shabby of him, and *not* what I would have expected from one of his sensitivity, for you remember he particularly said he had changed his mind about painting her un-draped. I fear he is not completely reliable."

Clivedon stared at this mild reproof of the former favorite, and said he thought the fellow could be relied on totally to make a mash of anything he did, outside of painting. Their talk was interrupted by the arrival of the lady in question. She was led to the front door to view her team, another set of grays, not so different-looking from the last. "Oh, you found me new grays! Whose are they?"

"Yours now—you said you preferred grays. They're a tamer pair than Bradbury's, you may be sure. They come from a country gentleman who trained them himself, but I drove them through town a couple of days to accustom them to city traffic. They're sweet goers."

This mark of consideration, of time spent on her convenience, struck her most forcibly. "How very kind you are," she said. "You spoil me, Clivedon."

"It is a guardian's privilege."

"I think you mean unpleasant duty, but this goes beyond duty. How lowering for you to be seen driving this country-bred pair through town. Were they very *farouche*?"

"A trifle nervous the first day, but they are fast learners."

She took the reins and directed the team to Bond

Street, congratulating him on his choice. "These are obedient without being slavish, just as I like. Did I pay a great deal for them?"

"Ah, good! You are showing an interest in your money. You'll get the bill."

"Not till next quarter, I hope. Clivedon, I dislike to ask another favor of you when I am in such deep disgrace . . ."

"You're climbing out of the moat. What is it?"

"There's a bill in my reticule, just at my side there, if you wish to take it out. A jeweler you missed in your canvass to cut off my credit. But only a couple of pounds; he reset a ring for me. That is not the real favor, however. The thing is . . . oh, I see you have found Fannie's letter. Read it, if you like. She is getting married in the country, and I ought to send her a present."

He drew out the letter and read it through, noticing the abrupt wording, no invitation for Barbara to attend the ceremony, but several joking references to enjoying herself and not sinking into obscurity with her new guardian. "Odd she should have been eager to send you to me, if she thought you were to be so poorly entertained," he said curtly.

"It was *her* idea, was it? I wondered where you got the notion of taking me on."

"She mentioned to Agnes that you did not wish to go with her to Austria. That led me to hope you were ready for the polite world. It was my own idea for me to replace Lord Withers as your guardian. What sort of present have you in mind?"

"Diamonds certainly. Fannie loves diamonds, and hers are nearly all turned to paste with the high cost of living. A brooch, I thought. Not a terribly expensive one," she went on, as she sensed his dislike of giving diamonds. "She had a good deal of bother with me all those years. I daresay I might have been an expense to her as well. We never discussed money much. Maybe I should give her more than a brooch?"

"You were no financial burden to her. You had your

own monies, which paid for at least half the running of that establishment, I expect. A brooch will do well enough."

They parked the phaeton and went to Hamlet's to select the gift. "I'll arrange to have it sent to her. One can hardly send diamonds through the mail," he said, taking the parcel and putting it in his coat pocket. "Shall we walk a little and see who is on the strut?" he asked.

"Lucky I can't afford to buy any parcels to burden you with, or folks would be saying I had attached you as my new gallant, Clivedon," she teased him, taking his arm to stroll down the street. This was a diversion not formerly engaged in by them, though they had often driven out together, and attended parties. She found it enjoyable to be seen in this new familiar light with her guardian.

"Fine talk, after you have already burdened me with a package of diamonds," he answered.

"Very true, but no one will *know*, so you are safe. You have my permission to tell anyone we chance to meet that we are on our way to Waites to have a tooth drawn. That will provide you an unexceptionable excuse to be seen with me, for naturally I would not go except under duress."

"Naturally! A good thing you reminded me. I'll have him give your teeth a going-over, since you mention it."

"Let us drop into the apothecary while we are about it, and order a mustard plaster, to complete our pleasant outing," she suggested playfully.

They continued for a block in this jocose vein, suggesting hair shirts and Bath chairs to each other till they saw a small crowd gathered around a shop window, looking at the cartoons of the day.

"I wonder what Prinney has been up to today?" he said, and went to have a look. When he heard the word "Babe," he knew he had misjudged the subject of the squib. Tall enough to see over others' shoulders, he saw a depiction of Lady Barbara, arising like Venus from the waves, with her hair her only garment. He tensed and looked down at her, scowling.

"What is it? What's the matter?" she asked.

"Stay here. I'll be right back."

She worked her way to the front of the little throng, just in time to see the cartoon being pulled from the window by Clivedon. She looked in dismay, catching a glimpse of the subject matter and an impression of an angry face behind the window. She saw him rip it into pieces and fling it to the floor, saw him utter a few angry words to the proprietor, while she withdrew to the back of the crowd, hoping she was unrecognized. She had graced dozens of shop windows in her flaming career. She had been shown climbing onto the Czar's knee as he sat on his throne during the royal visit, she had been depicted as leading Wellington into battle after her Paris visit, she had been shown on horseback, and this very season there had been one of her sideswiping Lord Petersham in her phaeton, but she had never before been shown naked. She had rather enjoyed being Society's daring darling, but this went beyond a joke. Clivedon was right; she had been closer to ruin than she knew, and wasn't sure she hadn't slipped off the razor's edge with this exploit.

He was out in a minute, taking her arm to walk briskly away. "You saw it?" he asked. She nodded her head mutely. "I'm taking you home at once," he said in a hard voice.

She was too distraught to make any reply, certain she was in for another lecture. When they went to climb onto the carriage, Clivedon took the driving seat. She was very relieved, for she was too overcome to drive now. She sat silent beside him, waiting for the attack to begin. "I'll sue," he said, after they had gone half a block.

"What?"

"I'll sue him for defamation of character."

"That would create such a lot of talk," she said hesitantly, envisioning courtrooms, crowds, more scandal, and more cartoons.

"Yes, you're right, of course. That would do more harm than good, make it a *cause célèbre*. Better to hush it up, but I'll threaten him in private, and it will prevent a repetition of this sort of thing. You won't want to be seen on the streets today, with everyone talking about this. I'll take you home and go back down to see if there are any more of them on display, and be rid of them if there are. Now don't give up," he said bracingly, attempting a smile, for her benefit, she knew. "You have more pluck than that. It was a damned piece of insolence on the fellow's part, but it is early, and not many can have seen it yet. A pity your every move is of so much interest to the vulgar. What can account for it, do you think?" he asked, positively smiling now, and with really something that sounded strangely like admiration, or pride, in his voice.

She was stunned to see that his anger was not directed at herself for once. He seemed preoccupied as they went home. At the doorway he said, "You haven't any other little rigs running that I ought to know about, have you? Quite sure you weren't recognized by anyone last night?"

"Only you and Romeo. You don't think he might take into his head to tell anyone?"

"God only knows what that bleater might do. I'll go and put a flea in his noble ear this minute. All we need now is Gentz landing into town to claim you for his bride."

"No, I wrote him. That is—sent him a copy of the retraction, in case he should see . . ." She stumbled to a stop. Why was she lying? "Actually, he wrote me asking about it, and I sent him a note explaining."

"That was well done," he congratulated her, when she was sure he'd browbeat her for writing to Gentz. "Don't worry, my girl, we'll pull through yet. Oh, what an infernal nuisance you are," he said, but in a joking way. "I hope you're worth all the bother."

She knew she wasn't. She had never felt more worthless in her life. It was unpardonable to be putting her relatives to so much bother and embarrassment. Lady Withers would hate the shabbiness of this latest bit.

The cartoons (there were two others) were got rid of before many had seen them, and the matter appeared to be at rest. Lord Romeo was warned to keep silent about his last outing with Barbara and accepted it calmly. But then, he never got excited much about anything except beauty and ugliness.

"I shan't say a word. I do not want my wife to wear a bad reputation," was his reply.

"I don't give a tinker's curse about your wife, whoever she may turn out to be, but you will leave Lady Barbara alone," Clivedon told him.

"When I marry her, *you* will leave her alone."

"She's not likely to marry a . . ." He could think of no comparison bad enough to convey his sentiments.

"A cobbler should not judge above his last," he was told. "I do not like you in the least."

"The feeling is mutual, I assure you."

"It was you who wrote my father, giving him a very wrong opinion of my renovations. I do not forgive you for that, nor for trying to keep me from Barbara. Please go away. You disturb me."

One always left Lord Romeo with a feeling of futility, unsure whether he had understood one's point, but quite certain his own had been made.

Eighteen

If ever a sliding woman was restored to respectability, that woman surely was Lady Barbara Manfred. The infamous Babe was no more in evidence. She instituted a régime of propriety that old Queen Charlotte would have admired. She took to inserting lace fichus into the necks of her more dashing gowns, frowning at anyone who called her Babe, driving at a strict trot twice in the direction of Mecklenberg Square to read the Bible with her cousin, Lady Graham. When she was told she read too quickly, she slowed her reading down to a trot too, and received that strict dame's strongest approval; she was declared to be tolerable. She was so determined to be decent that if she hadn't been on the catch for a husband, she might very well have given up receiving morning callers and stayed home from the balls. But her main goal now was to find a husband before the Season was over, and time was running short.

Ellingwood came soon to apologize for the fracas of the water party, and this uninteresting specimen was looked on with a new favor. Clivedon had often mentioned him as the sort of man she should be looking out for, and she learned to discover wisdom in his utterances. To be sure, he only said what everyone else said, but there was something in conventional wisdom, after all. Everyone couldn't be wrong, and it was her old flouting of convention that had set her on the road to perdition. He invited her to drive out the next afternoon, and when she received a gracious nod from Lady Withers, she accepted with alacrity.

Clivedon came to call just as she was on her way out the door. She smiled at him in a meaningful way, to show him how she was heeding his advice. He quirked a brow at her, but seemed pleased, she thought. He was less pleased when the performance was repeated the next day, and gave up any pretense of a smile when she quoted Ellingwood that evening before dinner. He dined with Lady Withers at her home on that occasion, in company with a large party. His approval was not so pronounced as Barbara thought it should be either when she went to sit with the Dowager Countess Anstrom and her sister, Lady Nathorn, both these ladies being sisters to Ellingwood's mother. He raised a brow at her in a sarcastic way that did not indicate approval but mockery, while he himself went to talk to a Miss Chumpton, who was young, pretty, and not at all a backward sort of a girl. In fact, the two of them behaved in a way that caused the countess to look down her nose in disdain and proclaim Miss Chumpton "a froward creature."

As there was an assembly to be attended that same evening, the party at Cavendish Square broke up early. "Are you coming with me or Agnes?" Clivedon asked Barbara.

"Lady Nathorn and Lady Anstrom have asked me to go with them," she replied, looking for a bit of appreciation that she had gained favor with this pair of Tartars.

"What!"

"They are Charles's aunts, you must know," she explained in a low tone. Ellingwood had become Charles during the course of a few outings.

"I see," he answered, very briefly and with the utmost indifference. Then he turned to Miss Chumpton to compliment her on a gown that was every bit as daring, and as pretty, as a certain green Italian silk he had found unacceptable for his own ward to wear in public. Still Lady Barbara continued civil.

"It is indeed lovely," she said to the lady. "Along with Clivedon, I have been admiring it all evening."

"Thank you," Miss Chumpton said with a little frown, wondering that her two admirers should be glaring at each other instead of looking at the gown for which they expressed admiration.

Ellingwood had not been to dinner at Withers', but he was at the assembly waiting for Lady Barbara to arrive. He rushed up to her, greeting her with both hands out. She had the strangest feeling he was going to seize her in his arms, which was not at all his usual way of proceeding. Certainly he was working himself up to a proposal, and she *did* wish he could be a little more dashing in appearance. There were an even dozen that exceeded him in elegance, and a couple of dozen who outdid him in conversation. But he was eminently respectable and eligible, and seemed inclined to favor her, so she smiled and welcomed him warmly, while the Ladies Anstrom and Nathorn glared their approval. This was expressed in one jerky nod of the head, rather like a pair of owls. She saw from the corner of her eye that Clivedon was already present, and appeared to have unburdened himself of Miss Chumpton, though he had certainly brought her in his own carriage, quite unnecessarily, as her mother was at the dinner party at Cavendish Square. When she went to the floor with Ellingwood, however, Clivedon soon followed with another lady to join their set, and at the next dance led Miss Chumpton forward. As he seemed to be keeping a close eye on her, Barbara was fastidious that not so much as a wayward smile escaped her lips. She was nice to the point of insipidity.

The evening was well advanced when at last Clivedon found her unpartnered for a dance. "Enjoying yourself?" he asked. She thought the stiffness in his voice was very likely the result of having stood up with Lady Angela, for despite the most marked lack of interest, she continued courting Clivedon, and had got herself on friendly enough terms that she had received an invitation to Lady Barbara's ball.

"Very much," she told him brightly. "And you?"

"Oh yes. I can relax tonight, with Romeo nowhere in sight and Ellingwood to keep you in line."

"You don't have to worry about anyone keeping *me* in line. I have now got myself under control. I wonder where Romeo is these days? I haven't seen him since the Cyprians' Ball. Don't bother to grin at me! I am careful not to mention that point in front of anyone but *you*. As you know all my past vices, I speak frankly."

Strangely enough, this remark brought forth the first smile that had been on Clivedon's face for over an hour. "It must be pleasant for *you* to be able to relax for a minute and be yourself too," he said.

"I don't find my new demeanor so heavy a burden as you think. I have been enjoying myself very much all week."

"Tell me," he asked in a confidential tone, "whose company do you prefer, Charles's or his aunts'?"

"Not nice, Clivedon. I thought I might have gained the reward of a compliment from you for my tractability."

"You have done better than that. You have gained a more tangible reward."

"Yes, I adore the new team. They are beautiful goers."

"I wasn't referring to the grays," he said with an expression on his face that was hard to read. If she didn't know him better, Barbara would have said there was mischief in it. "Carefully concealed in this inner pocket, there are a couple of cheroots waiting to be sampled. Shall we sneak out to the garden?"

"Clivedon! Are you *testing* me?" she asked, angry with him. "What a low stunt! You don't believe I have changed after all."

"I know you have changed the neckline of your gowns, for the worse," he mentioned.

"I have changed more than that. I have changed my-

171

self, and shall prove it to you. If you wish to blow a cloud, find yourself a gentleman."

"Or a more dashing lady." He looked off in the general direction of Miss Chumpton. "Congratulations, Babe," he said, and turned to walk away.

"I thought you were going to dance with me."

"No, I was going to go out and smoke with you, but if you have lost your taste for it, certainly I shan't encourage you to misbehave. Ellingwood would dislike it."

She knew well enough this was true, but it was no thought of Ellingwood's proprietary interest that angered her. Why had Clivedon suggested it? *Was* he testing her, or, more surprising still, was he serious? And he was calling her Babe lately all the time, just when she had ceased to deserve the opprobrious name. He usually called her Barbara before, except when he was angry. The whole affair put her in a very bad mood, that was not improved when that Grecian phenomenon, Lord Romeo, made a belated entrance to the assembly and walked directly towards her.

"How beautiful you are," was his opening speech. "A constantly recurring delight every time I see you. I am always surprised that reality outpaces the dream. You are wearing a very modest gown this evening, selected by the Philistine, I venture. It does not do justice to the contours of those heavenly shoulders, but its modesty appeals to me after the past several days. I am sated with debauchery. I have given myself to Dionysus and Bacchus. Dare I hope you have been wondering why I have not been to see you?"

"I haven't missed you," she answered sharply.

"I have missed you desperately." As he spoke, Clivedon returned, for, having seen the fellow enter, he was wary to guard his charge. "A harlot like Adele is enchanting for a few days, but I am fatigued with her cold, professional lovemaking, and want you now."

Barbara cast an eye on Clivedon, hoping he might rescue her, but he made not the least move to do so. He stood listening, interested but no more. Romeo ignored him completely.

172

"It is hardly likely to make you attractive to me, to brag of your doxie," she said angrily, knowing that the last word was not a polite one, and regretting it had slipped out, as it caused Clivedon to perk up his ears.

"I had hoped you might be jealous," was her suitor's simple reply. "Most girls are, but you are valiant, my Barbarian. The gods gave you that heroic quality of accepting me just as I am, without trying to change me. I admire it very much."

"You are easily pleased," she told him.

"On the contrary, I am nearly impossible to please. Only perfection can long please me. Adele gave me decreasing pleasure after the first night. Only you will please me for eternity." Then he turned to recognize Clivedon. "As you are officially my lady's guardian, I suppose I must humbly beg your permission to stand up with her. May I?"

Barbara waited for the expected refusal, foreseeing it might take the form of Clivedon standing up with her himself. "That is up to the lady," her guardian said.

It angered her sufficiently that she took Romeo's arm and went to stand up for the next waltz. Over the weeks, he had mastered the dance, taking "a fine Bacchanalian pleasure in it," he said, as it gave him an excuse to hold all the girls in his arms. Being naturally graceful, he performed well. The two made a lovely picture, moving in harmony to the stirring melody of the waltz. There were several heads turned to admire them, and there was one disgruntled gentleman who stalked into the garden to smoke a cigar, alone.

"When shall we elope?" Romeo asked her, as soon as he had got her away from Clivedon.

"Adele might not like that," she mentioned.

"One's mistress has nothing to say with regard to one's wife. Besides, I am through with her. It was a very temporary alliance. I gave her a hundred pounds. Do you think it was enough?"

"I expect she earned more."

"The sum was suggested to me by a gentleman friend. She seemed satisfied. But you don't. My heart, you know

173

it was always *you* I loved. Are you free to elope this Friday?" he asked punctiliously.

"I'm afraid Friday is out," she answered, lured into smiling at his foolishness. "Friday happens to be the day of my ball. I can hardly miss it, when my chaperone has gone to all the bother of arranging it."

"I am not allowed to come?"

"You know they don't want you hanging around me, Romeo," she said, laying the blame on the others to soften the blow.

"I know it. But I know as well that Lady Barbara, who the common people call Babe—insufferable name—is not likely to be stopped for that reason. You have a Jovian disregard for public opinion. It is one of your chief attractions, your disregard for convention. Only you, my beloved, would have dared to attend the Cyprians' Ball. It was an honor to accompany you. Are you quite determined not to leave before the ball?"

"Yes, quite determined. I value convention more than you know."

"You are making me jealous again," he said, sounding tender. "Is there someone else? You don't know what agonies I suffer with this jealousy, the more for the baseness of the passion. It is unworthy of me, but my hubris is dealt a blow as well. I must try to think of *your* feelings, to put them before my own. I wish I could be less selfish. Has Clivedon been turning you against me?" he asked suddenly.

"To tell the truth, Romeo, he seldom mentions you."

"He hopes to make you forget me, as though the moon could forget her dog star. He has been a great trial to me throughout this London visit. Even with Adele I had to hear his virtues extolled. Virtue rather. He has only one in her eyes, and that his wealth. It was he as well who wrote to my father and spoiled my little surprise, interfering man. He has no taste. He had an appalling Clitias forgery in his study, which I was happy to destroy for him."

"Kind of you," she answered ironically. Romeo was strangely annoying tonight, but with Clivedon ducked

174

back in from the garden after a dozen puffs of his cheroot, she did not intend to show it.

"Will you come to my house after the dance tonight?" Romeo asked innocently.

"Are you having a party?"

"A party *à deux*, just you and I. I would meet you in our garden after they take you home, and be sure to get you back before morning."

"I'm afraid you overestimate my daring, Romeo. I wouldn't dream of doing it, nor of eloping either. In fact, I shall very likely be marrying someone else before the season is over."

"Clysedale!" he said, stopping all movement and staring at her with strangely dilated eyes. "He means to force you to have him. I knew it all along."

"Don't be foolish," she said, jerking him back into the steps of the dance.

"He will not get away with this," she was told in an ominous voice. "Don't fear I'll let him make you do it, my dear. I shall protect you."

"Clivedon has no intention of marrying me. I didn't speak of him."

"You can't mean Ellswood? I have heard his name mentioned in connection with yours, but you would never be so lacking in taste. He is a wooden mannikin. Clivedon is at least an eloquent mannikin. He can rattle me off in a very high style, a style worthy of Zoitus."

"I know just what you mean," she laughed, though she hadn't a notion who Zoitus might be, nor did she care.

"Is he cruel to you, my dear heart? Shall I kill him?"

"He is not the least bit cruel. He is very kind, and I wish you will not kill him," she replied, as though she urged a child not to bite a dog.

"I must own I am glad you don't want me to. I have never killed anyone. It would be very Grecian of course, quite in the best dramatic tradition. I admire the Greeks in the plastic arts, indeed in philosophy and everything else but their drama. There is a streak of violence in that that frightens me, though the comedies are very well done. I adore Aristophanes, but when we get to the likes of Medea . . . I have always loathed Medea," he admitted.

"I wonder what she would have thought of you?" she asked, smiling at this peculiarly mild strain in him.

"I daresay she would have loved me. Most ladies do. Adele said I was a very accomplished lover. I was happy to hear that my style pleased an Englishwoman. But of course she is not a lady. Perhaps I should take an English lady as mistress for a week . . ."

"Please don't bother on *my* account."

"You *are* jealous," he said, and smiled softly. "Do you know, *that* pleases me too? Everything about you delights me. It would be immoral if we are not allowed to marry. The gods in their heavens would wreak vengeance on the perpetrator of such a foul deed. But we shall overcome all obstacles, my Divine One."

It was with very real relief that she heard the waltz come to a stop. It was also a relief when the assembly was over, and Clivedon could at last stop following Miss Chumpton's every step, making a cake of himself over the girl, and not once having the common decency to stand up with his own ward. She went home to relive the more lively moments of the evening before sinking into sleep. No image of Lord Ellingwood, whom she had definitely decided to marry, was in her head as she lay down that night. That was all settled, and there was no need to bother with that. She smiled a little at Romeo, frowned at Clivedon's unusual behavior, offering her a cigar, and apparently succumbing during the course of one dinner party to Miss Chumpton, for whom he had shown not the least partiality all season. And she had a perfectly horrid laugh too.

Nineteen

Lady Withers was extremely happy with the success she had achieved in leading her cousin away from the shabby precincts of hell's fire. As often as she had a word alone with her brother she congratulated him and herself on it, till he grew tired of hearing the words "perfect lady."

"Nothing could be more gratifying to me than to see her so well behaved when we go out together. I never have cause to blush for her, Larry. She puts on no gowns I must hint her out of, nor does she go a step out of her way to draw the attention of her ex-friends, but is polite without being friendly enough to encourage them to come to call at Cavendish Square. She will make a charming addition to our circle next year, she and Ellingwood. I wonder where they will live."

"Ellingwood?" he asked. "Don't think she'll settle for that dull dog."

"You are *quite* mistaken, dear. Dullness—that is, a little less vivacity than before—is what she seeks now. She is out with Charles this minute. You'll never guess what! He has taken her to call on Lady Anstrom and her

177

family. It is certainly a prelude to a formal offer. His aunts have both called on me on separate occasions, and expressed—in a roundabout way, you know—their approval of the match. Both her fortune and family quite unexceptionable of course, and in that way a very good wife for Charles. Lady Graham had something to do with it, certainly. An old crony of Charles's aunts, and she has put in a good word for Barbara. Those two visits to Mecklenberg Square have paid handsome dividends. Who ever would have thought—"

"I can't quite picture Lady Graham giving Babe a good character."

"She only cut up one lark while there."

"She has a few more under her belt since."

"Yes, but Charles was with her at the water party, and it is as much his fault as anything that she went on the raft."

"What have Charles's aunts to say to her late engagement to Gentz?" he asked, in a sardonic mood.

"They do not go much into Society. They lay the whole affair in the colonel's dish, where it belongs, very likely."

"You actually think Ellingwood will be calling on me?"

"I know he will, and I think you must ask him to call you Larry. Or Laurence at least. Oh, I would be so happy if we could announce her engagement at the ball. A fit climax to the season, and it would mean she is settled decently for life, and we could all stop worrying about her."

"You can't seriously think she has changed her spots in the space of a month!"

"But she has, and she tells me she is more content than ever she was before. Haven't you noticed she is *calm?* Not so eager and bubbling as she used to be. It was an inspiration on my part to have her. It is what she lacked all along, someone to take a little interest in her. Tact and tenderness, as I suggested from the start. She speaks of going home to Drumbeig for the summer, which would be a very good thing too—the marriage, I mean—for her to have someone to oversee her estate. Lord Romeo could never have been trusted to do it. He would have turned it into a Parthenon. My only regret in the matter is that we didn't think to have her when first her father died, for if we had, she would never have run amok. However, all's well that ends well, as they say," she ended up cheerfully.

"Don't count on it. I'm not sure we've seen the end of Babe yet."

"I wish you would not use that name, dear. Barbara dislikes it. You are in very poor spirits for a gentleman who has done precisely what he set out to do. Several times you have urged Ellingwood forward, and now she has decided to have him, so why are you in the devil's own mood? You should be happy for her."

"I am happy," he said, with a black scowl.

His sister was too busy on this, the day before Barbara's ball, to quibble, though she observed he was not in his customary spirits. Trouble with one of his flirts, of course. It was always woman trouble when Larry took to sulking. He was still protesting to be happy, and showing it in the same way, when Ellingwood brought Barbara home from the visit to Lady Anstrom. There was something on Clivedon's face that made Charles decide to delay the pending interview one more day. He had the perfect opportunity to speak, for Barbara had gone to remove her pelisse, and Lady Withers with great tact went out behind her to clear the way. When the suitor tried to make a few polite remarks before getting on with his business, he received such a blighting set-down that he suddenly remembered a commission he had to perform for his aunt, and asked Clivedon to make his adieux to Lady Barbara.

"I'll tell Babe you had to leave, Lord Ellingwood," he was told. And there was a deuced odd thing too. Clivedon had called him *Lord* Ellingwood three times in as many minutes, and he always used to call him Ellingwood.

"What—has Charles left already?" Barbara asked, when she entered the room.

"Yes, he asked me to tell you he had an errand to perform. So, Lady Barbara, have you found a captain to steer your frail barque after all?" he asked, in a tone not far removed from a sneer.

"I believe I may have," she answered pertly. "A lady
179

may be managed quite as easily as a man, you see, if the gentleman knows what he is about. Why are you staring so? You told me once that a lady might manage any gentleman, and I am merely pointing out that the reverse is also true. Even *I* am manageable, after all, by the right man."

The sneer was markedly accentuated at this speech. "I wonder how much success Charles would have had if I hadn't tamed you for him?"

This was said in a way that would have raised the temper of a much more docile lady than Lady Barbara, who did not consider herself quite broken to the bridle yet. "He has a talent for it. I think he might have contrived without your help," she answered tartly.

"Odd a young gentleman of twenty-five years should be so talented."

"Talent is by definition an innate gift, is it not? With a little cooperation from the barque, we will see it safely landed yet. Did he speak to you before leaving?"

"Yes, he said two or three times that it is a jolly fine day out."

"You know what I mean."

"You refer to making an offer for you? The subject did not arise. You think he intends to do it, when he manages to screw up his courage?"

"I trust he does. Surely he did not mean to set me up in a love nest when he spoke of my going to him. He *never* calls me Babe," she added with a saucy look.

"The slow top!"

"*You* are the one who said it showed disrespect!"

"Did I, Babe?"

"Oh you are hateful! You don't *want* to see me settled. I have learned from *you* not to live up to everyone's worst expectations of me. You said I should marry someone nice, and I shall."

"I am quite certain I did not use the meaningless word 'nice.' Nor do I wish to see you anchored to an anchorite."

"He's not like that! Not hermitish in the least."

"He's the dullest dog in the country. Watch what you

are about, or, in your effort to show me a lesson, you'll end up in the role of Lady Ellingwood. How does that strike you?"

"I'm not trying to show you a lesson! Clivedon, *you* suggested Charles yourself."

"*You* said he was immature and hadn't an original word to say."

"Well, I've changed my mind."

"So have I."

She stared at him in disbelief. This contradiction of his former views was so sudden she felt for a moment the floor was shifting under her feet. One of the major reasons she had undertaken to change herself was to please these relatives, and this was the way he reacted. "Kind of you to let me know!" she said angrily. "Don't you think you've left it a little late?"

"I didn't realize you were such a fast worker, but I should have expected it of Babe Manfred."

"As you are so intimately aware of my *true* character, you had better not goad me too far. There is more than one way to get married, and I don't fancy you would care for any but the proper, established mode, as my behavior now is to reflect on yourself."

"Hinting you mean to dash up to Gretna Green and get married by the smitty? You'll have uphill work getting Ellingwood moving in that direction. The wealthy aunts would disapprove."

"He's not the only man in England."

"Surely, as you speak of marrying him, he is the only one you love."

"This marriage has nothing to do with love, and you know it!"

"Does Charles know it?"

"He loves me! I'm marrying him because *you* convinced me it was the only course open to me. You told me I was a step from ruin."

"You were."

"Well, then!" She looked to see some recognition of her logic, and saw only an intransigent mask. "I come to see it's better than being *your* ward in any case. I'd rather marry a donkey than spend one more week under your dubious protection."

"In that case, send Ellingwood to me, and it will be arranged at once."

The scorching reply she was preparing died on her lips. She looked at him, too confused to continue.

"Well?" he said. "I can forbid it, you know."

"You risk creating a greater scandal than I have ever done, if you refuse such an unexceptionable match, one that has your sister's approval too, with no reason."

"Call it a caprice on my part," he suggested loftily.

"A conundrum is more like it. You are incomprehensible."

"Babe, you *know* he wouldn't suit you," he said, seeming to simmer down, though there was still a good head of steam waiting to blow.

"Why did you suggest him, then? What were you about all these weeks, but trying to get me married to him?"

"It wasn't my intention to see you gallop to the altar with the first man who asked."

"Actually, that would have been Romeo."

"Don't mention that lunatic's name to me."

"You two have one thing in common at least. He feels precisely the same about you. And you didn't make him leave last night, either, when he asked me to dance. I come to think you want me to do something foolish. Don't push me too far with this capricious guardianship of yours, Clivedon."

"What is it you have in mind? Dancing nude in the streets? Announcing an engagement to an actor? Or becoming one yourself. Yes, that's more like it, front stage center. Fairly amusing. Right in your old style. The donkey, I fancy, would bray, but the rest of your audience would applaud the return of Babe."

"Have you finished? I hope so, for I have finished with being Babe. You have thrown her in my face for the last time."

"Do you know, I come to think I like her better than the new Lady Barbara, so encumbered with fichus and calls on dowagers."

"Lady Barbara is greatly flattered at the comparison, but quite frankly, she will not heed your implicit advice to make a spectacle of herself. There will be no dancing in the streets to entertain you. If you wish to see me dance, come to my ball, and you'll see me open it with my bridegroom."

"You mean to have him, then?"

"Unless you have someone else in mind for me for the next week or so? Don't be shy to tell me if you have changed your mind," she said with as much sarcasm as she could find.

"You have already admitted you don't love him."

"At least I understand him. He isn't a moralist one day and a—a *fiend* the next."

"Now, surely it was yourself who told me variety is the spice of life. How will you take to such a bland diet as undiluted Ellingwood, I wonder."

"I'll provide the spice, if that is what worries you."

"God pity Ellingwood! He doesn't know what he's letting himself in for."

"He's not deaf or blind."

"Only dumb, alas, but then, he can't help that."

"He knows well enough what I have been in the past. Unlike yourself, he has some confidence that I can continue, with his help, to be what I am now."

"I wonder if that confidence isn't misplaced," he suggested in a conversational spirit.

There was no sense to be made of his conversation today. In a final, uncontrollable fit of pique, Babe surfaced and said, "Go to hell!" then turned and stormed from the room.

"See you there, Babe," he called after her, and laughed as he slammed the door behind her, but the laughter did not long remain on his lips. He took two hasty steps after her, then turned back, hit a chair with his fist and uttered an accomplished and original curse, before going to take a fairly polite leave of his sister.

Twenty

When Lord Ellingwood went to call on Clivedon the next morning, the latter's secretary was very surprised indeed to be asked to inform the caller his lordship was not at home, and not expected home that day. "He sent around a note yesterday to make the appointment, sir, and you directed me to tell him you would see him at eleven."

"I've changed my mind."

"It was an important matter, you recall, sir."

"You mistake your duties, Smythe. You are my servant, not my advisor."

Mr. Smythe left in confusion to do his duty. He realized Clivedon was in a pelter over something, and though he was a good-natured employer in the general way, one did not argue when he was out of sorts. Smythe did not trouble to tell his employer when the next gentleman called. If he had turned Ellingwood from the door, he would not want to see Lord Romeo. The instant the strangely persistent young artist was got rid of, Clivedon sent to ask who had called.

"You turned young Rutledge away without telling me!"

184

Clivedon asked, at his most arrogant. "Go after him at once. In future you will be kind enough to inform me when my friends call, and let *me* decide whether I wish to see them."

To Mr. Smythe's infinite relief, Lord Romeo had got no farther than the edge of the street, where he stood gazing at the red brick façade of Clivedon House, envisioning its revision.

"His lordship is in now, sir," Smythe said, feeling very foolish indeed.

"Oh, good," Lord Romeo said, and smiled sweetly. "I hope he is in a good mood."

"Not exactly, sir."

"Angry?"

"Rather."

"He's seen me, then. It cannot be helped."

Clivedon looked less angry than calculating when the young gentleman was shown in. "What is it you want now?" was his blunt greeting.

"I am leaving town almost immediately. I know you dislike me, but still I feel the honorable thing to do is to come and ask you for Lady Barbara's hand, as I am going to marry her."

"Lady Barbara's hand is taken."

"You're making her marry *you!*"

"It is another gentleman who has done us both out."

"Elderwood?"

"Close enough," Clivedon told him, smiling a smile that held an invitation, or a challenge. "She prefers him to us, it seems."

"I had not thought you were quite so stupid," Romeo replied. "I was afraid you might beat me out, but she cannot prefer Elderwood to me, or even *you.*"

"Thank you."

"That cannot possibly be misconstrued as a compliment. The man is a wooden dummy."

"I tend to agree with you."

"Enough to make me doubt my opinion, but no . . . You are in a position to prevent her making this match."

"I fear any prevention on my part might lead her to a

185

different, and in my own view worse, mistake. I would not agree to her marrying *you* under any circumstances."

"I know you hate me. It is jealousy, of course. I hate you too. Always have. You're so . . ." Romeo stopped and looked at his host with unveiled hate.

"Spit it out."

"When I struggle to be brief, I become obscure."

"Quoting Horace today, are we?"

"I enjoy to wander in the groves of academe."

"And carry back the fruits to enliven your chatter. But you surely didn't come to bring me this basket of quotations."

"Ah, I see you have got that dreadful forgery patched together again. Are you interested in the original?"

"No, I have come to admire my broken forgery. Is it Art we are to discuss?"

"Art and Love—the two eternal verities. You have given me your views on my Beloved, now we shall discuss Art. You mentioned once being interested in procuring my portrait of Aphrodite. It happens I require ready cash. Do you still want it?"

"I'm interested if the price is right."

"I make a gift of it to you, for the nominal sum of one hundred pounds."

"Magnanimous," Clivedon replied, with unsteady lips. "You're not likely to be long in need of ready cash, with such gifts."

"It was a gift that occasioned the shortage. I have discharged my mistress and gave her a hundred. It has left me short for my trip."

"How soon do you plan to leave?"

"Right after . . . Tomorrow, I think."

"Returning to Greece, are you?" Clivedon asked, settling down to an appearance of friendliness.

"Ultimately. My *psychë* cannot long endure this alien climate."

"You will want to visit your parents before leaving."

Lord Clivedon found it a strange experience to see that innocently open face try to assume a veneer of cunning. "I didn't say I was going home. It happens I have other business in the country. Some orders for—for Grecian artifacts."

"You'll have to have yourself drawn and quartered for removing them from the country of their origin. The Clitias vase too, that you peddle so assiduously, will be a loss."

"I ought not to let it out of the country, really. The fact is, the Greeks do not appreciate their heritage. Plenty of owls in Athens, of course, if you follow my allusion. But these baubles I speak of are not on the scale of the marbles stolen by Elgin. Do you think he would be susceptible to a plea to return them?"

"I wouldn't suggest you waste a moment on the project. They were stolen at a price of thirty-five thousand pounds."

"I haven't time to raise that kind of money. I daresay it would take days."

"Maybe even a week," Clivedon agreed blandly.

"You wouldn't care to consider setting up a fund . . . No, I see you would not. I'll send the painting around. Can I have the money now?"

"I will give it to your man when he delivers the painting."

"Is it that you don't trust me, or that you don't have the sum, and are embarrassed to say so?"

"How have you survived so long, I wonder," Clivedon said, arising to show his caller out the door.

There were a number of calls at Clivedon House that day, every one of them handled in a manner displeasing to the master. Ellingwood dashed to Cavendish Square to ask where he might find Lord Clivedon, which got Lady Withers over to Grosvenor Square within the half hour. Smythe went to inform his employer his sister wished to see him, most urgently, and had his ears scorched for saying he was at home. "Tell her I am out, and will be out all day."

"I have already intimated you are at home."

"Then you had better un-intimate it. And before you make any more of these colossal blunders, I am also not home if Lady Barbara should call. Do you think you can remember that, Smythe, or shall I have a sign painted and hang it around your neck?"

"I shall undertake to remember it, milord."

It was not unnatural in the face of this confusion that Smythe should turn a mere acquaintance away, but he was dressed down nevertheless for not allowing Mr. Empey entrance. The portrait was delivered within the hour. Taking no chances, Mr. Smythe, with ill-concealed impatience, told his employer that he had asked the man to wait, till he discovered whether or not Lord Clivedon was home at that particular instant.

"Ass. Give him a hundred pounds, and bring me the portrait at once."

The painting was brought in, and for the next half hour Clivedon tilted back his chair, locked his door, and sat gazing at it, with a musing smile on his face. Smythe, with the worrisome chore of announcing Lady Millington, tapped nervously at the door, and was told in a shout quite audible to the waiting lady to get rid of her. And if he pestered him again, he may consider himself discharged, and write himself up a cheque for a week's wages.

"What can have happened to Larry?" Agnes wondered, when she returned to Cavendish Square. "The very day of your ball, and Ellingwood not allowed in to see him. We wished to announce the engagement tonight. I shall give him permission myself, Barbara. I am your chaperone, after all, and it is not as though Larry will object. He will think it an excellent match for you. I can't imagine where he is gone. Chasing off after some piece of horseflesh, I expect."

"You had better wait and let Clivedon decide," Barbara suggested. "He will be here for dinner before the ball, and Charles can speak to him then." Barbara felt strangely listless. Her desire to become Lady Ellingwood was not acute enough that she worried about Clivedon's breaking the appointment. In fact, she was rather relieved to have the sealing of her fate delayed a little. Was it possible Clivedon meant to insist she pass another Season in London? There was no possible way she could make any other match in so short a time as the week that remained of the Season. It was likely this uncertainty that made her feel so wretched. "I have a headache, and seem to be running a little fever. I am going to lie down to be recovered for tonight," she told her chaperone.

It was exactly the sort of nuisance that was bound to crop up, that the star of the evening should fall ill, with four hundred guests invited. All of a piece with the cream curdling and the servants spilling a batch of grease on the carpet in the dining room. She was strongly advised to go to bed at once and stay there till she felt quite well. Lying down had not the least good effect. The headache worsened, but by late afternoon, groggy with laudanum and determined not to miss her ball, she got up from bed and went to her window to sit looking out on the little rose garden, which Romeo called "their" garden. She opened the casement window and brought a chair to it. The cool breeze felt good against her feverish cheeks. For half an hour she sat on, sipping a cup of tea, and imagining she felt somewhat better. She mentally compared Romeo and Charles, not at all pleased with the prospect of spending the rest of her life with either, but determined not to go to Drumbeig with a hired companion.

While she sat having her tea, a call came from below that Lord Clivedon wished to see her. She didn't feel up to it. She knew Lady Withers was at a meeting of one of her charity organizations, and knew that Clivedon was aware of it, for she had complained a dozen times of the inconvenience of having to go out on that particular afternoon. He wished to badger and pester her some more with his incomprehensible and ever-shifting views on her marriage. She was so weary she was afraid she'd do whatever he suggested, only to be rid of him. She felt so drained she would even marry Romeo, if that was what he wanted today. After he left, the green Italian crepe was brought to her door, with a note from Clivedon, succinct and offensive:

Babe: I wouldn't want you to have your last fling in too modest a gown. You have my permission to wear this one. Save me a waltz, if your toes are in a dancing mood. Clivedon.

Her toes were not in the mood; neither was her head. She ripped the note to bits and threw the gown on the bed, then sat on it. He expected her to do something outrageous tonight—even the gown would outrage Lady Anstrom and Lady Nathorn. She was determined to show him she had changed. She put on the white crepe de chine agreed upon with her hostess, added the gaudy, unattractive corsage sent by Charles—pink roses with an excess of lace and ribbons—had her hair carefully arranged, not in coils. Her color was high, too high, from the fever, and her eyes held a febrile glaze as well, which in no way detracted from their beauty. How could she look so vibrant, when she felt as limp as a dishrag? She was too upset to be much surprised or disappointed when Clivedon sent a note excusing himself from the dinner party. Something had come up, but he would be at the ball. What could this mysterious something be? Not chasing after a new horse, for he had come here this afternoon. Whatever it was, it would prevent Charles from speaking to him before the ball. Her engagement would not be announced that night.

Clivedon ate at home alone, in thoughtful silence. It was the more usual custom for Smythe to accompany him at the table on those rare occasions when he took dinner at home alone, but, to the secretary's relief, no invitation came to him this evening. Cook's nose was out of joint when a nearly full plate was returned to the kitchen. The butler tried the claret himself to insure it was not corked, for his lordship had not finished even one glass. His valet examined his clothing with a nervous eye, for a charge of carelessness to this paragon had been issued on the last occasion when Clivedon left his dinner on his plate. No such charge was laid this evening. He donned his satin knee breeches and white silk stockings without the usual tirade against this antique outfit, shrugged himself into the close-fitting black jacket, selected from the case held out to him a discreet diamond tie pin, all without a single word. "I'll be late," he said just as he stepped from the room. Then he turned back to add, "Tell Smythe I want him at home this evening. I may have need of him."

This titillating speech caused a good deal of discussion after his lordship had left. Was it a matter of a challenge having been issued? Nothing else of sufficient importance to account for the day's unusual proceedings occurred to any of the hirelings who sat around the kitchen table arguing the matter. Smythe wasted half an hour cleaning and oiling his dueling pistols, and the valet went through closets selecting a suitable dark jacket, choosing his own least favorite, in case of bullet wounds.

While this went forth, Lady Barbara sat at dinner with Lord Ellingwood, who found her an unusually silent partner. "Do you not feel well, Barbara?" he asked.

"I feel perfectly wretched. I hope I am not going to be ill."

To forestall this, she went to the little study after dinner, to sit alone and rest. She turned the lamps down low; the bright light hurt her head. With the door closed behind her, she first sat on the sofa, but had soon put her feet up, arranged a pillow under her head, and was carefully arranging her gown to prevent unnecessary creasing. She was still perfectly uncomfortable, and felt that in some way it was all Clivedon's fault. She began to wonder if he was ill too, as he hadn't come to dinner. She found it impossible to picture him ill, or any other way but in perfect command of the situation. She decided he had stayed away on purpose to prevent Ellingwood's speaking to him, so he didn't know whether he was going to allow the match or not. She was not pleased or angry. She didn't feel up to either being engaged or giving a refusal. It was too much bother. She closed her eyes, and when she felt sleep creeping in on her, she succumbed gladly to it. Maybe a half hour's rest would cure her of this lethargy.

In less than half an hour, she was rudely awakened. The lamps had either gone out or been extinguished. She lay in darkness, hearing furtive footsteps, feeling a cool blast from the open door that led to the garden. The footfalls came closer. "Who is it? Who's there?" she asked, not greatly alarmed, but annoyed at the stupidity of servants, to be bungling about in the darkness instead of lighting a lamp.

A hand was clamped over her mouth, while a second person grabbed her hands and tied them in bands that felt, incredibly, as smooth as silk. The gag soon being tied over her mouth too was soft and rich, even scented, with a tangy, delicious perfume. Still weak, she hardly put up a fight. She was lifted in strong arms, while the second figure, seen to be smaller in the dim light from the moon at the doorway, held the door. The first man was seen to be wearing livery. She thought it was the dark green livery of Lord Clivedon's household, but it was the wrong design. No, it was the gray of the Duke of Stapford's servants.

Soon all doubt was removed. In the garden, smiling softly on her, stood Lord Romeo, with a soft woolen shawl to throw over her. "Rejoice, we are victorious!" he greeted her. "I am sorry to have to do it in this manner, my dear heart. I have arranged all to provide you as much comfort as possible, but we really must elope now. I'm afraid Clivedon suspects. It was necessary for me to see him today. He positively forbade our marriage, so he knows I must use force."

Speaking was impossible in her condition; she could only look a look that attempted to express her wrath, and kick her feet. All the rest of her body was confined by the silken bands and the man's strong arms. "Don't vex your delicate feet, my dear," Romeo told her, then held a foot, as though it were a hand, while she was carried out the gate that separated the rose garden from the yard backing it. The strange party hastened into the dark shadows between two houses to see her abductor's carriage waiting in the street. A door was held open while she was placed inside, amidst a heap of flowers. Romeo got in beside her, the door was closed, the servants took their perch above, and the team of four bolted away, while she writhed to get out of her bonds.

"Flowers for my lady," Romeo said, taking a rose (with thorns) from the seat and placing it on her lap. "A conceit on my part—a whimsy if you like—to greet you with flowers. A pity they don't show in the darkness. It looked lovely this afternoon."

She attempted to make some sound, that came out very

much as a growl, due to her gag. "You are angry that I took you away before the ball," he began softly, persuasively. "The hour had come. Time passes, and I sleep alone. Clivedon means to make you marry Ellingwood. He told me as much today. You think it only spite that I was not invited to your party, but that did not enter into it, though I am glad to have kept you away from the ball. You may imagine what agonies of jealousy my *psychë* would have been subjected to this night, to think of you in other men's arms. He would have announced your engagement to the mannikin, and who knows, he might have induced you to accept. It grieves me to say the man has some influence over you, but it will be my task to change that. I will see my Aphrodite again in all her splendor, without pieces of lace stuck into her bosom, and wearing her old wanton smiles of yore."

Again she tried to speak through her gag, tried to wiggle her arms free, but Romeo made good his boast. He was accomplished at arranging a runaway match. She was missing her own ball, fled from the house, without a word to anyone. With her history, no one would believe it had not been her own doing. It would be the crowning exploit of the infamous Babe Manfred. She was ruined.

"Don't struggle, my beloved. I don't want a scratch on those arms. I used the softest bands I could find—this beautiful blue silk, purchased this afternoon to match your eyes. And the blanket—isn't it soft?—comes from Greece. I have scented it, as well as your gag, with verbena for your delight." He sniffed it, and smiled. "Don't worry your head about a thing. I have made all arrangements. I have got plenty of money—got it from Clysemore, a beautiful ironic touch, for which I congratulate myself. We shall have a luxurious journey. I have arranged all in advance. Rooms at a little inn just west of Chertsey. I had to leave their preparation in the hands of my servants, for I hadn't time to go myself, but there will be music, wine, and a feast. Tomorrow we shall proceed to my father's home in Hampshire to receive his benediction. From there, safe from Lord Clydeholm, we shall be married and go together to Greece. Ah, Greece in early summer with you! I am ravaged at the exquisite contemplation of it."

Again she tried to argue with him, but he only put his arms around her shoulder and kissed her eyes. "You feel warm. I shall take off the blanket," he said, and did it, with infinite tenderness.

She now felt uncomfortably cold, but there was no telling him anything with a gag in her mouth. "Do you wonder how I hit on this excellent scheme?" he asked, in a conversational tone meant to lighten the tedium of the journey. "I took a page from the Romans. They were clever too in their own rude way. The Rape of the Sabine Women, you recall? I have decided to rape you."

An angry, incoherent sound came from her throat. "My love, don't let any base thought enter your head. I do not refer to actual physical rape in a criminal sense. To seize and carry off is the true meaning of the word. When the Romans were deprived of wives, they attended a Sabine feast and carried off the women. What fun it must have been! But as I was not invited to your feast, I had to contrive to do it in a slightly different manner. The effect will be the same. The Romans and Sabines eventually came to amicable terms. In fact, the Sabines migrated to Rome and they became allies. Men do not quarrel irrevocably over women—only over power and money. We shall migrate to Greece, and if Clivemore follows us, I shall perhaps kill him after all," he added, to contradict himself.

She was tired, weak, and so upset she could struggle no more. She sunk against his arm and gave away to despair. A hot tear started in her eye. Romeo soon discovered it, for his hands were gently brushing her hair and cheeks as he spoke. "My beloved—my delight—don't weep! Don't mar your eyes with red streaks. I want you perfect, as you always are." When she remained quiet and unstruggling, he removed first the gag, then the arm bands, pointing out to her at each step what a fine quality they were, to do homage to her beauty. Then he selected in the darkness a handful of flowers and placed them in her lap.

"Romeo, please take me back," she said, but in a small voice.

"Never!"

"You must. I'll be ruined if you don't."

"I have taken care of all that. From my father's home I shall write to Clivesmore and explain the whole, so that no blame can attach to you for anything."

She saw there was to be no arguing, no bargaining with him, and started scheming instead. "Where are we to stop for the night, did you say?" she asked.

"We shall break the journey halfway, just beyond Chertsey."

"That is so far away. Could we not stop sooner?"

"No, alas! Clivehague might come after us, or Ellingwood. No, not Ellingwood. He would not have the temerity."

"But I am awfully thirsty."

"Dear heart, I have taken care of all contingencies. I have brought along a bottle of ouzo," he said, and pulled from the pocket of the coach a bottle of some liquid that he passed to her. "I forgot to bring glasses!" he exclaimed, mortified at this solecism. "Forgive me. No, it is unforgivable. But pray try to find it in your heart to forgive. Here, drink it from my hands," he offered, uncorking the bottle.

"No—don't. Never mind."

"Perhaps you would deign to try a sip from the bottle?" he suggested, pressing it forward.

To be rid of him, she tipped the bottle up and tasted a liquid she was very sure was never meant for human consumption. It was surely poison, it tasted so strong and so foul. She spluttered and pushed it away.

"You don't like it," he said, unhappy. "You must learn to like ouzo. My friends will be offended if you do not. But I too disliked it at first. It is an acquired taste, like Mozart and cold soup. Really it is excellent stuff. It can make you drunk so very quickly. Do have some." Again he pushed the bottle towards her, but when she declined, he took a long draw himself.

Disliking the prospect of a drunken abductor, she took the bottle and lowered the window to throw it out.

"Why did you do that?" he asked, suspicious. "It is a

195

trick. You mean to leave clues for Clivesdale. But he'll never see it in the dark, and by tomorrow morning it will be too late. We shall have spent the night together."

"I am not spending this or any other night with you."

"Pray relieve your mind of rape, my love. I regret having used the word, for I see you are squeamish. It is the malign English influence on your free spirit. I have booked two rooms for us, and mean to hire a woman at the inn to set up a truckle cot in your room, to satisfy Clyesmore and the proprieties. You are perfectly safe with me. All your troubles are over now. Relax, my beloved."

It was more illness and defeat than relaxation that sunk her to a few moments' silence. When Romeo began to regale her with tales of the beauty awaiting her eyes at home in Greece, she let him ramble on, and put her own wits to better use. She must make him stop *long* before Chertsey, preferably within ten minutes, to insure some hope of getting back to Cavendish Square before her ball was too far advanced.

Twenty-One

"Larry, what is to be done? I can't find hide nor hair of Barbara!" was Lady Withers' distracted greeting to her brother when he arrived at Cavendish Square for the ball. So great was her distress that she uttered these horrified words even before she got him into a private study, thus revealing the shabby truth to her butler. "Not here to greet the guests, and *who* is to open the ball?"

"Flown the coop, has she?" he asked, undismayed. "Did she leave me a note?"

"Of course not. That is—I haven't found one, and if she wrote to anyone, it would be myself. I am having her room searched this minute, and Harper questioned, though the woman says she hasn't seen her since dinner, but she might have *heard* something. Ellingwood says she was feeling ill at dinner, and went into the little study to rest a minute. She did look pulled, but she had been complaining of a headache, and naturally everyone has a headache at her own ball. My own head is splitting this minute. The study door was ajar, and I thought she might

197

have wandered into the garden for a breath of air, but there are no signs of disturbance at all."

"How long has she been gone?"

"A quarter or half an hour—I can't say for sure. I personally have not laid an eye on her since dinner."

"We must tell Ellingwood she is gone," he said, turning to the door that moment to seek him out.

"*Tell* him? Are you mad? He is the very one must not learn she has bolted. She must be found and brought back."

"I disagree. It would be infamous to let that poor boy become engaged to a wild filly like Babe. I shall tell him this minute."

"You *are* insane. It may have a perfectly innocent explanation, and to lose him only over a trifle . . . I wonder if she would have darted over to Fannie's place for any reason. Hop into your carriage at once and check it out, Larry. I'll stave off Ellingwood and the others. Say she is feeling ill—it will not be surprising, as she *was* looking peakey at dinner."

"I'll go and have a look," he agreed, not nearly so upset as his sister felt he should be. As he went into the hallway, Ellingwood accosted him.

"I hope Barbara is all right?" he asked, worried.

"Having a little lie-down," Lady Withers assured him, with an uneasy smile that would not fool a child. "We expect she will be feeling better soon, and have sent for the doctor . . ." She realized suddenly that Ellingwood was not looking at her. His eyes had gone past her shoulder to Clivedon, who stood behind her, shaking his head to refute her careful story.

"Larry!" she squealed, her tact deserting her.

"It is too late for lies and patching up," Clivedon said bluntly. "Babe has tipped us the double, Ellingwood. Run away. Typical, of course. She's been too tame of late. I knew she was planning something."

Lady Withers plunged into her evening bag for her vinaigrette, for she would *not* faint. "Larry's little joke, you must know," she said weakly, and, easing herself behind her brother, she delivered a sharp poke in his back.

"We'd better go after her, Ellingwood, and see if we can get her back," Clivedon continued unchecked. "You still want to marry her, I hope. Sorry I was out this morning when you called. Permission granted, of course."

Ellingwood was looking very uncomfortable indeed. "I have no desire to force her, if it is my suit that has set her off," he said. "Is—is that why you wouldn't see me today?"

"No, the fact is, young Lord Romeo has painted up that picture of her coming out of the pond naked, and I had the devil's own time convincing him not to display it at Burlington House. Couldn't talk him out of it," he said, shaking his head. "But you must have a go at him. I think a duel is your best hope. He's gun-shy."

"Larry, you didn't tell me that!" his sister gasped. "Oh, dear . . . But she has not run off at all, Charles. She wandered into the garden . . ."

Ellingwood's head turned from one to the other, his face a perfect mask of horror.

"Agnes, my dear, you disturb yourself for nothing," Clivedon told her. "Charles is not likely to go blurting out the truth to others. If he means to have her, it is time he become initiated into the rites of covering up Babe's scrapes. The chore will fall to *him* now, thank God. This is the last time you and I will have to scramble over the city trying to find her, and exert our wits to make up some story to whitewash her."

"Larry!" Agnes squealed again, in fainter accents, as she saw she was beaten.

"Really, I hardly know what to say," Ellingwood said, looking dazed. "Not much good at this sort of thing—duelling. I had no idea . . . thought she was all over that . . . Lady Anstrom would not like . . ."

"We shan't tell your aunts, of course," Clivedon agreed. "Good God, if they ever learn half the truth, you may whistle their fortunes down the wind. You'll have to learn to hide Babe's carryings-on from them. You don't suppose it's Gentz she's run to again, Agnes?" he asked, turning aside from Ellingwood, who stood trembling at the closeness of his escape.

"Of course not! Romeo is more like it."

A servant approached, bearing in her fingers several pieces of paper. "I went through her correspondence as you suggested, milady," she said, handing the letters to Lady Withers, who snatched at them eagerly.

"Might as well give me these bills," Clivedon said, helping himself to a few sheets. "God knows how she shall pay them. Badly dipped."

"Oh my God, there's one from Gentz," Lady Withers moaned, all discretion tossed to the winds. "Look here, he addresses her as his dear Bride."

"Any from Romeo?" Clivedon asked, carefully putting his thumb over the date of Gentz's letter as he took it from his sister.

"One from Fannie and some invitations. Ah yes, here is one from Romeo, making an assignation to meet her in the garden."

"Maybe I should just return to Lady Anstrom," Ellingwood said, backing from the room hastily.

"That might be best," Clivedon told him. "We don't want her to become suspicious. Shall I go ahead and announce the engagement, by the by? It would help distract attention from her absence. Or would it do just the opposite? We'll say she is not feeling well, and try to get her back before the ball's over . . ."

"No!" Ellingwood pleaded. "No—I—I think not, Lord Clivedon. I'll just run along—do as you say and try to cover for her, but I don't think—I mean it was never actually settled . . ."

"Can't take the pace?" Clivedon asked archly. He received no verbal reply, but the white, frightened face staring back at him was answer enough. "There's another one got away," Clivedon said to Agnes with no attempt at secrecy. "It seems the chore of finding her is to be mine alone. Gentz, do you think, Agnes, or Romeo this time?"

"I have no idea," she said. "Whom shall I get to open the ball?"

No one seemed to have any ideas on that point either, but she went with Ellingwood to put on a brave face and make excuses for the absence of the guest of honor.

Clivedon wasted not a moment in going to Fannie's house, nor in worrying about Gentz. He went instead to Stapford's London residence, to confirm that Lord Romeo had gone to visit his father. This he ascertained by asking the butler in a fairly disinterested way whether his lordship had left for Hampshire yet, and received assurance that he had left that same evening.

"It's very urgent. I hope I can overtake him. He was to procure for me a certain vase from Greece."

"He arranged to stop the night at the Twin Oaks Inn, just beyond Chertsey," the servant told him, smiling, for while he was unaware of any kidnapping, he knew well enough his master had spoken of finding a buyer for the Clitias vase, and had in fact mentioned Lord Clivedon in that regard.

Still, Clivedon thought it better to take no chances of a foul-up, and took the precaution of going to speak to Smythe before leaving. "I want all roads covered, especially the Great North Road towards Gretna Green. Take that one yourself, George." Mr. Smythe was Smythe when he was not in disgrace, and occasionally George when he was in high favor. "I've written notes and put my gaudiest seal on them, with orders for the local magistrate to stop them if they are caught, and hold them, preferably *in jail*," he finished with a smile. "Send my valet towards Dover. The Greek may have a barge waiting to take her immediately to Athens. I'll go west myself. I think Stapford Hall the likeliest destination. Don't bother driving all night. Stop at a couple of tolls, and if they haven't passed, return here and wait word from me. They can't be far ahead of us."

"Yes, sir. Is there anything else?" Smythe asked stiffly, still remembering the morning.

"That's all I can think of. Enjoy yourself. I plan to. Good night, George."

He handed him two sealed notes, took up his drab greatcoat with several fashionable collars, his hat and cane, and strode out the door, merrily whistling a country tune.

Clivedon headed his carriage west and was soon out of

the city. He stopped at the first toll, and was informed that a crested carriage containing a young gentleman, an invalid wrapped in a blanket, and a great quantity of flowers had passed an hour ago. The flowers convinced him he was on the right track. The gatekeeper was surprised and gratified to receive a gold coin of a large denomination. Surprised too that the carriage proceeded at a leisurely pace, as though its owner were not at all eager to overtake his quarry. Nor was he. He had no notion of returning in time for any ball. He went on for an hour, after which time he had covered eight miles, though he could have gone faster. He stopped at the toll booth again to inquire for the passage of the vehicle he was following, and was amazed to be told it had not passed.

"It must have!" he exclaimed, feeling suddenly the surge of panic.

"Nothing anything like it," he was told simply. "We don't get that many crested carriages that I'd be likely to forget it."

"But there's nowhere else it could have gone."

"Happen it pulled in at an inn."

"No, not yet."

"Accidents *do* happen," he was reminded.

He knew well enough they happened to Babe, and with a vision of her playing coachman, he had his carriage turned around to retrace its steps at a much faster speed than that at which it had been advancing. Good God, he'd have to stop at every inn and coaching house along the way. He wondered as he went along whether Romeo, that bizarre article, had sent a flower-decked carriage out of London to confuse him. Was he crafty enough for that? He had no idea, but realized he had never quite plumbed the depths of that strange young mind. "Damn his eyes! And damn that girl. I'll beat her!"

Twenty-Two

Lady Barbara had not the least intention of going nearly so far as Chertsey before making a first stop. Her abductor, however, was uncommonly heedless of her every polite request. Neither rest, food, drink, nor a delicate mention of some unspecified physical discomfort was sufficient to slow him down. "We don't want to give Clivehorn a chance to catch up with us," he told her. "He'd follow and steal you from me if he could."

She quickly considered the efficacy of a bout of illness, which would need very little simulation, against a fit of amorousness, which would require a great deal, in bringing him around to do as she wished. "I am feeling very hot, Romeo," she said in a small voice. Her head was indeed feverish.

"I am burning with desire," was his answer, in a voice that sounded somewhat scorched with passion. "It is the excitement of running away that heats the blood. It is always so. Flight is the great aphrodisiac. My love, my beautiful Venus, it won't be long now. Soon we two shall

203

be one." His warm hands caressed her arms, her shoulders.

She wrinkled her brow in the darkness, and opted for passion as a reason for having the coach stopped at an inn. "You call that *soon?*" she asked in a voice that held something of the sulky and sultry combined. From an inn she could escape. In the middle of a dark highway in a carriage galloping ahead at a rapid pace, it was impossible.

His fingers tightened painfully on her shoulder. "*One* day, my goddess," he crooned. "I knew the flight would arouse you to passion. I wish you hadn't thrown away the ouzo. You are fire and ice, moonbeams and sunshine. Oh, how I look forward to possessing you."

"That's still a long time," she pouted, and took his caressing fingers in hers.

He squeezed them fervently, then lifted them to his lips to kiss. "My splended Barbarian, I am aflame with the need of you."

"Oh, look, my love, there is an inn just ahead," she pointed out. "We have not formally pledged our troth. We should do so, in champagne. Only it affects me so wickedly—just like ouzo does you. I get tipsy and so foolish after a few glasses."

"Do you, my little pet?" he asked with an eager interest. Then, in his usual guileless way, he went on to give the show away. "Only we are not married, and it would not be at all proper for me to take advantage of you, much as I want to. Of course, we are to be married tomorrow. One day can make very little difference. You are already mine, and I am yours, totally, completely, eternally. Forms and services and signing papers are for the hoi polloi. Aphrodite has no need of such trappings. You will be mine tonight."

"How quaint the place looks," she pointed out. "There is something Grecian about it, is there not?"

He was too besotted to mention the lack of any Grecian features in a half-timbered Tudor structure. Indeed, till he had the carriage stopped, neither of them saw more than a bunch of lighted windows and a torch to awaken passersby to the driveway leading in. They drove up to the inn door to alight, and the carriage was taken around to the stable by the groom. Romeo selected a handful of the less-withered blooms for her to carry with her. "We shall make a potpourri of these, and burn them as incense to Janus," he told her.

"What a splendid thought, Romeo," she answered, trying not to wince as a thorn pierced her fingers.

"My wife and I want a bedchamber right away," he told the proprietor.

"A private parlor, my dear," she corrected with a gentle smile. "You are not forgetting our champagne."

"To be sure, it slipped my mind. You need your champagne first. A bottle at once, my good fellow. A large bottle, and a private parlor."

They were shown into a cozy room, where he helped her off with the woolen blanket she had around her shoulders. "I must slip out to comb my hair and freshen up," she told him, smiling to forestall suspicion.

"The landlord mentioned there is a water closet here, *en suite*," he told her. To her utter consternation, this convenience was available without leaving the private parlor. She had no choice but to enter. There was no window to aid her escape. There was a mirror, which showed her a feverish face and a pair of dark, staring eyes, along with a hairdo greatly disheveled, and a badly wrinkled gown. She tidied her appearance, while scanning the room for a weapon. A water pitcher was impossible of concealment; a chair the same. There was nothing. She would have to return and find one in the private parlor. She began to wonder at this point whether she was likely to get help from the city. For some inexplicable reason, it was not the man who professed to love and want to marry her she thought of, but Lord Clivedon. He had not been seen all day, had excused himself from the dinner, and might very well miss her ball, for all she knew, but it was he that she thought of as possibly coming to her rescue. As it was by no means certain, however, she planned to do the thing herself. She had handled equally difficult situations in the past, but none of equal importance to her.

Squaring her shoulders, she settled herself down to calm determination. Her feverishness and headache lessened to a manageable extent, and other than a strange itching on her back and arms, due, she thought, to the blanket that had covered her, she felt much better. A glass of champagne to steady her nerves, and she would strike her amorous Romeo a blow that would, she hoped, knock him senseless for at least an hour.

When she emerged into the parlor, he had already poured two glasses of the wine, and sipped one tentatively. "My Aphrodite!" he greeted her, with an exultant smile, quickly handing her the other glass. "We shall lock arms and drink a love toast. To the goddess of my heart," he proposed in his low, sweet tones, then linking his arm through hers, they both drank, while he stared at her with eyes that would melt stone, so hotly did they glow. With their heads nearly touching, half a glass was gulped down, giving them both courage.

"Drink it all up, my dear," he urged, holding the bottle in his hand to replenish her glass to the brim. "Two glasses, you say, make you drunk?" he asked, ever transparent.

She smiled shyly. "Don't rush me, or I'll get the hiccoughs," she cautioned playfully.

"Oh, please, don't do that! I abhor such low physical effects when I am trying to make love. I like to think of it as the merging of two souls, not bodies. Adele belched," he told her sadly. "It ruined the evening for me. Take your time, love, sip slowly. I don't want you to hiccough. And I wish you will put some powder on that spot on your neck, my dear. A pity you had to throw out a spot so close to your bosom, tonight of all nights. That snowy, immaculate bosom."

She sipped again, ignoring all his foolish chatter and skimming the room for her weapon. It was totally incredible, but there was not a jug or poker to help her. There were no andirons by the cold grate. The only crockery was a bowl on top of a cupboard that nearly reached the ceiling. With a sinking heart, she glanced back to him, to see him trying to get another ounce into a nearly full glass in her hand. The champagne bottle was large. He had asked for a big one. It was still full enough, too, to carry considerable weight.

"Romeo, my love," she said, "you must drink from my slipper. It is not a Grecian custom—well, one could not drink from a sandal—but in England, you know, it is the custom for a gentleman to drink from a lady's slipper."

"That's disgusting!" he said at once. Then he went on in a more conciliating line. "It sounds very unsanitary. And it would not be at all comfortable for you to have to put on a wet slipper. You would not like it."

"You don't love me," she said, tossing her head and pouting.

"I adore you."

"Do it then, for me."

With an eye less smoldering, quite annoyed in fact, he set down his glass and bent down to undo her slipper. She reached out for the bottle, which movement he regarded closely. She feared he had tumbled to her stunt, but he said only, "Damme, you've got a spot on your *hand* now. I hope you are not subject to spots, Barbara. They are not at all romantic."

"No, I never get spots," she assured him, and, raising the bottle high as he bent to unbuckle her slipper, she lowered it on his head with all the force she could muster. It did not break. A quantity of champagne bubbled over him and her own gown, unnoticed. She was too concerned at the dreadful, hollow, ominous sound the bottle made as it hit his head, for all the world as though his head were empty. He fell over with an unromantic grunt, into a heap at her feet. She leaned over to examine him. He was perfectly inert. When she lifted a hand, it fell limply as soon as she released it. His head, too, lolled on his shoulder in a terribly dead-looking way. She looked at the door, and escape, then she looked back at Romeo, who appeared of a sudden as vulnerable as a baby. She didn't want to leave him quite helpless like this. For a moment she tried to rouse him, all in vain. She was seized with the idea that she had accidentally killed him, or at least hurt him worse than she had intended, and ran to the door calling the landlord.

"Lord R—my husband has fainted," she said, frightened. "Pray call a doctor at once. Quickly."

"What's happened to him?" he asked, walking forward to the heap on the floor. "He's been koshed! You hit that cove yourself, miss."

"Call the doctor at once, you silly man. Why should I hit my own husband?"

"Husband—pshaw. Lover is more like it. You don't wear no ring, I see. We get plenty of your kind in here."

She fixed him with an imperious eye, to hide her anxiety. "If he dies, you will be hanged," she told him, feeling a dreadful quiver that it was herself who was for the gibbet after this night's work. Even Clivedon had never prophesied this fitting end for her. "Go, I say!" she commanded, as he was not impressed with her threat. "It was likely your poison wine that killed him. Get a doctor this instant or I'll have you reported."

At last he stomped off, muttering disapproval of the habits of "Lunnon ladies." She went into the hallway and garnered up a serving wench and a rough man-of-all-work to help her get Romeo lifted onto a sofa, still completely unconscious, to fetch her *sal volatile* and brandy, while she knelt on the floor, fanning him with a tattered magazine and occasionally speaking to him, urging his silent lips to speak. She was so distraught and worried that she made a silent promise that if she had killed him, she would marry him, without recognizing any incongruity in this moral bargaining. She only wanted to make up in some manner for what she had done to him. When five minutes had passed without bringing any doctor, or any sign of life in Romeo, she began to tremble in fright. A turmoil worse than she had felt all day was taking place within her, threatening nausea from sheer fear. This was what came of her wretched way of carrying on. She ended up murdering a sweet, helpless boy, who only loved her and wanted to marry her. Tears welled up in her eyes, and slipped down her cheeks, as she lifted his head tenderly in her hands, speaking softly to him, apologizing, urging him to speak, to recognize his own Aphrodite.

When she heard a firm tread at the door, she turned anxiously, expecting a doctor. "Thank God you've come!" she said, then stopped, struck to silence.

Clivedon stood one pace within the room. He did not look angry, as she expected. His appearance was of a man who beheld a ghost, the sight of which froze him to the spot. One foot was extended, indicating a long stride, with an arm to balance, but he stood stock-still, staring at the scene before him. In a heartbeat he had resumed motion towards her. "Babe, what is it?"

Her first shock at seeing him was overcome by a wave of great relief. "Oh, Clivedon, help me! I think I've killed him," she said, and pitched herself into his arms to heave two convulsive sobs before recovering her voice.

"Hush," he said, in a low but commanding voice, bending his head to hers to conceal the word from the servants. She could perceive no point in trying to hide it, when the corpse lay before them all, but sensed some purpose in him, knew him well enough to trust him. How glad she was to let him take over her problems once again. The third sob was a sigh of relief. The idea came to her that she had reached a calm port after a stormy voyage. Weary and worried, she wished she could close out the world and stay forever in his arms.

Clivedon glanced at the prostrate and very pale body on the sofa, at the goggling servants, at the champagne bottle on the floor, its contents making a dark mark on the carpet, and formed an idea of what had happened. "We'll handle this now, thank you," he said to the servants. They stood on, staring, till he said more forcibly, "Go!" Then they straggled from the room, looking over their shoulders in fright.

"What happened?" he asked, releasing her and going to the sofa to lift a wrist and feel for a pulse. He put his head down to Romeo's heart to listen for a beat, and exhaled a very relieved breath at what he felt and heard.

She babbled incoherently about kidnapping and drinking champagne from a slipper and accidents, mingled with animadversions on her own infamous conduct, but indeed she had not meant to hit him *quite* so hard.

"All right—self-defense at the very worst," he assured her. "He kidnapped you and was forcing you to yield to him."

"Yes—but not exactly *forcing*," she corrected scrupulously. "I mean—I gave him the idea to get the carriage stopped before we had gone all the way past Chertsey, for I knew I would never get back in time for the ball if we went so far. Oh, how stupid it seems now, to have worried about missing a *ball*," she said wistfully. "It's like you once said, Clivedon, I got manners and morals all mixed up."

She was interrupted by a low moan from the sofa, as Romeo's hand came up, reaching for his head. Without more ado, Clivedon reached down for the champagne bottle and poured the remains of its contents over the abductor's head. He sat up, spluttering. "*You!*" he said in a grim voice, looking at Clivedon with a black scowl. "You *Nemesis!*"

"Oh Romeo! Thank God you are alive!" Babe declared, and ran to take him in her arms.

His arms went around her possessively, while he looked at Clivedon over her shoulder. "My dear heart, forgive me," he said. "What very bad form, for me to have got drunk. Champagne does not usually affect me so quickly. Pray go away, Clyesdon," he added politely.

Babe opened her lips to correct Romeo, but received a warning stare from her guardian, who spoke up rapidly. "Very bad *ton*, to become drunk in mid-seduction, Romeo," he said.

"I agree. It never happened to me before. Next time I shall be more careful. You can go now, Cliveston. I am taking Barbara home to meet my family." To Barbara he added, in a voice nominally lowered, "I think we had better wait till after the wedding, my pet. I really do not feel at all the thing. I'm not up to it tonight."

"Romeo, I am not marrying you," she told him. "I

never said I would. In fact, I have told you dozens of times I would not. I am going home with Clivedon."

"You are disgusted with me," he said simply. "I hardly blame you. A gentleman who makes such an appalling mess . . ." He stopped and examined her critically. "You have got a spot on your cheek now. That is three spots you have got tonight, I noticed one on your hand before, only I hesitated to harp on it as we were about to . . . If you are not planning to stay perfect, Barbara, I hope you will tell me."

"I was never perfect, you ninny!" she pointed out.

"In the pulchritudinal desert of London you appeared so to my famished eyes. But with all those spots . . . and really, it was not nice for you to try to seduce me before the wedding, either. I was shocked, but so eager to have you that I gave in, and even tried to find excuses for it."

"I was not seducing you, you silly twit. I was only trying to get away from you."

"You called me your love, for the first time, tonight."

"You called me your wife in front of the innkeeper, but it doesn't mean I am. How could you be so stupid as to think I'd marry you, after you kidnapped me and tied me up—"

"With silken bands, verbena scented," he reminded her. Then he picked up her Grecian wool blanket and sniffed it, with a satisfied sigh. "Lovely," he told her.

Clivedon stood back, listening in amusement while they bickered. "It is that stupid old blanket you wrapped me up in that is causing these spots. I feel itchy all over to remember it."

"It never gave any other girl spots," he retorted. "And it is improper to call a blanket stupid. A transferred epithet, I think?" He looked to Clivesdon for confirmation of this grammatical irrelevancy.

"I daresay Adele was so busy belching she hadn't time to grow a spot," Barbara retaliated.

"Maybe I will marry you," he reconsidered. "You are very beautiful when you are angry. Yes, I will. Clivesmore, you are a man of the world. Explain to Barbara why I had to kidnap her. It was only partly showing off that I am a man of action and resolution. I had to teach her, as well, that she is under my control, subject to obey my orders. I can't have a wife who sets herself in opposition to me."

"You're carrying off the wrong girl, I can tell you," Clivedon warned him.

"Obey *you,* you spouting popinjay. Whip you is more like it," Barbara replied, incensed.

"I don't want an intransigent wife. There is no record of the Sabine women being so unruly."

"He meant to rape me, like the Sabine women," Barbara said aside to Clivedon, with a wrathful eye.

"You may count yourself lucky you weren't hammered into a wooden horse," he informed her.

"Ah, the Trojan War—an apt analogy, Clivesmare. Excellent. Fair Helen, launching a thousand ships . . ." His eyes played over Lady Barbara, lingering on her lips. "I wonder if Helen was a dutiful wife."

"You don't want a wife. You want a caryatid or a demmed statue," Barbara answered hotly.

"I don't like to hear you use vulgar language, my dear."

"You'll hear language that will curl your *psychë* if you ever pester me again. Clivedon, please take me away, before I hit him again."

"Did you hit me?" he asked, then smiled. "Ah, you can be a Fury too, you Infinite Woman. But does this mean you have ceased to love me?"

"Love *you?* I love—I love *Ellingwood* better than I ever loved you."

"Isn't she glorious when she's in a temper?" he asked of Clivedon.

"Resplendent, except for the spots," he answered, surveying her critically.

"If I hear another word about spots!" she exclaimed angrily.

"I expect you'll hear quite a few words about them before the night is over," Clivedon said. "Ah, here is a caller—the doctor, I hope?"

The doctor stepped into the room, took one look at Lady Barbara, and diagnosed her instantly. "Measles," he declared. "A good deal of it going around. Best get to bed, milady."

"She has been trying to get there all evening, I understand," Clivedon mentioned, with a rallying glance to the angry lady. "But there were a host of unforeseen difficulties."

"Aye, I daresay you've been feeling poorly," the doctor told her. "The worst of the fever and nausea are over once the spots are out. You'll be feeling pulled for a day or two yet."

"Perhaps you would be kind enough to have a look at this fellow while you are here," Clivedon suggested. "He—fell, and struck his head on a caryatid. We cannot remain long, and would like to know he is in no danger before leaving."

"Did I fall too?" Romeo asked, interested in his recent past. "That's why my head aches so. I know how Zeus felt, before Pallas Athene popped out of his head, fully armored."

Barbara cast a worried glance at him, fearing he had run quite mad at last. "More Greek stories," Clivedon told her quietly aside.

The doctor examined Romeo's bump, prescribed a paregoric draught and a good night's sleep, and gave him permission to resume his trip in the morning.

"We'll leave you, then," Clivedon said, putting a hand on Barbara's elbow.

"About the Clitias vase, Clysedale . . ." Romeo mentioned vaguely.

"Thank you, no. The patched-up forgery will do well enough for me. I really don't care so much for the Greek ideal as you do."

"Extraordinary, that lack of discretion exhibited in your possessions. But then, there was always a streak of the barbarian in you. I attributed it to jealousy."

"How very wise of you."

"So I am to lose my little Barbarian," Romeo said, with a touch of sadness. "Zeus does not bring all men's

213

plans to fulfillment, alas! Still, there is that ravishing wench at Taunton . . ."

"I pity her!" Barbara said, and, with an indignant look at her erstwhile suitor, she stalked off.

Twenty-Three

"How do you feel?" Clivedon asked as he tucked Barbara into his greatcoat for the trip home.

"Better than I have all evening. I wanted to *die* earlier, at dinner, and when he kidnapped me. I daresay coming down with the measles didn't help. Why have you kept yourself so scarce all day?"

"I called on *you* this afternoon, so you must refer to my missing Ellingwood this morning."

"He was very angry with you."

"Were you?"

"I was too sick to be angry with anyone, but where were you?"

"Hiding in my study with the door locked, to prevent having to either give him permission to propose to you or forbid it, till I had a chance to propose to you first myself. A slight unfair advantage, of course, but I felt, in all honesty, I had earned it. It was your refusing to see me that created this little contretemps."

Barbara's heart leapt in her chest at the words, but

when she spoke, she did not acknowledge having heard them. In a high, nervous voice, she said, "I am in a worse pickle than ever, missing my own ball. Your sister will never forgive me. Just when I was trying so hard to be respectable."

"And deaf," he added, undeceived.

A nervous laugh escaped her. "Oh, you are joking, Clivedon. I am much too disreputable for you."

"I used to think I thought so, once upon a dull time. Lately I have had to reconsider the matter. My *psychë* was not content with that old decision. In fact, I have lately found you much too nice in your notions to suit me. Not wanting to smoke a cigar! But your latest spree leads me to hope you are not totally converted to the acceptable mode."

"But it was not my fault!"

"Oh no, it was mine. I all but begged Romeo to do it. I knew you didn't care for *him*, and had to make you see Ellingwood was not your type at heart either. He is not pleased with you, Babe."

"Pray tell me what you are talking about. How did you know Romeo would kidnap me?"

"By refusing him permission to marry you. His dramatic soul was bound to be incensed enough with that to lead him to an elopement. I had to finance it myself, but I shall enjoy to have the portrait. There will be one thing in my barbarian house of which he approves, at least. Maybe two—if he doesn't win the female at Taunton, he will be falling in love with you again."

"Why were you always after me to behave politely, then? It was you who nagged me into it."

"Naturally I wanted *some* semblance of behavior in my wife, at least a token that she was—no, I daren't use the word 'biddable.' You'll hit me. For your own peace of mind . . . Wrong again. I shall take a leaf from your last suitor's book and blurt out the unvarnished truth. I was making you over for *me*, not anyone else. I wanted you to treat *me* with respect, and didn't give a damn how you acted towards the rest of the world."

216

"Is it possible we are discussing Richmond Park, Clivedon?"

"Entirely possible. I have been angry for two years, being insufferably proud, and my anger perhaps grew a little out of proportion. Yes, I wanted some petty revenge too. Lady Graham was a revenge, and a mistake of which I am greatly ashamed. For the rest of it, it was a necessity which happened to coincide with my own wishes. Your health was suffering with so many late nights, and your reputation with the association you had with Fannie's raffish friends. The gowns, while ravishing, were too dashing for a spinster, and the nags, of course, a positive danger to the whole city."

"How about my money? I think that's the only thing you've left out."

"Naturally I wanted your dowry intact! How can you ask? We'll need every penny of it to bribe our way out of future scrapes."

"Well, I think it was very petty of you to hold a grudge for two years, only for missing a date," she said, reverting to the least heinous of her crimes. "You might have given me a chance to explain."

"Was there an explanation?"

"Of course there was! I had to bring you to heel, to have you eating out of my hand like the others."

"Let it be well understood, dear Aphrodite, I do not mean to eat of your fingers *like the others*. I am not a tame squirrel. I want no servility from you, nor will I give any. You will behave more or less as a lady should, and if—*when* you run amok, *I* wish to be the first to hear of it. It will not be necessary for you to tuck any more lace doilies down the front of your gowns, and in fact I had hoped to see that green outfit tonight. Why didn't you wear it? Afraid Ellingwood would disapprove?"

"Oh, dear! What is to be done about Ellingwood? I have as well as said I will have him, to show you a lesson."

"Not to worry. I convinced him you are beyond his poor powers of handling. He was mighty relieved I had managed to escape him all day, I can tell you. You never saw such a frightened hare when I told him he might have to challenge Romeo to a duel."

"Oh, he knows about the kidnapping, then."

"Not at all, he thinks it was a dash to Gretna Green."

"I hope he hasn't told anyone. What story has your sister told at the ball?"

"You are ill."

"If we hurry, we might be back in time for the last dance."

"Long before it, but do you think you will look your best in polka dots?"

"Ah, my measles! I feel so much better now that the spots have blossomed that I forgot all about them. Romeo didn't much care for them, did he?" she asked, and laughed softly.

"Romeo is an inveterate fool. And so have I been. I still am, wasting this precious opportunity. Evening star, I want to kiss you."

"You'll have to ask my guardian, Lord Clivedon," she informed him in a prissy manner.

"Call me Laurence," he said, reaching out for her in the darkness.

"Clivedon!" she repeated in a louder voice. "Don't touch me. I've got the measles."

"I noticed. And you will call me Laurence, or I shall wring your beautiful neck, as I have been wanting to all these days," he said, putting his hands around her neck and tilting her chin towards him. "To hear you speak of that Greek puppy as 'fascinating,' and to see you planning to marry Ellingwood when you *knew*—"

"No, I was not at all sure!"

"Liar," he mumbled in a caressing voice. "You have known ever since you stood me up two years ago."

"I wonder what would have happened if I hadn't."

"This is what would have happened, before the day was out, Aphrodite," he mummured in her ear. Then he lowered his head and kissed her gently on the lips, a warm, tender embrace. "But, as two years have passed

218

since then, and you are a confirmed jezebel, *this* is what will happen now," he added ominously. He attacked her much more vigorously, with a ruthless embrace that left her breathless.

"Babe. Oh Babe," he said in an unsteady voice. "I have been ten times a fool. Get rid of those spots at once, you hear? I'm going to marry you before you fall into any more scrapes."

"I wish I could be rid of them. So *lowering* to have the measles at my age. But really, I feel fine, Laurence."

"Only fine? You should be feeling ecstatic, like me. Am I slipping?" he apologized, and kissed her again. "Better?"

"Much better! That was Homeric, or do I mean Herculean?"

"Damn your eyes, you're thinking of that Greek at a time like this."

"I was only thinking how glad I am to be rid of him. He hated the Cotswolds, you know. Can you imagine anyone hating those hills? And I was thinking too, maybe we could go there for our honeymoon."

"Persuade me," he suggested, and showed her the best manner of doing so.

*　*　*

Lady Withers' hysteria was reaching an uncontrollable height by midnight, when her company was going in to dinner. She actually emitted a shriek—so tactless—when she was called to go abovestairs by her butler. She was assured as soon as she was in the privacy of the hallway that the sight awaiting her there was pleasant, however, and had settled down to babbling incoherency by the time she reached Barbara's chamber. "You have found her, thank God. I pictured a runaway match with Gentz, or a *fatal* accident. Oh my dear, you are all covered in *spots!*"

"You noticed that, did you?" Laurence asked. "At least we have got our excuse for Babe's missing her party tailor-made for us. Now we can announce the precise nature of her illness. Is she still ill, by the by?"

"Yes, and that pesky Lady Angela has asked a dozen times to be allowed to see her, just for a moment. She suspects, of course . . ."

"Excellent! Let her come," Clivedon declared. "She'll put an ad in the paper for us, and the world will know what happened."

"I hope she catches them from me," Babe said, and gurgled happily at the thought.

"Better slip into a dressing gown first, Babe," Lady Withers suggested. "Oh, my dear! What did I call you? I beg your pardon, Barbara. It is my poor head . . . Clivedon, you can't be here when Lady Angela comes up. You might just come into the ballroom and make an appearance, for the looks of it. With the two of you gone, you know, it looks so very odd. It has even been suggested the two of you were together. Lady Angela, I think, mentioned it . . ."

"The trouble is, I may be coming down with the measles myself," he objected.

"What, are you ill too?" Agnes asked.

"I feel strangely light-headed," he lied happily.

"You both caught them from Boo, of course. I hope I am not next."

"I have been out of commission all day, you recall, so my absence will surprise no one," Laurence said. "I'll just hide in the closet till Angela leaves. Bring us some champagne, will you, Sis?"

Barbara threw a dressing gown over her gown to hide it from Lady Angela, and closed the door of the closet on her groom. She reclined gracefully on a chaise longue, and soon had the exquisite pleasure of seeing Lady Angela start back in fright and beat a hasty retreat from the room. She feared she had not got close enough for contamination, but resisted the impulse to go after her.

There were several who had no heart for staying in a house cursed with measles, but plenty of others who were willing to take the risk. The Ladies Anstrom and Nathorn and their nephew were amongst those who elected to leave. "Did you find her?" Ellingwood asked in a quiet aside on his way to the door.

"Yes, Clivedon got her back. She is abovestairs this minute."

"Wasn't sure Lady Angela wasn't in on the cover-up," he said, nodding in a commiserating way. "Where had the girl got to, anyway?"

"She had wandered into the garden, feeling warm, you know," Lady Withers explained. He looked at her, disbelief written all over him.

"I see," he said, and nipped smartly forward to hold the door for his wealthy aunts, who had no opinion of a lady who would be ill for her own ball.

Abovestairs, Clivedon opened the door onto the balcony that graced Lady Barbara's room and took the champagne out to it. He lit a cigar as he looked out on to the street. "The little party is breaking up," he pointed out, as several carriages were being brought around to the house front.

"Laurence—look—there is Mrs. Harkness getting into Balfour's carriage. They *are* having an affair; I knew it."

"Lucky dogs," he replied, pulling her to his side to kiss her ear.

"No one ever talks about *her*. I don't know why they all pick on *me*."

"Jealous as green cows, every one of them," he assured her.

"I think there was some jealousy in it," she answered.

"Certainly there was, and there will be a good deal more when they read tomorrow that you have captured *me*."

"Should we announce it so soon? I mean, after Ellingwood . . ."

"To hell with Ellingwood," he answered, and setting aside their two glasses, he pulled her into his arms. Looking over the railing towards the street, she exclaimed, "There is Lady—"

"Never mind, love," he said, and kissed her quite long, till he began to feel a little curiosity as to the unstated lady's name. Glancing to the carriage, he recognized her and her escort. "That's a new romance."

"And she a widow with three children. It's shocking," Barbara said in a righteous tone.

"Shocking," he agreed censoriously, and passed her his cigar.